Tempting a Knight

Hell's Knights Book 1

Leann Ryans

Copyright © 2022 Leann Ryans
All rights reserved.
ISBN 13-9798832959863

Cover by Dazed Designs

No part of the book may be reproduced or transmitted in any form or by any means, electronic or mechanical, including photocopying, recording, or by any information storage and retrieval system, without permission in writing from the author.

Leann Ryans
Tempting a Knight
Hell's Knights Book 1

Interested in find out more about me and my books? Check out https://leannryans.com where you can claim a free short RH story for signing up for my newsletter.

Table of Contents

Chapter One 1
Chapter Two 7
Chapter Three 13
Chapter Four 21
Chapter Five 29
Chapter Six 41
Chapter Seven 53
Chapter Eight... 65
Chapter Nine 79
Chapter Ten... 93
Chapter Eleven 101
Chapter Twelve 111
Chapter Thirteen 117
Chapter Fourteen 127
Chapter Fifteen 137
Chapter Sixteen... 147
Chapter Seventeen.. 157
Chapter Eighteen 171
Chapter Nineteen.. 181
Chapter Twenty... 193
Chapter Twenty-One... 203

Chapter Twenty-Two 215
Chapter Twenty-Three 229
Chapter Twenty-Four 241
Chapter Twenty-Five 251
Chapter Twenty-Six 259
Chapter Twenty-Seven 269
Chapter Twenty-Eight 279
Chapter Twenty-Nine 285
Chapter Thirty 295
Chapter Thirty-One 303
Chapter Thirty-Two 313
Chapter Thirty-Three 323
Chapter Thirty-Four 329
Chapter Thirty-Five 341
Chapter Thirty-Six 345
Chapter Thirty-Seven 357
Chapter Thirty-Eight 363
Chapter Thirty-Nine 371
Chapter Forty 383
Epilogue 393
Thanks 399

Chapter One

Brooke

What do you do when one of the baddest alphas you know decides he wants you during your next heat?

You find a bigger, badder alpha to take it instead.

Or you try to.

Tension crawled down my spine as I forced myself to keep my chin raised, though I didn't meet the gaze of the male in front of me. My plan was insane. Completely desperate and ill-advised, but it was the only thing I could come up with to save myself from Arik.

"You want to what?"

The alpha's tone was neutral, as if he was asking me the weather and not to repeat the most embarrassing thing I'd ever had to say. It didn't matter that I'd known him once, he'd changed since then. Become dangerous, according to some. Bikers weren't to be trusted.

Sucking in a deep breath, I squared my shoulders and met his dark gaze.

"I want to offer you my next heat. It should begin in about a week, and I—I'd appreciate you tending me through it."

Not an ounce of emotion showed on the alpha's face as he stared down at me. The noise of the garage seemed to have stopped as I spoke, but I refused to look around to see how many others were watching.

Massive arms rose to cross over a broad chest, white t-shirt doing little to hide the muscles and dark ink swirling beneath. Grease and dirt smeared his forearms, the tang of it blending with the virile, musky scent of him, teasing my nose even amidst all the other smells in the shop.

"Do I know you?"

The rumbled question sent a shiver through my core. His already deep voice had dropped further, the only sign he'd registered what I was offering. What I'd be submitting to if he accepted.

I'd known the alpha in front of me because he'd been best friends with my older brother, but I doubted he had ever noticed me back then, and that was a long time ago anyway. I had been just an awkward girl who'd yet to present when my brother got in trouble with one of the local gangs and was killed shortly after, but I remembered how close the two of them had been before the issues started.

"I'm Vincent Frost's sister."

I saw a flash of something in those chocolate eyes, but it was gone too fast for me to be sure what it was. Surprise? Grief? Arms dropping to his sides, he took a step closer, my own feet moving me back before I could resist the instinct to retreat from the powerful male.

"You shouldn't be here."

The way his voice scraped my insides had me taking another step back, heartbeat fluttering in my throat. I'd known it was crazy to approach Sebastian, but I was grasping at straws to save myself from what was coming. Arik was the last alpha I'd let use me, even if denying him meant my death.

I needed help.

I bit my lower lip to stop it from trembling. Blinking back tears, I dropped my gaze to the stained concrete, trying to come up with something to convince Sebastian to agree. This was the only plan I could come up with.

Before I could think of a valid reason, a large hand landed on my shoulder, startling a small yelp from my throat before I could choke it back. Spun around to face the open garage doors, I was thrust forward by the hard grip.

Chuckles followed as Sebastian marched me out of his shop. The size of it proved how well the business had done, and it provided a place for his motorcycle club to hang out during the day. I didn't know much about the Hell's Knights, but they were discussed in whispers just as much as the Purists. The main difference was that Sebastian's club was more inclusive, and respected, and feared more by criminals than the average person.

Sebastian didn't release my shoulder until I cleared the building, and I took two more steps before turning to face him again once he let me go. His ridicule would be better than what I'd face with Arik if I didn't find a way out of his plans.

Leann Ryans

"Please."

The whisper was pathetic, and shame burned my cheeks as I resorted to begging. Omegas were desired, shifter or not. They bore whatever they mated with, so there was plenty of interbreeding. I should have had alphas fighting over me, not be begging one to take pity on me and see me through my heat to save me from another.

The problem was finding one who didn't answer to the Purists, wouldn't claim me, and wouldn't enjoy hurting me.

Movement to the right caught my attention but I ignored it to keep my gaze locked on the alpha in front of me. Even if they were Knights and a better choice than Arik, they weren't who I was here for. It was hard enough to place my trust in a man I barely knew, but who my brother had trusted.

"Just for this cycle, then I'll figure out something else before the next. I'm not asking you to claim me or do anything more. Just a couple days."

Sebastian's eyes narrowed, features hardening, but he remained silent. The figure who'd approached from the side stepped into my field of vision, another grease-stained alpha, though smaller than Sebastian. His stringy hair was slicked back from a narrow face, grin sporting missing teeth despite being around my age.

"I'll tend you through your heat, pretty. You say when and where, and my knot is yours."

A shudder rolled down my spine at his leer, the way his eyes focused on my breasts as he adjusted his crotch making my stomach surge. The scent of something wet and dirty rolled off him, gagging me further. I parted my lips to form a denial, but a harsh growl rumbled through the air before the words could emerge from my throat.

Hands clutching my belly as it spasmed, I fought to stay upright under the weight of an alpha's displeasure. As civilized as people tried to pretend they were, we were still animals at our core, and instincts were impossible to ignore. There were different kinds of growls, but this one was clearly full of rage, and it took a moment before I realized it came from Sebastian but wasn't aimed at me.

Dark eyes locked on the second male, lips pulled back in a snarl as his canines elongated, the noise continued until the other alpha bowed his head and backed away, apology lost under the grating noise assaulting my nerves. Trembling, I stared at the ground and sucked in great gasps of air when it finally faded away, drenched in sweat and on the verge of tears.

I didn't notice Sebastian move closer until his boots appeared on the concrete in front of me. Dragging my gaze up his body until my head tipped back, I was hit once again with how large he was. Human alphas were big, but shifter alphas tended to be even more massive.

Unlike the other male who'd approached, Sebastian's scent wasn't revolting. It wrapped around me, filling my lungs with each inhale and making my eyes try to roll back in my head as I shuddered.

The omega part of me knew this was a strong, dominant male, and was ready to roll over and present for him at the first sign of acceptance. The wholly female part enjoyed all that was before me. He was everything an alpha should be. Everything I desired rolled into one delicious package that I shouldn't want beyond what I needed him for.

"Go home, Brooke, this isn't the place for you. You're better than this. Vincent would be disappointed."

Chapter Two

Sebastian

My teeth were clenched so hard my temples pounded as my fingers bit into my biceps. I could feel the tips of my canines cutting into my bottom lip, and my nails had sharpened into claws when Tom approached. If I uncrossed my arms I'd reach out and drag the little omega closer to get a better taste of her scent, but she didn't need an alpha like me in her life, despite her request.

Her cheeks flamed red, lush lips parting at my jab. I didn't like shaming her, but my words were nothing more than the truth. Brooke Frost was too good for anyone in my garage, my club, or this whole damn city. Her sweet innocence didn't belong here.

I let out a huff as she turned in silence and stumbled back to the car she'd arrived in. She had seemed familiar when she walked through the open door and called my name, but I hadn't placed her until she mentioned her brother. She'd changed a lot in the past few years.

Another stab of pain shot through my chest as I forced myself to turn away. Vincent had been my best friend growing up, the garage our shared dream, but now I was running it without him because of what I was, and a dumb decision I'd let him make.

I'd tried to talk him out of joining the Purists, but he hadn't listened. Had insisted on working for them despite what they stood for. I knew he'd never shared their ideas of human superiority, but seeing him associating with them had left a bad taste in my mouth. He'd said it was the best way to make the money we needed for the garage, but I'd known they were involved in dangerous shit, and we should have stayed clear.

But Vincent had been right. He made a lot of money. Fast. Every penny of which went to his funeral less than a year after joining the gang that targeted shifters like me and the humans associated with them.

I shook my head and stomped back to the bike I was working on, lifting my gaze to see the others still watching me.

"Back to work."

They jumped at my barked order, eyes turning back to the vehicles in front of them. I was generally laid back as long as the men got their shit done in a timely manner, but I wasn't in the mood for prying eyes, or twenty questions. Brooke may not be my sister by blood, but she was the closest thing I'd ever had to one, and I'd beat any asshole who thought to take her up on her offer. I wouldn't trust any of them not to claim her and trap her in this shitty city on top of the hell she'd catch for bonding with a shifter. The Purists were too prominent here to let that happen.

I could see the questions burning on the tips of their tongues. Queries about why I'd turn away an omega offering herself to me. Even if they guessed she was pure human, they didn't know she was my dead best friend's little sister and part of the pain I'd carried every day.

And I hadn't known she was an omega.

I'd seen Brooke as a child of course, all knobby knees and awkward smiles. She'd grown into a hell of a woman while my head was buried in the garage, and a part of me soured at the thought that I'd failed Vincent by not keeping an eye on her after he passed. Even without being an omega she'd have drawn attention from any male she passed, and with a pair of human betas for parents, I doubted she'd had an easy time with boys while growing up. I should have been there to protect her.

Growling under my breath, I tried to push thoughts of Brooke aside. I didn't know why she came to me with her request, but it was damned uncomfortable to crawl around a motorcycle with a boner jammed into my zipper.

Balls pinching as I shifted to reach for a bolt, I cursed and threw my wrench to the ground. There was only one way to solve my current problem so I could focus, and I stomped my way to the bathroom, hating every second.

Yanking my cock out of my jeans the second the door closed behind me, I didn't waste any time. Taking it in a punishing grip, I jerked up and down the length, hissing at the pull before spitting to give myself a little lube.

I tried to keep my mind blank, but it was impossible not to think of Brooke. Her full pink lips as she asked me to tend her through her heat. The way her baby blue shirt clung to her breasts, full, and more than enough to fill my palm. Her hips had swelled out her white leggings, swaying when she walked and making me want to leave my dirty prints all over them.

I let out another string of growled curses as I came, one hand shooting forward to brace against the mirror as rope after rope of my seed painted the sink and the floor in front of me. Black fur had broken out along my arms, showing how on edge I'd been.

My knot didn't even have a chance to swell as I strangled the demanding thing and forced it to finish draining. Groaning at the thought of having to clean up the mess, I reached for the paper towels and turned on the water as I fought back the shift. At least I'd be able to focus and do my job without an erection trying to rip through my jeans.

And hopefully Brooke wouldn't come back, though my cock twitched in disappointment at the thought.

Ignoring it, I cleaned the sink and floor beneath before tossing the paper towels in the bin. There was nothing I could do about the smell, but the men knew better than to mess with me when I was in a mood. Any idiot dumb enough to open his mouth would get the shit schedule for a month and be scrubbing the garage from top to bottom. There was enough dirt collected in the rafters to keep them busy for a week.

Brooke had to be insane coming to me after all these years, making that kind of request. Omegas had their pick of partners. She knew I was a wolf. She'd always seemed like the good girl type who'd settle down with a quiet beta human and have the usual two point five kids and the white picket fence. Preferably somewhere outside the city, after getting a degree from a college her brother and I had been too dumb and short sighted to attend.

Insane... Or in trouble.

Frown tipping down the corners of my mouth, I stepped out of the bathroom and fought to subdue the sudden urge to track her. The Brooke I remembered hadn't been an omega. She'd been quiet, and shy, but smarter than her age suggested. Not someone who'd come to a biker garage asking a virtual stranger to fuck her while she was at her most vulnerable. She knew better than to trust that easily.

Adding up the years in my head, I was honestly surprised she was still in town since I'd have expected her to be in college already. She was plenty smart enough to make it. Given the chance, she should have gotten as far from here as she could, so why hadn't she?

Possibilities turning over in my head, I went back to work on the bike. My hands knew what to do even if my mind wasn't on the repair, and there was nothing to stop the distraction I was chasing.

What if something had happened? Was she in trouble?

I clenched my teeth and set to finishing my work as fast as possible. I wasn't going to be able to rest until I'd checked on Vincent's family and was sure everything was okay.

I just needed to do it without running into his little sister again, or I might lose control of my baser urges and accept her offer.

Chapter Three

Brooke

"You're getting closer."

The words billowed against the side of my neck, the stench of smoke on his breath making me gag. I was pressed against the wall so hard I was surprised I hadn't become a part of it, but it wasn't enough to save me from Arik.

He sucked in another breath with his nose buried in my neck, the rumble he released on exhale not affecting me the way Sebastian's had. Arik made my skin crawl, but there was nothing I could do to avoid him when he cornered me at work.

The bell above the entrance jingled, announcing the arrival of another customer. I'd been trying to stock the shelves when Arik arrived and waylaid me, so I couldn't see the person who entered.

"I-I need to get back to work."

Arik's hands pressed against the wall on each side of me, hemming me in. Footsteps moved through the aisle next to us, but he didn't seem to care that we may have an audience. He pictured himself as above everyone else, and anyone who knew who he was wouldn't interfere on my behalf. Even if they didn't, it wasn't likely someone would be willing to put themselves between an alpha and omega, even if the omega seemed to be in distress. Alphas were too powerful to risk enraging if they didn't have good control.

"Mmm. Just a few more days and that sweet little pussy's going to be mine. You'll be milking my knot for days."

Shame at his crass words flooded my cheeks. There was no disgrace in being omega, but there were certain parts that weren't necessarily the way I would prefer them to be. I'm sure many omegas felt the same.

A shudder rolled through me before I could fight it, but he must have mistaken it for a shiver of excitement. Arik expected any woman he gave attention to be thrilled about it, but I'd heard the whispers when he wasn't around. About how he left women broken and damaged, weak from exhaustion and neglect. Some never recovered.

And those were just the betas he took to his bed. The only omega I'd heard mentioned hadn't survived her heat with him, though everyone was careful not to place blame for the tragedy after he killed her mother for doing so.

I wasn't going to be one of his discards, but it wouldn't do to tip him off before I had a plan in place. He wouldn't think twice about locking me away until I was so lost in my instincts I didn't know or care who the alpha mounting me was. I still didn't know what I was going to do to avoid him, but I had to figure out something. I was running out of time.

He finally lifted his head from scenting me. Only a thin strip of deep blue ringed his pupils, the first sign of my rising pheromones. For an alpha, the scent of an omega in heat was like a drug, the markers announcing their fertility giving the alpha a high some couldn't resist. It was the only reason he wanted me.

Well, besides what he could do to me during my cycle.

A ding came from the front counter, the customer ready to check out and calling me back to my post. Swallowing the bile threatening to spew from my throat, I jerked my eyes away from Arik's and focused on the floor.

"I have to get up there."

I barely heard my whisper over the thudding of my heart, but the alpha finally dropped his arms and straightened. Sliding along the wall to avoid brushing against him, I took the opportunity to escape, rushing behind the counter as I tried to compose myself.

Keeping my eyes downcast, I mumbled a greeting and rang up the customer's drinks. When another entered and got in line behind them, I risked a glance up, catching a glimpse of Arik striding toward the door. I didn't breathe easier until he'd walked out and climbed into his black SUV, pulling out and driving off in a reckless spin of flashy wheels.

The rest of my shift passed in a blur, the afternoon picking up as people got off work. By the time my coworker showed up to relieve me, my feet were aching, and I was ready to go home, but stepping into the apartment I shared with my parents only reminded me how much trouble I was in.

My mother was a nurse and worked twelve-hour shifts in a hospital downtown. Adding in her travel time, she was gone from eight in the morning until ten at night. My father worked the late shift at a warehouse and left at six, not getting home till almost four in the morning, so I was alone most evenings.

Even if they happened to be home when Arik came for me, they couldn't stop him. My parents were betas. Smaller and weaker than Arik, there was nothing they'd be able to do to protect me from him, even if he was cocky enough to arrive alone. If he came with his usual posse of alpha goons, it would be dangerous for them to even try, and I didn't want to think about what he might do to them.

I sighed as I slipped off my shoes and walked toward the tiny room in the back. I'd shared it with Vincent once, my parents unable to afford a three-bedroom apartment with the price of housing in the city, but I'd had the space to myself after he passed. It took some getting used to, but I'd made it mine over the years.

Dropping onto the edge of the twin bed I'd had for as long as I could remember, I stared into the mirror of my vanity. My dark hair was pulled back in a ponytail but the few whisps that had escaped highlighted the paleness of my skin. My dynamic left me on the short side, but assured I had the curves an alpha desired. I'd been teased about my *breeding hips* by other girls in school often enough, though I'd managed to avoid attention from the boys by keeping my nose buried in my studies.

Looking around the small room at the books and knick-knacks I'd collected, I couldn't stop my lips from trembling as I fought back a wave of despair. I'd give anything to go back to the invisible, geeky girl I'd once been, but it was impossible once I'd revealed as an omega. My dynamic may not be as rare as we'd once been, but there were still less of us than there were alphas and the more populous betas.

Slaves to our biology, it was unusual for an omega to make it through their teens or early twenties without being claimed and bred by the dominant dynamic. At twenty-four I was an oddity, but I'd always been careful. I'd used beta pheromones to hide mine in school when I could get them from the community clinic, and stayed away from alphas when I was close to my cycle.

A long-time friend from school had turned out to be an alpha, but he'd preferred partners of the same sex. When my first heat came after being told I was too old to receive free care any longer, he'd offered to tend me through it despite my gender, and we'd both taken precautions to be sure nothing unexpected happened. Luckily, I didn't cycle often, but I'd continued to go to him for each heat, and he'd helped me through them. When he moved away at the beginning of the year, I had been sad to see him go, but I'd figured I'd just lock myself in my room for my cycle and suffer through it.

Until I ran into Arik.

I knew who he was before he ever walked into the little convenience store I worked for. He was part of the Purists, and one of the reasons my brother was dead, according to rumor. Son of a higher-ranking member, Arik liked to throw his weight around, and Vincent had mentioned him more than once as being the cause of a lot of problems, though I hadn't known at the time he was a gang member. I'd caught glimpses of him with Vincent back then, but that had been before I'd revealed and given Arik any reason to be interested in me.

I'd known I was in trouble the moment he strutted into the store with his band of thugs and leaned on the counter. He'd opened his mouth to demand something as he drew in a deep breath. Eyes widening, a sick smile crossed his face moments before his hand caught my arm in a bruising grip, dragging me half over the counter to him so he could scent me better.

I suppose he thought he'd been wooing me ever since. Not a week passed when he didn't show up at some point during my shift, and I'd ran into him enough outside of work to be convinced he was following me. I was so distracted trying to keep an eye out for him I hadn't noticed the first signs of my approaching cycle until it was too late, and he'd picked up on them too. There wasn't much I could do since I had to work, and he knew where to find me.

Shoving those thoughts aside, I stood and walked to my closet to change. I had no plans other than to put on my pajamas and make myself noodles for dinner, until my eyes caught on a slip of red fabric hanging in the back of my closet.

It was a dress a friend had talked me into wearing one of the few times I'd gone out in the past couple years. I usually didn't have much time for socializing, but it had been her birthday and I'd agreed to go to a club with her since I hadn't been able to visit after she'd moved deeper into the city. When I arrived at her house in my typical jeans and t-shirt, she'd had a fit and forced me into the skintight thing, then declared it fit me so well I had to keep it.

Heat filled my cheeks at the memory of looking into the mirror the first time after she'd stuffed me into the dress. I'd never seen myself as anything other than plain, but with the fabric hugging my hips and squeezing my breasts into obscene mounds, even I had to admit I turned heads.

Breath catching in my throat, the spark of an idea began to grow. It was a terrible idea, risky in ways I didn't like, but anything had to be better than waiting for Arik to show up and drag me away.

Even tempting an unknown alpha.

My heart fluttered at the thought, a wave of fear rolling through me, leaving goosebumps in its wake. I didn't have much time left, a few days at most before my scent grew too ripe to go out in public, and I was running out of options. I'd gone to Sebastian because my brother had trusted him and I'd hoped I could as well, but any alpha not associated with the Purists who could keep me away from Arik for those few important days would do. I was terrified he'd do more than use me during my heat and I'd end up tied to him forever.

I backed until I could sit on the edge of my bed again, eyes locked on the scrap of red taunting me. If I was careful and went somewhere outside the Purist's territory, I might be able to find an alpha willing to tend me through my heat without claiming me. A shifter would be safer since there was no way they'd be connected to Arik. I could convince them to use the same precautions I had in the past, then stay with them through my cycle, and if Arik found me afterward, I could claim another alpha got to me first and wouldn't let me leave. Maybe I could even fake a call to him asking for help to escape before I was too lost in hormones.

He would be angry, but he wouldn't be able to do anything about it until my next heat rolled around. It might put my parents at risk if he came looking for me, but I could warn them. It would buy me a few more months, and all I could hope was that Arik would lose interest before then.

Chapter Four

Sebastian

Vincent's family hadn't moved, and it wasn't hard to find my way back to their apartment. I'd spent enough time there as a teen that it had become a second home. As tiny as the place was, it had still been better than what my drunk father had been able to provide.

I killed the engine of my bike as soon as I rolled into the parking lot, walking it up onto the sidewalk beside the stairs. There were a couple young guys lingering at the corner of the building who shot me a look, but the scent on the breeze told me they were beta. While the neighborhood was filled with hard-working middle class barely scraping by, it wasn't part of the ghettos where I'd worry about leaving my motorcycle unattended. It would take more balls than the kids had combined to risk pissing off an unknown alpha like me with my vest proclaiming I was part of one of the many gangs in the city.

Glancing up the stairwell, I wondered what to say. Vincent's parents had worked a lot, but they'd still known me. With my own mother dead before I could remember her, Mrs. Frost was the closest I'd ever had, and a pang stabbed through my chest at the thought of how long it had been since I'd stopped by. I'd thought I was doing them a favor by staying gone, but looking back, I could see I was only running from my own grief and the reminders they represented.

The echo of my boots on the stairs followed me up to the third floor. I still wasn't sure what to say by the time I was standing outside their door. The lingering scents on the landing assured me it was the right apartment, but I hesitated before raising my hand to knock. There were traces of other scents, including the sour stench of another alpha lurking beneath the sweetness that had risen from Brooke when she'd come to me.

A low growl escaped before I could stop it, claws extending from my fingertips as the thought of her with another male caused my fists to clench. Jealousy flared, igniting my instincts. Brooke was clearly unmated and wouldn't have come to me if there was a potential mate in the picture, but maybe she'd gone to another after my rejection.

I had to fight back the possessiveness that rose at that thought, the animal side of me struggling to break free. Brooke was too good for any of the assholes around here. She needed to be off at college getting an education to get her ass out of this city for good, not settling for what she could find here.

Still breathing heavy and trying to control my temper, I waited until I could push back the shift before rapping my knuckles on the door in front of me. Standing out here wondering what-if wasn't going to get me anywhere, but having them answer the door with me in were-form wouldn't help either, and it was getting late. I still had to open the shop in the morning and wanted to get home, but I needed to be sure Vincent's family was okay before I'd be able to sleep.

I heard soft footsteps on the other side of the door, causing my breath to catch in my throat as I waited. They stopped, but there was a long pause before the sound of the deadbolt sliding back reached my ears.

"Sebastian?"

Wide green eyes stared through the crack that had opened and threatened to swallow me whole. Brooke's mane of dark hair was pulled back in a crooked ponytail, a red mark on the side of her face showing I'd likely woken her, but she was still beautiful. Seeing her was a punch to the gut and I had to swallow over and over before I found my voice.

"Brooke."

Her name was almost a groan, and I had to peel my eyes away to search over her head for her parents as she opened the door wider. No sounds of movement came from behind her, only the drone of a television in the background, and the protectiveness I'd felt before knocking surged back to the fore.

I was stepping over the threshold before I made the conscious decision, forcing Brooke to move back or risk being pushed out of the way. Searching for signs of anyone else, my gaze landed back on her when I confirmed there was no one besides her in the apartment. She still clung to the door, staring up at me with her mouth hanging open but no words coming out.

"Where are your parents? Why are you alone?"

The questions came out sharp and held the edge of a growl, my wolf side surging inside me again, and I watched a shiver roll through her as her fingers tightened on the metal she held. The door might have been sturdy enough by most standards, but I knew if I'd wanted to, I could get through it, and the thought only pissed me off more. She wasn't safe in the apartment alone if another alpha caught her scent and decided he wanted in. Even a human alpha could get through in moments if he tried hard enough.

"They—They're at work."

She glanced toward the clock in the kitchen before her head turned back to me. She didn't raise her eyes above my chest, pink tongue slipping out to wet her lips and test my resolve.

"Mom should be home in an hour."

I choked back the growl that tried to escape. The poor girl didn't deserve my shitty attitude, especially when she was close to her cycle. I'd only cause her pain.

I fought to subdue my instincts and think clearly. Each breath I dragged in was torture, telling me exactly how close she was to tipping into heat, and I had to curse my cock as it throbbed against my zipper once again.

"Why are you opening the door for an alpha when you're home alone? Why are you opening it for anyone? It's not safe."

I couldn't stop the words from spilling out. She was putting herself in danger and the entire situation had me on edge. She may not be my mate, but she was still a member of the most precious dynamic, and the little sister of my best friend. I couldn't resist the need to protect her.

Those emerald eyes flashed up to mine before flinching away. My chest clenched at the loss, the green more vivid than any I'd ever seen.

"I-I thought you'd changed your mind."

The whisper was almost inaudible and the flush of color rising from the loose tank top she wore distracted me just long enough for her to dare another glance up. When what she'd said registered my cock gave an eager twitch and I had to clench my fists to keep from throwing her over my shoulder and carrying her off to do exactly what she was asking for. The girl didn't know how hard it was to control myself.

"I did not. I came to see how your family was doing since it's been a while."

Been a while. I almost rolled my eyes at myself, but my irritation was still too strong. I had to force the words through clenched teeth, and the way her shoulders drooped and her face fell almost broke me. The pain in her expression before she turned her head away sent a spear through my heart, the acrid scent of shame rising between us, and it was all I could do not to reach out and force her to face me again so I could assure her it wasn't because I didn't want her.

No, I definitely wanted her. Her lush little body was everything a man dreamed of. Rounded in all the right places, she had plenty of meat on her bones to grab ahold of as I plowed her. All omegas were desirable, but Brooke seemed to have an extra allure that had my teeth itching to dig into her slim neck.

I had to pull my thoughts away from that path as my erection threatened to rip right through my jeans. I knew I was leaking, my boxers clinging to me in a way that pinched and assured me walking down the stairs was going to be hell.

"My parents are fine. I'll let them know you stopped by."

Brooke refused to look up at me, mumbling to the carpet as she shifted more behind the door. It was a clear dismissal, and the alpha part of me hated it. I'd hurt the little omega, and now she was rejecting me.

Which was exactly what she should be doing. She never should have come to my shop making an insane request like she had. The area where my garage was located was not much better than the ghettos the Purists ran, and as close as she was to her cycle, she needed to be keeping herself locked away before she attracted the wrong kind of attention.

I forced myself to turn toward the landing outside, stepping through the doorway before looking back over my shoulder. I could see the wet track of a tear sparkling on her cheek, and once again I felt like I was letting my friend down. He may not be with me anymore, but he was still part of who I was, and only the prick of my claws digging into my palms kept me from making things worse.

"Be safe, Brooke. Vincent wouldn't want you tangled up with someone like me. He wanted you to do better."

The soft explanation was all I had to offer. She shut the door between us without another word, turning the lock as soon as it closed. My skin shivered with the urge to shift to my wolf and mark the area with my scent as a warning to other alphas. The human side of me knew the idea was barbaric, but the animal part insisted it was necessary to keep Brooke safe.

I hesitated outside the door until I heard Brooke's footsteps fading away into the apartment before I dragged my feet to the stairs. My legs were dead weights, instincts screaming I was making a mistake leaving the omega unprotected, but I had no other choice. I couldn't wait around outside her apartment to be sure she didn't leave, even if that was what I wanted to do.

My bike was where I left it when I made it back down to the ground floor, the kids still lingering at the corner of the building. I gave them a nod when they glanced my way as I swung a leg over the saddle before my eyes were pulled up to the third-floor window. Soft light shone through the blinds in the front room, my thoughts still caught on Brooke inside alone. There had been pain in her emerald eyes from my rejection, but there was something else as well. A sense of desperation that pulled at the alpha in me to protect her, but from what?

I walked the motorcycle backwards off the sidewalk, moving into a dark corner of the parking lot where I could keep my eye on the window and the base of the stairwell. Brooke had been right about her mother returning within an hour, and I watched as Mrs. Frost made her way up the first few steps. There was more grey in her hair than I remembered, and it hit home how long it had been since Vincent's funeral. Years had passed without me being brave enough to mend the rift I'd created. I'd lost myself in working and trying to make the dream we'd had a reality, but even now after I had, it still felt empty without my friend there to share it.

Rolling out into the street, I kicked the bike to life. I'd planned to go straight home but there was too much on my mind, so I let the wind try to chase away the pair of wide green eyes haunting me as I road through the city. It didn't work, and eventually I gave up, falling into bed only to dream about what I wanted to do to a certain little omega I shouldn't touch.

Tempting A Knight

Chapter Five

Brooke

Usually, I only had to deal with Arik once or twice a week, but unfortunately for me he'd apparently decided I needed to be checked daily now. He had me pinned behind the counter, uncaring that he wasn't supposed to be back there.

"I think I should pick you up tonight. We could go ahead and get you prepared for what's coming."

My racing heart stuttered as what he said penetrated. Jerking my gaze up to his, horror sent a wave of ice through my veins. There was no way I kept the terror off my face, but he was too busy staring at my heaving breasts to notice. He didn't possibly mean to prepare me in the way that a considerate alpha would.

"Y-you can't. M-my parents are expecting me tonight."

They wouldn't be home, but my brain couldn't supply any other excuse while most of it was screaming in panic. I knew I was pushing things too close since the other alphas who came in had showed signs of scenting me, but I needed all the hours I could get before my heat hit and I wasn't able to work. I hadn't expected Arik to corner me again and try to take me early.

"So?"

His blunt response ripped right through my flimsy reasoning.

"I-I promised to have dinner with them before my cycle begins. It's not really time yet, and the beginning is always rough. Don't you want to wait until I'm past the… fussing?"

Arik's brow wrinkled as he finally raised his eyes to mine. It was clear he cared nothing about the beginning stages of an omega's cycle, when a mate, or any decent alpha, would help prepare the nest an omega needed to feel secure.

"You're a nester?"

The disgust in his voice was thick, and the question showed how little he truly knew about omegas. All omegas built nests to feel safe when they were at their most vulnerable, but I'd heard he was the type to deny the need. He didn't care about the trauma it could cause.

Straightening, Arik let his gaze wander over me again. I didn't respond, breath held as I waited to see if the excuse would work to buy me a little more time.

"Yeah, just call me when you're past all that shit. I don't have time for the whining and nitpicking."

Dragging my eyes from his face, I let myself draw in a ragged breath of relief. I didn't see the hand extending toward my hair, or expect the sudden tug as he pulled my head back. Scalp protesting as his other arm banded around to crush me to him, his lips descended on mine as they parted to release a cry of pain.

I clawed at his chest without thought as he thrust his tongue into my mouth. Slimy and unusually cold, he tasted like old tobacco, alcohol, and something bitter as he invaded. I couldn't stop my protests despite the muffling of his lips, but Arik either didn't notice, or didn't care. It took every bit of my strength to keep the tears at bay as he plundered my mouth and ignored my struggles.

I retched as he released me, stumbling back into the shelf behind me, but Arik only chuckled. He took my chin in his hand before I could get oriented, forcing my eyes up to his as I blinked to keep the moisture away.

"Don't forget to call. If I feel like it's been too long I'll come pay you a visit, and we wouldn't want Mommy and Daddy to get in the way, now would we?"

The whimper that escaped was beyond my control, my entire body shuddering in revulsion. I had no choice but to give a small nod, resisting the urge to sniffle as his cruel smirk was aimed at my upturned face.

A honk from outside the shop drew his attention and he finally released me, turning to stride around the counter. He paused before walking through the door, pinning that soulless gaze back on me. Even after taking an interest in me, Arik hadn't shown any sign of knowing I was Vincent's sister, but his next words shattered that delusion.

"Your parents already lost one child who didn't know his place and consorted with the wrong people. Make sure you know where you belong when I come for you, so they don't lose anyone else."

My throat closed as the door swung shut behind him, eyes clenching to hold back the flood that threatened to come. My pulse pounded in my head, the blood rushing in my ears drowning out the sounds of the cars on the street outside. I'd been a fool to think Arik hadn't checked into who I was, even if he hadn't recognized me at first.

Despair filled me as any hope I had of avoiding what he wanted was crushed beneath the weight of it. Even if I found some random alpha to hide me away during my heat, I'd be leaving my parents unprotected when Arik came looking for me. He wasn't the type to take being thwarted well, and I knew he had no qualms punishing anyone he thought was involved in taking away something he wanted.

My knees hit the tile floor, the counter giving me a sense of seclusion despite the windows lining the font of the building. Unable to hold them back any longer, tears tracked down my cheeks to drip onto my knees as the fear finally won. I was scared to give in to Arik, especially with him knowing I was Vincent's sister.

Yet I was scared to leave my parents to answer for me avoiding him as well.

Images of coming home to a bloody apartment filled my mind, the mangled bodies of my family so vivid in my head I could almost scent the copper in the air.

And what he'd do to me once he found me would be twice as bad. I'd wish for death long before it came. I had seen it happen.

The fear.

The bruises.

The vacant stare.

The wasting away as the mind shut down in an attempt to protect itself.

Arik wasn't one to lock away the women he abused. No, he dragged them out, smirking and bragging about how he'd 'broken them in' and turned them into 'proper women who knew their place'.

He'd broken them for sure. One after another, going back for as long as anyone I talked to could remember. A few managed to hold themselves together long enough for him to lose interest and move on to his next target, but they all bore the scars.

Sobs shook me as I knelt behind the counter until I'd finally cried myself out. By the time another customer entered the store I'd been reduced to numbness.

Wiping my face, I pretended to adjust things on the shelf beside me before forcing myself to my feet and focusing on my job. It seemed pointless to be worried about losing it, but it was all I had to cling to. It was supposed to be what saved me from this city and this life, buying me a way into a life as far away as I could afford, but after four years of working and trying to save, I still had little to show for it. The cost of living kept rising while wages stayed the same, and half my checks went to my parents so we could keep our home and put food on the table.

Pulling my thoughts away from the well-worn worries, I pasted on the best smile I could manage and finished my shift with as little thinking as possible, but the walk home left me with nothing to distract myself. Nothing, except the mass of muscle that had forced its way into my apartment the previous night before my mother returned from work.

Sebastian had denied me twice, yet it was impossible to keep him out of my head. I'd had a crush on him back when he was a teenager, but seeing the alpha he'd grown into made him more irresistible. Just thinking of his dark eyes locked on me sent a pulse of desire through my core that couldn't be ignored, yet he'd been clear he wasn't interested in helping me.

But his actions raised questions. It seemed odd for him to come by the apartment after so long, and the anger once he realized I was alone had been obvious.

Just as obvious as the bulge in his jeans when my gaze had dropped from his.

My breath caught in my throat as I remembered the size of the outline. It had taken my stunned brain a moment to realize what I was staring at, and even once I had I hadn't been able to pull my gaze away. Slick dampened my panties again at the memory and my stomach spasmed in a reminder that I didn't have much time until I'd need what he had. Until I'd cry and beg for an alpha's knot, even if it was an alpha I despised.

Tempting A Knight

Once again, I circled around to the debate between giving in or protecting myself. Sebastian could have other members of the Hell's Knights protect my parents when Arik came looking for me, but without that option I wasn't sure I could leave them to face Arik. The only other thing I could think of was to send them away during my heat as well, but where would they go? They still had to work and had no money to spare for hotels.

I gritted my teeth as I stomped up the stairs toward my front door. It was ridiculous that I even had to worry about this, but I couldn't deny that I didn't have any other options. I was sick of feeling like a trapped mouse waiting for the cat to pounce.

Tossing my things on my bed, I turned to the closet to change out of my work clothes. Stripped down to my underwear, the little red dress in the back of the closet caught my attention once again. The idea to tempt a strange alpha into tending me held a lot of risks, but it was still the only one I could come up with that didn't leave me a sitting duck.

My eyes moved up to the box at the top of my closet. The one stuffed with every bit of money I'd saved over the years. I knew it was stupid to keep cash in the house when it could be broken into and stolen, but a part of me had never trusted letting it out of my control. I wanted it where I could see it and assure myself it was still there. Seeing numbers on a screen just wasn't the same.

I knew exactly how much was in the box. I kept a running tally, adding to it from each check. I'd only had to pull cash out the one time our toilet had broken and the landlord refused to fix it, claiming it was due to our neglect. There was more than enough for me to book a room for my parents somewhere in the city for a few days. They'd resist, but I was sure I could convince them to go if they knew who it was that would come looking for me.

My hand reached for the dress before I'd made the conscious decision to go through with the idea. The first step was finding an alpha who didn't know Arik had laid claim to having me, that I felt safe enough with to risk going into heat. Once that was accomplished I'd worry about convincing my mother to take the money and leave the apartment until I returned. Dad would follow her lead.

I hoped I had enough time. I was already sweaty even though I knew the house was cool, and the ache in my lower back wasn't from being on my feet all day.

I shimmied and tugged my way into the dress, chest heaving by the time I had it pulled up to cover my breasts. They strained the fabric, threatening to spill over at any moment, but there wasn't anything I could do to fix it. Nothing else in my closet would accomplish what I wanted to do.

Swiping on a light coat of makeup I usually didn't bother with, I took my hair down from the ponytail I wore to work, letting the dark mass fall around my shoulders. Pulling some of it to the front helped tone down the obviousness of the cleavage created by the tight dress, but there was nothing I could do about the way it clung to my hips or stopped indecently short of mid-thigh.

Tempting A Knight

Scrutinizing myself in the mirror, my critical eye screamed I'd be giving every male the wrong impression, but I rationalized that it was the impression I wanted at the moment. I may not be soliciting them for money, but the alphas still had something I wanted in exchange for what the dress promised. My scent would only assure them it was a guarantee, and I worried for a moment that I may end up with more than I bargained for.

I chewed on my lower lip as I stared at myself, wondering if it was too much. Alphas could get rowdy over an omega in heat, and I wasn't trying to start fights. My heat could come on in a rush and cause major problems. I'd have to be careful where I chose to go to avoid too large of a crowd.

Shaking my head, I pushed the worries aside. I'd take the car to be sure I had a way to leave when I was ready, and so I wouldn't have to deal with people on the buses. Most bars had a bouncer or someone who knew how to handle trouble, and I'd have to trust in that to keep things from getting out of hand.

I grabbed my purse from the bed and dug out my phone, trying to decide where to go. The clubs deeper in the city would be too crowded, and anything close-by was likely to have someone in it that knew Arik. The last thing I wanted was him showing up.

Pulling up a map, my eyes zeroed in on the last place I'd gotten directions to. Sebastian's garage was a bit of a drive, but that also meant the area was outside the territory claimed by the Purists. It wasn't the best area, mostly frequented by the shifter community. Not that I had the same prejudice against them as Arik's gang, but they tended to be larger and stronger than human alphas, and I wasn't sure I could handle one if things got out of hand. Despite the shiver it sent down my spine, I knew nowhere I was likely to go would be any better.

Biting my lip again, I zoomed in on the road I'd taken to his garage. I'd passed a couple bars between here and there, and one of them would have to do. It was a Thursday night and hopefully wouldn't be too busy, but I also didn't want a bar that was almost empty. It took a little swiping, but I finally settled on one that seemed large enough to give me options without being crowded.

My eyes caught the time as I tapped on the location to get directions. It was later than I'd realized, and while my mother wouldn't be home in time to stop my drastic plan, I also didn't want her to worry if she returned and I was still gone.

Shooting her a vague text about going out and knowing she wouldn't see it until after her shift was over, I tossed my phone back into my purse and pulled the strap over my head. I didn't own any heels, so the black flats I'd gotten for my birthday two years before would have to do. After debating on a jacket, I decided it was too warm to bother with it, especially when it would add to the things I'd need to keep track of.

My heart was pounding as I locked the front door and made my way down to the car. All of us shared it since my father's old truck had broken down, but we didn't use it often to save on the cost of gas. I worked close enough to walk when the weather was decent, and my mom and dad both took the train so they didn't have to worry about parking in the city. While the bar I was going to was on a bus route, using it would leave me at the mercy of the bus schedule and add an hour to my trip each way.

Not to mention having to wait at stops in the dark in a skimpy dress.

Sliding behind the wheel, I sucked in a deep breath and squared my shoulders. What I was doing was risky, but it was the only option I had left, and I was almost out of time.

Leann Ryans

Chapter Six

Sebastian

By the time I finished up the last vehicle on the schedule for the day it was well past dusk. I usually didn't have to stay after closing time to finish up, but the customer was a friend, and I knew Bill needed his truck to get to work in the morning.

It didn't hurt that focusing on the problem of fixing the old rust bucket also helped keep a certain omega from my thoughts.

I'd tossed and turned every night, waking with an aching erection that refused to abate even after spilling myself in the shower before coming to the garage. I hadn't been able to keep thoughts of her out of my head until the truck was hauled in and old Bill begged me to do what I could. Bikes may have been my specialty, but regular cars and trucks were the staple that paid the bills.

Wiping my hands on a dirty rag, I slammed the hood with a creak of old hinges. I was amazed the thing still ran at all and wasn't surprised none of the younger mechanics had known how to fix a carburetor. Manufacturers had stopped making cars with them for a reason.

"It's all done. You're good to go."

The old man sitting on a chair in the corner startled from his doze. I didn't know how Bill had slept through my cursing and the noise of fixing the truck, but he'd been snoring away in the corner for a couple hours. Offering me a smile sunken in wrinkles as he reached for my hand, he shook it before turning to eye his old truck.

"You always have worked miracles on this baby, but I thought she was a goner this time."

Bill had been a friend of my father's when I was a kid. In truth he'd been more of a father than the man who shared my blood, and he'd been the first to let me and Vincent help when he worked on his truck.

The very same one sitting in front of me, stirring up old memories. It seemed the world was determined to remind me of the past.

Watery brown eyes turned back to me as I ignored the tremor in the man's hand. At his age he should have been resting comfortably at home, not worrying about how he'd make it to work each day so he could pay the bills, but less and less people were able to retire these days. Especially in the city.

"What do I owe you?"

His gaze moved to the clock over my shoulder, and I knew he was trying to figure up how much the repair was going to cost. I had a flat hourly fee that was added to the cost of supplies for most work, and after spending the entire afternoon and evening on the truck, he'd be looking at a bill higher than he likely made in a month if I charged him full price.

"It's on the house."

Bill's brow furrowed as the grip on my hand tightened. I knew he didn't have the money to cover the repair, but he'd also argue with me about it all night if I didn't head him off.

"I had all the parts I needed collecting dust in the back, and it kept me busy. She was what got me on the path that led to this shop, so I owe you for all of it. I'm just happy I could get her running again. That's enough for me."

Bushy white brows rose again as Bill's lips ticked up in the corner.

"Kept you busy? Girl trouble?"

I huffed and dropped Bill's hand. He started chuckling as I stepped away to clean up my tools and put them back where they belonged. If it was anyone else, they'd have backed off when a growl left my chest, but Bill knew me too well and ignored my bluster.

"She must be special to have you all worked up. An omega I'd guess."

My eyes snapped to him at the word omega, but I forced them away again. His chuckling continued as he crossed to the driver's side of the truck and the door creaked open for him to get in.

"Omegas are special, boy. Don't try to force her into anything she doesn't want."

I dropped the last wrench into its place in the drawer of my workbench, turning back to watch as Bill climbed into his seat.

"I'm not trying to force her into anything," I grumbled.

For an old man his ears were still sharp, and a grin split his wrinkled face.

"Then you're really in trouble. I'll have Martha bring you over some lunch tomorrow."

His door slammed before I could respond. Martha's cooking was terrible, but I knew Bill meant well. Someone at the garage would be desperate enough to eat it.

Raising my hand, I gave him a wave as he backed out, watching his headlights swing onto the road as I rolled the garage door shut. Flipping off the lights and making sure my office was locked, I made my way out of the shop and headed for my bike, but I didn't want to go home. There was nothing there to keep me occupied, and despite working late, I wasn't tired yet.

Knowing most of the guys would have headed to The Hangout after they got off work, I kicked the engine to life and pointed the bike in that direction. As far as bars went it was a decent place, and we'd claimed it as ours years ago when the club first started to grow.

I'd never meant to create a motorcycle club, or biker gang as many referred to us. It started out as a few single alphas who worked together and enjoyed riding our bikes together once we were done. As the garage's reputation grew, so did our numbers, and somehow they all looked to me when we came across shit that didn't sit right.

Like one of the other gangs trying to force people out of their homes to take over the property, or drugs being sold on school grounds. Eventually we became known as Hell's Knights, since everyone here agreed we lived in Hell, and the locals came to us when there were issues that couldn't be handled through other channels. We were their knights in... fairly dented and dirty armor. Good cops were few and far between on the fringes of an overpopulated city, but people knew they could count on us to help.

They also knew we could be found at The Hangout most nights, and I groaned as the parking lot came into view. It was a Thursday night and shouldn't have been too busy, but music and people spilled out the door as I rode by to park my bike beside the others already in the lot. Something was going on to have the crowd boisterous enough for me to hear them outside, and I only hoped it wasn't any of my guys getting into trouble. They were mostly well behaved, but every once in a while we had someone with the Purist mindset stumble in and realize what we were.

Swinging my leg over the saddle, I sighed as I strode toward the doors and prepared for whatever was happening inside. I generally let the guys do what they wanted and stayed out of their business unless it affected the entire group, but pissing off the owner of our favorite spot for wrecking his bar was one of those things where I'd step in if I had to.

Leann Ryans

The dim lights and pounding music hit me as soon as I walked inside. It took a moment to adjust so I could look around, but it didn't take long to see the center of the commotion was by the bar. There were too many people between me and whatever it was for me to tell what was going on, but at least it didn't appear to be violent.

Yet.

Most of the guys were mine or regular patrons, but I noticed a few new faces as I waded through. It took a few elbows and growled threats to force my way to the bar, but the moment I did I knew exactly what the issue was.

I saw red.

A slinky red dress clinging to a set of breasts and hips that had my mouth watering, to be exact. I didn't need to see those large green eyes to know who it was stealing all the attention and causing the pack gathered at her back to slather like a bunch of prepubescent whelps. I just didn't know what the hell she was thinking coming here.

Dressed like *that*.

A snarl surged from me before I could stop it, catching the attention of every male pressing in around her. Those closest to me stepped back even as a few returned my growl. Brooke didn't get the chance to turn before my hand was tangled in her hair, chest pressed to her side as she sat on the barstool chatting to the alpha on her right.

No one but me was close enough to hear her whimper or feel the way her body shuddered. She tried to look for who was holding her, but I didn't give her enough slack, pulling her head back as I leaned down to her ear.

"What the fuck do you think you're doing?"

I never took my eyes off the male across from me, his lips pulling back to bare his growing canines as I manhandled Brooke further from him. The other men beside me were ones I knew, men I'd trusted to watch my back when we went up against other gangs, but this one was a stranger and clearly didn't know he should back the fuck off before I really got pissed.

My growl deepened as Brooke's scent filled my lungs and she whimpered again. She was practically at the peak of her heat, and I had no idea why she was out in public instead of staying home like the good girl she was.

"Sebastian!"

Her squeak was laced with pain but the possessiveness flooding my veins didn't care that I was hurting her when there was a rival so close. Her pheromones called to my instincts, pulling forward my wolf and my baser nature. The female was too close to her estrous, and there were other males nearby. The only thing that mattered was getting her away where I could have her to myself.

"Sebastian, please!"

Her plea brought back a bit of sense as her blunt nails dug into my arm, until the other male reached out to grab her wrist and keep me from pulling her off the stool. Another snarl ripped from my throat, my free hand shooting forward to take a similar grip on his wrist. I felt the bones grind under my palm, knowing it hurt though he kept it from showing. Most of the men around us had backed away, but Carl, the man I considered my second and who helped me run the garage, took hold of the stranger's opposite arm when he went to reach for where I held him.

"I was here first. She was talking to *me*."

The alpha's protest was pathetic, and my lip curled up in derision, showing my own canines as I fought to keep my claws from extending and hurting Brooke.

"I don't give a fuck. Get your hand off her."

"She's not claimed."

Brooke wiggled between us, her fingers trying to ease the hold I had on her dark hair, but my focus was still centered on the threat on her other side. The man opened his mouth to say something else, but Carl leaned in, whispering in the man's ear words I didn't catch over the music. His jaw snapped shut but it was another moment before he released Brooke's wrist and jerked from my hold. I let him go, eyes still locked on him as he took two steps back and dropped his arms to his sides.

"Pussy isn't worth it, even an omega's. Go fuck yourselves."

The guy spat on the floor next to Brooke's chair before turning away to shove through the men still ringing us. They'd given us space but were there watching, waiting to see what would happen. When my gaze swung to them, the ones who knew me found other things to turn their attention to, the ones who didn't following their lead when they realized the show was over.

Without releasing my hold on her hair, I dragged Brooke off the barstool. Her hands tugged on my wrist, protests flowing from her mouth that I ignored as I marched her through the bar. She had to stumble along beside me, bent over and staring at the ground as she fought my hold, but I was too pissed to care how uncomfortable it was for her. Once again, I'd found her putting herself in danger.

When had she grown so stupid?

Curses dropping from my lips as I slammed open the door and stepped out into the night, her sobs finally penetrated the fog in my head. Sucking in the cool night air, I stopped beside the wall and pulled her upright before releasing my hold, reigning in my wolf who wanted nothing more than to force the omega's submission here and now. She tried to dart away but I didn't let her, crowding her against the side of the building and pinning her in with my arms. The wood siding flexed under my fingers, old paint flaking away as my claws burst free and raked it. I let it take the brunt of the anger still coursing through me as I sucked in one deep breath after another filled with her scent, the mix of fear and arousal doing nothing to calm me.

"You still haven't answered."

The words came out so rough I almost couldn't understand myself. Brooke's head was down, hair almost black in the moonlight, hiding her face from my view. I could smell the salt on her cheeks from tears, but there was no way I was letting her get away without telling me what she was doing here.

The little omega remained silent, her trembling visible despite the lack of lighting where we stood. Part of me raged at her defying my demand but I knew growling at her wasn't going to get what I wanted. Blowing out another breath, I forced my heart to slow its angry pace as I rolled my neck and dropped my arms so I wasn't hunched over her.

"What are you doing here, Brooke?"

Her chest rose on a shaky breath, breasts threatening to spill over the scandalous top. The sight stole my attention until her chin lifted and moonlight sparkled off emeralds. Dragging my gaze up to hers, I waited, but she still refused to speak.

Sighing, I took a step back and crossed my arms over my chest, doing my best to look bored while I fought with the urge to take her over my knee and spank the answer out of her. The mulish look she was giving me reminded me of nothing more than her brother when he'd decided to be stubborn about something, and eventually my patience wore out.

"Is this about what you came to me for? Is that why you're here dressed like a cheap whore?"

A flash of pain crossed her face, painted lips popping open in a shocked O before she snapped her jaw shut again. A spike of guilt pierced my gut before her expression turned angry and my ebbing fury returned despite her beauty.

Or perhaps because of it.

"You refused me, so of course I need to find someone else!"

Her hiss made my fists clench, the confirmation that she'd been looking for another alpha drowning out everything else. I knew there was no reason to be so angry over what she was doing, unclaimed omegas did it all the time, but a part of me couldn't stand the idea of her being with another alpha. With any other man. I couldn't stop myself from lurching toward her again, knuckles slamming into the wall at her back as fur popped out along my arms, bones creaking as they tried to shift, and I leaned down to be eye level with her.

"No, you don't need to find someone else. You need to go home and lock yourself in your room until your heat's over like the innocent girl you are. You're going to cause a riot!"

Leann Ryans

Chapter Seven

Brooke

His roar made me flinch, but no matter how scary he seemed, I knew Sebastian wouldn't really hurt me. Nothing more than my pride anyway.

"I can't! He'll find me there, and he'll hurt Mom and Dad if I don't go with him!"

The words escaped before I could stop them, tears filling my eyes again and threatening to spill over. His remark about my dress hurt, but the fear of Arik was what had me on the verge of crying.

Sebastian pulled back but I kept my eyes level with his chest instead of looking up to follow his.

He didn't understand.
He couldn't.

As an alpha he was on top, nothing threatened him, while my omega dynamic left me at the bottom of the heap, weak and naturally submissive. I could only resist for so long before biology took over and made me give in when Arik came for me. I wouldn't have a choice.

"Who?"

Sebastian's voice rumbled over my head, the threat in it sending a pulse between my legs. I was shamefully damp after his face-off with the other alpha inside, despite Sebastian's rough treatment. The presence of so many virile males had driven me closer to true heat, and hormones were trying to take over. Being the center of attention at the bar had been uncomfortable, but the men had mostly been careful about touching me as they crowded closer. There had been an odd sense of disappointment until Sebastian arrived.

"Who will find you?"

I closed my eyes and let my shoulders slump as the last of the anger drained from me. I didn't have the energy to sustain it.

"Arik. He wants to—"

My voice caught on the lump rising in my throat, threatening to suffocate me if I said the words. I felt the warmth of Sebastian's body move away but kept my eyes shut. His scent still surrounded me, leather, and grease, and his natural musk. A hint of smoke and fur. Somehow it was both reassuring and stimulating at the same time, and I swallowed to force out the rest.

"He wants me during my cycle."

It was so quiet I almost thought Sebastian hadn't heard me until a low growl filled the space between us.

"You mean Arik from the Purists? The man who killed Vincent; who murdered your brother?"

Sebastian's voice had gone hard and cold despite the noise reverberating from his chest. I opened my eyes to look up at him, and the fury burning in his gaze stole my breath. I remembered him blaming Arik at Vincent's funeral, but nothing could be proven. The cops wouldn't look into the death of a gang member, and no one involved with the Purists would speak out against another, and definitely not to a shifter. I didn't know if Arik had killed my brother himself, or simply had a hand in it, but it was one of the reasons I'd remembered who he was when he showed up that first day.

Unable to find my voice, I dipped my chin in confirmation. Sebastian had crossed his arms over his chest, and I could see the way his fingers bit into his biceps as his jaw flexed. His nails had become black and pointed, sticking out past his fingertips and digging into his flesh beneath the edge of his shirtsleeve.

"How do you know Arik?"

His tone had dropped a few more degrees, sending a shiver through me that cooled what was left of the reaction to two males fighting over me. I had to swallow twice before I could speak.

"He came into where I work. Realized what I am. He's been checking on me ever since, waiting for my cycle. He… He knows where I live. I didn't think he knew who I was, but he does."

A whisper was all I could manage. Sebastian remained frozen even after I stopped, eyes locked on mine. Only the flare of his nostrils and the rise and fall of his chest gave away that he was flesh and blood.

My lip trembled, more words spilling out since I'd already begun, but I couldn't complete the thought.

"I don't want… Don't want him to…"

Take me. Touch me. Use me. Hurt me.

It all jumbled together as my vision swam. I'd tried to be strong, to find another way, but I could only take so much. I couldn't let my parents be hurt, either by Arik or by having to bury another child. It was looking as though I had no choice but to give myself to the man I hated.

Raising my hands to wipe the tears away, I didn't see Sebastian move closer again. Strong arms wrapped around me, a large hand cupping the back of my head to press my cheek to a warm chest. My automatic reaction was to stiffen against him, but a moment later the softest noise vibrated into me, melting my bones.

Sebastian was purring.

The sound turned my thoughts hazy, rekindling the warmth in my belly as stress drained away. My hands turned to cling to his shirt as I buried my face in him, dragging his scent deeper into my lungs. He murmured something into my hair, but I didn't catch what it was, and I didn't want to pull away enough to ask. Whimpering as his arms loosened, I tightened my hold on him, but he only shifted his grip to my hair once again, tipping my head back so I had to look up at him.

"How did you get here?"

It took a moment for my addled brain to make sense of what he was asking. Brow furrowed, I moved my eyes toward the edge of the parking lot where I'd left the car.

Tempting A Knight

"I drove, but my keys are in my purse."

I hadn't realized until then that I hadn't grabbed it when he dragged me out of the bar, and the worry that flooded my veins cleared the last of the haze from his purr. I tried to pull away to head back to the door, but Sebastian's arms only tightened around me.

"I'll get it. It's not safe for you in there."

Looking back up into his dark eyes, it was hard to tell what he was thinking. Different emotions flashed across his face before his cool façade settled back into place.

Freeing one arm from around me, he pulled a phone from his pocket and pressed a button before raising it to his ear. It must have rung only once before whoever he was calling answered, because in seconds he was rumbling off orders.

"Brooke left her purse at the bar, get it and bring it out to me. Tell Tim to come too, I have a job for you."

He hung up and stuffed the phone back in the pocket of the leather vest he wore over his t-shirt, his eyes never leaving mine. Without light to differentiate the deep brown of his irises from the pupil, his eyes looked solid black, and another shiver rolled down my spine.

"Same car you drove to my shop?"

I nodded, not sure why he was asking. He finally released me as the door of the bar opened, taking a step back and scanning the parking lot before turning his attention to the two men who emerged. I recognized them, though neither had been the men to crowd close and talk to me. They both wore a vest that matched

Sebastian's, and I realized it must have something to do with their gang.

The slightly smaller blonde had my purse in his hand, and Sebastian moved between us when he held it out, taking it himself. I opened my mouth to protest when he dug inside, but the words died when he pulled out my keys.

"Jason, drive the white Jetta to the Cypress Apartments and park it in front of building 520. Hang around there with Tim and keep an eye on things. Make sure no Purists start poking around. If they do, call Carl for backup."

The blonde he called Jason grimaced but nodded, looking around the lot until he spotted my car. He strode toward it while the other turned to the row of motorcycles lining the front of the bar. I was about to ask what was going on when Sebastian returned his focus to me, pulling my phone out of my purse and thrusting it at me.

"Let your parents know you're safe but not coming home until your heat is over. You've already tipped over."

My eyes widened as my fingers fumbled the phone. I finally tore my gaze away from his when the rumble of an engine startled me.

Too scared to question him least he burst the bubble of hope growing in my chest, I rushed to do what he said. I sent another message to my mother, ignoring her response from earlier and contradicting what I'd sent her before. I knew it would cause questions, but I didn't have the time to explain.

I angled the phone toward Sebastian when he craned his head to be sure I'd done as I was told. Grunting in response, he took my phone back and crammed it into my purse, wedging the whole thing under his arm as he took hold of my wrist. Being dragged behind him was less uncomfortable this time, though he didn't bother to shorten his strides any more than he had the first time, and I didn't realize where he was pulling me until we stopped beside the last motorcycle in the line.

"Oh. Oh, no."

I shook my head, hands raising to fend off even the idea of straddling that beast. Sleek black body and chrome handles, it shone under the moonlight and the glow spilling from the bar. It was all power and beauty, and just as deadly looking as the alpha by my side. I'd never understood how someone could trust their safety to something that left them so exposed, and there was no way I was getting on that bike.

Sebastian turned to look at me with a brow raised. I could see his lips twitching like he wanted to laugh as I took a step back, but he managed to resist, crossing his arms over his chest again with a helmet dangling from his fingertips.

"You'd trust me to tend you through your heat, but not to give you a ride on my bike?"

I could hear the amusement in his voice and had to admit he had a point. The worst he could do in one case was wreck, and possibly maim or kill me, while he could do the same during my heat as well as claim and bond me, tying me to him for the rest of my life and taking away any thought of freedom. Dying might seem like the worst option, but I'd seen what could happen when there was a bad bond. It was a living death, the omega becoming nothing but a warped shell.

But for some reason, Sebastian claiming me didn't seem like such a bad thing, despite not knowing him well. Being bonded to Arik would have been torture, something worth dying to prevent, but although Sebastian was practically a stranger, I was sure he'd never hurt me.

I still wasn't getting on that bike.

Eyes darting around as I searched for a valid excuse, my gaze landed on my exposed legs extending from beneath the scrap of red fabric barely keeping me decent.

"I'm in a dress. I can't…"

I held my hands open next to my thighs before waving one at the seat of his bike. A sneak peek up showed Sebastian's eyes darkening as they focused on the tiny skirt before sliding down my pale legs.

"I'll be in front of you. No one will see anything."

The timbre of his voice had dropped again, some blend between purr and growl lining the words and sending sparks down my spine.

I was getting hot, and tiny cramps were fluttering to life in my belly.

Tongue darting out to wet my lips, I started to shake my head again, but he turned away from me, swinging a leg over the seat of the bike.

"C'mon Brooke. This is the only way you're getting out of here. Unless you want to go back inside and find someone not connected to Hell's Knights to give you a ride."

The sudden chill in his tone had me shivering as he locked those dark eyes on mine. He wore the same blank mask he'd had at the garage, as if he couldn't care less either way, but I could feel the tension between us. The danger in believing that offer.

My breaths came in short gasps, chest straining the crimson fabric stretched across it, the aggression in the air telling me he wouldn't really let me go back inside. For better or worse, I'd caught Sebastian's attention, and I doubted the alpha in him would let me take more than a step away before he'd be on me again.

My core clenched, lower stomach tensing around the ball of pain and need growing inside. I'd been too close to my heat to do this, to leave the house, and I was running out of time before things got a lot worse. He seemed to be offering what I'd come to him for, and despite everything, I didn't want him to change his mind. I'd had a crush on him since I was a girl, and regardless of the shitty circumstances that drove me to him, the idea of being with him, even if only for my heat, was thrilling.

I wanted him. I wanted him to want *me*.

Scooting one foot forward I licked my lips again.

"My parents—"

"I've got it covered," he interrupted before I could get any further.

It wasn't much, but I trusted him. Hell's Knights were known to be a group who helped people, only going after those who were doing others wrong, and since Sebastian was the one who led them, that meant he had to be good beneath it all.

Giving a short nod I shuffled closer. I could feel warmth radiating from the metal, or maybe it was from the man. Or maybe it was just my heat rising higher as I approached a virile male.

"And me?"

Tremors wracked my body as I forced myself to hold his gaze. Omegas were meant to submit. To bow down and accept what others did with us. I was willing to submit to Sebastian, eager for it even, if the wetness between my thighs was any indication, but I needed to be sure I wasn't reading things wrong. He'd already rejected me twice.

"I've got you."

The words were low.

Husky.

Hungry.

My core spasmed as need exploded in my belly. My entire body shuddered as my blood turned molten. If I waited any longer I wasn't going to be capable of resisting the things suddenly racing through my mind, and I wasn't one for exhibitionism, so with one hand on his shoulder to keep myself steady, I swung my leg over the back of the bike.

Sebastian's big hands curled around each thigh just above my knee, callouses sending crackles of sensation across my flesh as he pulled them up until my feet rested on the pegs. My legs were splayed wide around his hips, my dress riding dangerously high. Anyone close enough to look would see the scrap of drenched fabric covering my core.

Twisting, he handed me the helmet, watching as I put it on before reaching back with one hand to tighten the strap.

"Arms around me and don't let go. It's a short ride to my place, and I'll go slow for you."

I gave a quick nod, sliding my arms under his when he turned to face forward again. When the engine vibrated to life under us with a roar, I couldn't help the squeak that escaped, or the way I clung to Sebastian's muscled form. As distracting as his scent was right from the source, and the feel of his muscles playing under his clothing, the fear flooding my system battled my encroaching heat to dominate my thoughts, and I was no longer sure any of this was such a good idea.

Leann Ryans

Chapter Eight

Sebastian

This was such a bad idea.

But I really didn't care anymore.

Fury still burned in my chest at the thought of Arik trying to take Brooke. That murderous bastard shouldn't be breathing, much less thinking of laying a hand on my best friend's sister.

Brooke said he knew who she was, so trying to force her into giving him her heat had to be part of some sick, twisted game. That he threatened her family to get her to comply only confirmed he was still the same disgusting fuck he'd been when Vincent died.

Fingers tightening on the handle grips, I shoved all that aside to back my bike out of its spot. Brooke clung to me as if she feared for her life, and I was determined not to scare her any further. She'd been through enough, and the amount of trust she'd already shown me was staggering. I didn't know if I deserved any of it, but in this one thing, riding a motorcycle, I knew I could show her there was nothing to fear. They were just as safe as any other vehicle when proper precautions were taken.

We weren't going to talk about the reckless shit I did on my own.

Easing out of the parking lot, I took the turn wide, keeping the throttle back and going at a cautious pace. I could feel her trembling against me, her slim thighs squeezing my hips for all she was worth as her fingers dug into my belly. Despite her being behind me with the air blowing her scent away, I could still smell her rising heat, and it was hard not to think of her legs wrapped around me in a different way.

My cock throbbed in my pants, eagerly agreeing with the images in my head as we rolled down the street.

It hit me, then, that she'd only come to me to tend her through her heat to avoid Arik. If she'd have explained the issue from the beginning, I would have protected her without anything in return, but there was no way I was letting her back out now. I was too invested, too caught up in her pheromones and my instincts. No time to play the shining knight now.

I passed my shop and turned down the next street. For a long time, I'd lived out of the garage, but when a struggling older couple who lived nearby told me they were trying to sell their home to move closer to family, but couldn't due to the state of the house and a terrible housing market, it had seemed meant to be. The house had needed a lot of work and I was still in the process of repairing it, but it had four walls and a locking door, and that was what was needed right now.

I slowed as I approached my driveway, swinging wide to make the turn gentle. While Brook still held tight to me and her head remained buried against my back, the trembling had eased.

We rolled into the garage, but it took a moment after I killed the engine for her to lift her head, and another before she pried her fingers out of my shirt. Offering my hand for her to use to steady herself, I waited as she slowly uncurled and swung her leg over the back tire before tugging down the bottom of her dress.

Without the wind to carry it away her scent hit me full force, sending another painful surge of blood below my belt. My erection already dug into my jeans, and I wasn't sure I'd have enough blood left to stand if I didn't clear my head. Pretending to adjust the cuff of my pants on the side opposite, I leaned down and sucked in a breath of hot metal and exhaust fumes despite my wolf's protests before straightening and getting off the bike.

"C'mon."

I fought with the urge to reach out and take her hand in mine, instead giving a rough jerk of my head toward the door that led inside. If I touched her smooth skin again I wasn't going to be able to stop with just taking her hand, but she wouldn't be comfortable in the garage. She wasn't some club bunny to bend over a bike to be railed.

Her dainty footsteps followed me across the concrete and through the doorway into the main part of the house.

Leann Ryans

I suppose it was the dining room we walked into, but it currently only featured a crooked fan dangling from the ceiling above buckets of paint, drop cloths, and boxes of supplies I hadn't gotten around to using yet. As a human her sight wasn't as good as mine, and I worried she'd take a wrong step and trip over the mess.

"Wait here."

The only light shone from the bulb above the kitchen sink to our right, leaving the house in shadows. Not wanting her to see the mess I knew the kitchen to be any better than she already could, I moved to the left and fumbled for the light switch in the living room.

A glow came up on each side of the large screen tv at the end of the room, revealing the sectional separating the living space from the chaos of my dining room. The coffee table in front of it was scuffed and littered with crap, and I couldn't help the bite of discomfort that spread through my chest as I looked back at Brooke. She deserved better than this.

I watched her glance around before moving closer to where I stood at the end of the couch. The front three rooms created one long rectangle, so it wasn't hard to take in the whole mess in one glance. Across from me was the opening to the short hall where the two bedrooms and bathroom were, and that was the extent of the house. It wasn't much, but I never thought I'd need anything more.

"So, this is your house?"

Her nostrils flared, testing for the scent of anyone else. Those big green eyes blinked up at me, too much wonder showing in them for this paltry place. I gave her a nod and she looked around again before wrapping her arms across her middle.

"You've done well. Your own house. The garage. Vincent would be proud of you."

The pleasure that burned through me at her words was almost embarrassing. You'd think after him being dead so long I wouldn't care anymore, but Vincent had been my first friend. The first person to give a shit about me and show me not everyone's feelings were dead.

Clearing my throat, I glanced away before a low whine pulled my attention back to Brooke. She was clutching her belly, face scrunched in pain, and it brought me back to why we were here in the first place.

I knew I couldn't move too fast, despite what my aching cock demanded. She needed a place and time to nest, and I needed to make some preparations before I was too distracted.

Striding the few steps it took to cross to the hallway, I motioned for her to follow as I opened my bedroom door and walked inside. It might have been more diplomatic to offer the guest room instead of mine since this wasn't an intimate arrangement, but the other room would carry the lingering scents of the many club members who'd slept off a drunken night at my house, or crashed after helping with repairs, and the alpha in me couldn't abide their scent around the omega.

I moved through the dark room to the lamp in the corner, clicking it on before stepping into the closet. While the rest of the house may have been a mess, my bedroom was the one place I kept neat. Bed made, no lingering dishes or trash, no clothes on the floor. There wasn't much in it besides the king-size bed, a pair of nightstands, and a dresser, but it was clean and safe. The shutters over the window were locked, the back yard it looked out onto fenced and padlocked, and I'd take care of securing the rest of the house while I gave Brooke time to get comfortable.

The pile of extra bedding I had in the closet didn't seem as extensive as I remembered as I looked at it with the eyes of an alpha trying to provide for an omega, but it was all I had. If it wasn't enough I could make one of the guys bring us more, but hopefully she'd be satisfied, and I wouldn't have to wait even longer. It was getting hard to think with all the blood rushing away from my brain to other parts that thought their need more pressing.

Brooke was standing in the middle of the room when I came out with the bundle of fabric, eyeing the bed as though she wanted to dive into it but wasn't sure she should. When she heard me behind her she startled, spinning around to face me with wide eyes lost to black pupils.

"Make yourself at home, Brooke. You won't be going anywhere for a while."

Her brows lowered and those plush pink lips thinned into a narrow line until her gaze dropped to the bedding as I placed it on the end of the mattress.

Tempting A Knight

"This is all I have, but if you need more just let me know and I'll get it. I'm going to step out to take care of a few things and let you get settled."

She blinked up at me, pink tongue darting out and testing my resolve once again. Digging nails into my palms, I fought the urge to grab her and toss her onto the bed, to hell with her nest, but I knew she needed it.

Ignoring the itching sensation along my arms as my wolf pushed to the fore, I turned my back to her and forced myself to move toward the door. My hand was on the knob when I heard her whisper.

"Thank you, Sebastian. I know you don't really want me, don't want to do this, but—"

I'd spun around and cut her off before she could finish, hands buried in her hair as my lips crashed down on hers. Her body went stiff in my arms, my actions taking her by surprise, before she melted against me. Rocking my hips, I let my erection dig into her belly as I claimed her mouth, taking advantage of her gasp and thrusting my tongue in to stroke hers.

She was milk and honey. Sweetness and innocence. Everything I'd ever wanted and would never deserve.

It was hell to drag my lips away, my forehead pressed to hers as we panted for breath before I could speak.

"I've wanted you since you walked into my garage, but I knew you were too good for me even before I realized who you were. Vincent wanted more for you. Wanted you to go to college and get out of this shit city. Not be stuck here, and definitely not with me."

She pulled back, green eyes flashing up at me, her pupils shrinking at the mention of her brother as some of the haze of her heat cleared.

"I'm not too good for you, you were his best friend. That's why I came to you first. Because he trusted you. You know we don't believe in that Purist crap."

I leaned down to silence her again, not wanting to talk and give her the chance to make this harder than it was going to be. I'd never felt the urge to settle down and claim a mate before, but something about Brooke had me ready to take her and make her mine.

I was going to see her through her heat, but I had to let her go afterward. She didn't want me to claim her, and I wouldn't take the choice from her, but what she was saying was stirring things in my chest better left ignored.

Pressing light kisses to her plush lips before giving the bottom one a nip, I pried my arms away from her body and took a step back, shaking my head to clear it enough to think.

"I know."

I sucked in a breath, reaching down to adjust my aching erection and almost losing my control again when her eyes followed my hand and that pink tongue snaked out.

"Nest. I'll be back soon."

I waited until her eyes crawled back up to mine and she gave a nod of understanding before I turned to leave. The pheromones she was pumping into the air were growing thicker, and I had to escape while I still had the chance. The scent of her arousal had my mouth watering, but I couldn't just abandon the guys with no warning, and once her heat deepened and dragged me into rut with her, I wouldn't be able to function enough to tell them what to do.

Putting as much distance as I could between me and my bedroom door without leaving the house, I pulled my phone from my pocket and dialed Carl. We didn't go by the typical club titles, but if we did, he'd have been the VP. He was my right hand at the garage and during anything the club got involved in, but now he'd have to step up and take the lead.

"'Sup boss?"

Heaving a sigh, I dragged my hand through my hair as I tried to get my thoughts in order.

"Remember the girl from the other day? At the garage?"

"The one that sent you running to the bathroom to jerk off?"

The growl burst from my chest without a conscious decision, but I cut it off as his chuckle rolled through the speaker. He enjoyed screwing with me when he got the chance, but I didn't have the time to care about his teasing.

His laughter trailed away, and he spoke again before I got the chance.

"Heard she was at The Hangout tonight, too. You almost started a riot when you dragged her out like some caveman."

I rubbed the back of my neck, stomach flipping. I couldn't deny my actions.

"Yeah. Anyway, she's the sister of an old friend and she's in trouble."

"Bad enough to send her into a biker bar full of alpha shifters on the verge of her heat?"

His tone had turned sober, all joking gone. Carl was always one of the steadiest members of the club and the first to jump on anything involving women and children. None of us stood for that shit, but his issue with it was more personal than most. Even I didn't know the full story.

"Arik has been harassing her. Tried to blackmail her into spending her heat with him. He killed her brother years ago for associating with me."

Carl's hiss of displeasure was almost drowned out by the rumble of his growl through the phone. We all knew who Arik was, even if all the guys didn't know my personal history with the murderer.

"You got her?"

I turned to face the closed door, imagining what was going on inside while I paced out here.

Was she kneeling in the middle of my bed arranging blankets? Was she still wearing that red dress, or had she peeled it off in exchange for comfort? I almost groaned at the thought, wanting to be the one to take it off her.

"Yeah, but I need guys on her place. She lives with her parents, and he threatened them, and once he realizes she's disappeared he's going to be pissed."

Carl's only response was a grunt, but I knew he'd take care of arranging a watch for them. It was only a matter of time before Arik showed up, but we could hope he'd go alone and not with his usual posse of goons.

"Anything else?"

I scrubbed a hand over my face again, stubble scratching my palm.

"Take care of the garage and send one of the newer prospects to keep an ear out for Purist activity. Someone they won't recognize."

We tended to have a new guy show up every month or two to join us, so there should be someone the Purists didn't know that could watch their main hangouts and report back. We needed to know if they were going to be moving closer to our area so we could watch our own backs.

Carl grunted again and I could picture him drumming his fingers on the table like he usually did when he was thinking, his greying goatee bristling. It was a relief to know I had someone who had my back, and it wasn't until then I realized my brothers in the Knights were just as important to me as Vincent had been.

They were family. One I'd chosen when the one dealt to me turned out to be trash.

"Do you need someone on your place?"

Another growl built as my claws extended, gums aching as my canines grew at the thought of another alpha nearby while Brooke was in heat. Even if she wasn't my mate, it was still instinct to guard the omega and keep her away from other males. The possessiveness was difficult to ignore.

"If he had anyone tailing her, he might know where she is. I know you can handle yourself, but if he shows up with enough men, even a wolf in rut won't be able to stop him, and she'd be in danger."

Grumbling under my breath, I made the only compromise I could.

"Outside only. Anyone puts a foot in my house and they're going to lose it, along with their balls."

My growl underlined the words, the rumble impossible to hold back.

"Gotcha boss. I'll do it myself if it makes you feel better."

For a moment I considered it. If there was another alpha in the club who could give me a run for dominance, it was Carl, but he was also the one I trusted most to keep a level head and make the right decisions for the club.

Which was why I had to refuse.

"I need you available to help when Arik shows up at her parent's place. They were like family to me once. I don't want anything to happen to them."

"I got it. Go take care of the girl and I'll hold things down till you're done."

Carl hung up before I could say anything else, but my attention was already drifting back to the closed door separating me from Brooke. The conversation hadn't taken long so I doubted she'd be waiting for me yet, but I was already antsy to get back in there.

To get in *her*.

My cock kicked against my zipper, causing a wince at the tight pinch of my jeans. I couldn't remember the last time I'd been so hard, but I still needed to double check the locks and set the alarm so I could be sure we were as secure as possible.

I tested the windows and entryways, even sliding the bar across my garage door so it couldn't be opened. The whole process only took a couple minutes, so I paced around gathering the garbage piled on my table and counters. Empty beer bottles and takeout wrappers were relocated to the trashcan where they belonged, and there was a part of me that itched to break out the cleaners and do a better job, but the aroma coming from my room when I walked past wiped all other thoughts from my mind.

There was an omega in there.

In heat.

And it was time to take care of her.

Leann Ryans

Chapter Nine

Brooke

I stood staring at the bed, trying to gather my thoughts. They'd scattered when Sebastian kissed me. Even the cramps and fuzziness brought on by my heat had receded and left only the feel of his hands in my hair. His lips on mine. His tongue claiming my mouth.

It took a moment for me to realize the whining I heard was coming from me. Cutting off the noise, I lifted a hand to touch the bedding he'd set at the foot of the mattress. The fabric was a bit worn, but that only made it softer, the scent rising from them that of the male who my thoughts were centered on.

My movements were slow and halting at first, hesitant as I began my task, but instinct soon took over. I'd done this before, and my hands knew how to do it even without direction.

Pushing the pile of blankets onto the floor, I crawled to the center of the bed and stripped back the sheets covering it. Using the ones with the strongest scent of him, I began to build my nest.

Starting at the head, I placed the pillows in an arc, stacking them, before laying more halfway down the sides. The mattress was a bit stiff and lumpy, so I used some of the thinner sheets to even it out and create a layer that would conform to our bodies. I had to get off the bed to spread the top blankets and tuck them under the mattress, but in the end I'd created a snug little burrow, just large enough for the two of us to fit inside.

I was still smoothing and adjusting, my cramps growing harder to ignore as slick slid down my thighs, when the door to the room opened. The growl that sprang from my throat was automatic, my posture changing to defensive as my space was suddenly invaded.

The answering rumble that met me was quiet and reassuring, though it held the edge of dominance. I relaxed as Sebastian's scent reached me and the haze that had overtaken my thoughts cleared enough for me to recognize him and remember where I was.

"It's just me. The house is secure, and we won't be disturbed until I tell my men we're ready. Your parents will be protected while we're preoccupied."

A shiver rolled through me at his voice, the words barely registering. I knew I should be more focused on what he was telling me, but the stubble framing his mouth caught my attention, the thought of what it would feel like on the inside of my thighs caused my core to clench and more liquid to slip out to coat my folds.

My nest was ready, there was an alpha before me, and there was no reason to keep waiting. He could soothe the cramps, calm the ache, and ease the need.

I closed the space between us, raising a hand to lay on his broad chest without thinking. A purr vibrated the flesh beneath my fingers, the warmth of his muscles burning through his shirt as if it wasn't there.

And suddenly, I wanted nothing more than for it to be gone. I could see the ink on his arms, disappearing beneath the edge of his sleeves, and I needed to know how far it went.

Sebastian said something else but the words didn't register, my mind distracted by the feel of him as I slid my hands up his chest to push his vest from his shoulders. He caught it before it dropped to the floor, tossing it on the nightstand as I continued to run my palms over him, humming under my breath as the blood flowing through my veins burned hotter.

Stomach clenching with an intense cramp, I dug my nails into his pectorals, the groan he released sending more slick gushing from my core. Fingers gripped my chin, tipping my head back and forcing me to look up into eyes turned pitch black.

"You have no idea how much I've thought about doing this."

The rumbled words barely left his lips before I was spun around. I stopped myself from falling by bracing my hands on the mattress, mussing the blankets, but the worry left me as Sebastian pressed himself against my backside. His thickness throbbed between us as he leaned over my back to run his nose along my neck, drawing in a long breath before letting it out on another groan that had my entire body trembling.

I wanted him in a way I'd never felt with my friend. Even in the depths of heat there was a part of me that knew my friend wasn't the alpha for me, but all that I was preened under Sebastian.

Hips canting, I pushed back, grinding myself against the length trapped beneath his jeans. The fact that there was still clothing between us was frustrating, but his closeness kept me from protesting just yet.

The thought had barely crossed my mind when he straightened. Something warm and smooth touched my nape, sliding down my spine toward the top of my dress, but it wasn't until the sound of ripping fabric reached my ears that I realized it was his claws.

"Seeing you in this dress in front of those other alphas made me want to murder them all. It didn't matter that some of them were my men, my friends and loyal club members. I wanted to skewer their eyes with my claws and pluck them from their sockets to be sure they couldn't look at you any longer."

My skin broke out in goosebumps at the possessiveness in his voice. One last sharp yank had my dress loosening around me before fluttering to the floor. My breasts hung free, the outfit leaving me unable to wear a bra, so the only things left between him and I were his clothing and the lace riding up my bare cheeks.

I shivered again as he let out a low growl, the tip of his claw running under the edge of my panties before he released them and moved away from me. It took a moment for me to pull my scattered thoughts together to look over my shoulder to see why he'd stopped. My mouth watered at the sight of his t-shirt moving up his abs, exposing them row by row.

I was frozen in place as he whipped the fabric over his head, his chest finally fully exposed. A scattering of hair lent texture to his inked flesh, the trail growing thicker as it flowed down to disappear beneath his jeans.

When his hands moved to his belt buckle my core clenched, sending a gush of slick down my thighs. Sebastian's nostrils flared as he sucked in the scent and let out a groan on the exhale.

"You smell so sweet, omega. Do you taste as good?"

My breath caught in my throat, not allowing me to answer. All I could do was tip my hips further, presenting for the alpha standing behind me with his eyes locked on my lace-covered sex.

"You've always been such a good little girl, I bet you do taste sweet. Are you going to be good for me?"

His belt hissed through the loops of his jeans and I nodded so hard my teeth clacked. His rich chuckle poured over me as he stepped forward, reaching out to trail the tips of his fingers down my spine.

"Keep your hands on the bed. I can't wait any longer to taste you."

I watched as he dropped to his knees behind me, his hands braced on the outsides of my thighs. More slick left me, trying to tempt the alpha closer, preparing me for what was to come.

Sebastian's thumbs brushed along the crease under my bottom as he leaned in closer. I couldn't see what he was doing but I felt the warm gust of his breath on the backs of my thighs. I was left trembling, waiting for his touch, begging silently for him to hurry, but he seemed to be savoring the moment.

"You don't know how many times I've imagined this since you came to my shop. How many times I've brought myself to an unsatisfactory release wishing it was you I spilled myself in."

His voice was so rough and hungry it made my clit throb as I let out a whine. Cramps ravaged my belly, the thought of his seed wasted increasing my frustration.

"Sebastian…"

I lowered my chest further, wriggling my hips in his hold as I said his name. The anticipation had me panting with the need for him to touch me.

"Please!"

His chuckle was dark and half growl.

"Patience sweet girl. I have to make this memorable."

I was about to protest when a firm stroke followed the seam of my panties, the shock freezing the words in my throat. The lace was already soaked through, so it took another pass for me to realize he was licking me through the fabric.

I felt his tongue along the edges of the lace before he returned to the center. A gasp tore from me as his lick continued further than it had before, following my crease to the top of my panties. The edge of his teeth scraped against the base of my spine as his fingers curled over the sides of them and he began to drag them off me.

I was dripping, the mental image of what he must look like behind me making my nipples tighten as tingles spread through my body.

My panties dropped and hit the tops of my feet, but I didn't get the chance to step out of them. His hands spanned the back of my thighs, his thumbs pulling me open wider so he could thrust his tongue against the bundle of nerves hidden in my folds. My knees nearly buckled but his hold held me up even as his noises of enjoyment kept me shaking as he devoured me.

My orgasm came hurtling toward me, breaking open before I had the chance to brace myself. Lips parting on a cry of surprise, my hands curled in the blankets, fisting the fabric as my body tried to collapse.

Sebastian didn't end his attention, lapping up my release with slow licks and a purr that turned my spine to jelly. He was gentle on my clit, but each pass still made me twitch, the sensations too intense as awareness returned, the world slowing its hectic spinning from moments before. I tried to step forward, to get away from his seeking tongue, but his hands held me in place, his rough growl freezing my muscles.

Teeth nibbled my delicate flesh, teasingly threatening pain. The tips were sharp, the scruff on his face abrasive on my inner thighs, his nails digging in where they'd elongated, all combining to send a strange mix of heat and ice straight to my womb. Each breath I dragged in was flooded with the heady scent of him combined with the sweetness of my arousal.

It was intoxicating.

"Sebastian, please!"

While the same words earlier had been meant to entice, my whimper now was a plea for mercy. I was on the edge again, but the feeling was verging on painful.

He grumbled behind me, slowing further, though his tongue still ran across my skin. Catching every bit of slick that seeped from me.

His eyes were coal black when I finally saw them as he pulled away. His wolf was close to the surface, evident in his gaze and the extended canines peeking from beneath his upper lip. His brow ridge was more pronounced, his ears resting higher on the sides of his head and pointed, his cheeks hollowed as his jaw sharped with the appearance of a predator.

While I'd seen him as a full wolf once when we were younger, I'd never seen the half-form shifters could supposedly take. I hadn't even been sure it was true, but looking at him like that I knew it was. He wasn't there yet, but it was obvious he was struggling to hold back the animal side of him.

Tempting A Knight

I shivered as his palms moved up the backs of my legs to cup my bottom. He squeezed my cheeks as he held my gaze, claws flexing and pricking my skin as he stood.

Sebastian towered over me, the bulge in his jeans dragging my gaze from his. As close as I was and the way I was over-sensitized, imagining what was beneath those pants and what he planned to do with it almost tipped me over the edge.

Whimpering, all I could do was watch as he removed one hand from me to unbutton his jeans. The sound of the zipper was loud when the only other noise in the room was my panting and the constant low rumble rolling from Sebastian's chest. It seemed to take hours for the little piece of metal to part teeth and expose what was beneath.

I groaned when all I saw was dark fabric, Sebastian's snicker mocking my impatience.

"You act like you've never seen an alpha undress. I know I can't be your first."

His rich voice had my eyelids fluttering, threatening to close, but I wanted to see him too badly to let them.

"You're not."

The two words were all I could think to say, and Sebastian's face contorted with a snarl. Thrusting his pants down his legs, he reached out and spun me to face him, his fingers curling around my throat before the room quit moving around me. His face was inches from mine, his warm breath fanning over my ear as he leaned closer.

Leann Ryans

"You better not be thinking about them while I'm with you. I'm the alpha you came to. I'm the one that'll rut you through this heat."

Slick ran down my thighs as my core clenched, the utter dominance in his voice doing things to me that had the omega part rolling over and showing her belly. My friend may have been an alpha and able to satisfy the needs of my cycle, but he wasn't as dominant as Sebastian, and I'd never been attracted to him as I was the half-naked man standing before me.

"Yes, Alpha."

The words were a whisper, all I could get out with his knuckles pressed against my jaw, tilting my head back to meet his eyes. I could see the hunger there, the barely restrained need that matched my own, and it made my blood burn hotter.

His muscles rippled, bones popping as his wolf surged, struggling to take control before it settled again.

"You tempt me, Brooke. That's not smart, and we both know you're a smart girl."

Sebastian released his hold on my throat and took a step back, both hands going to the waistband of his underwear. He didn't waste any time, pushing them down and kicking them away in seconds.

It was impossible not to look. To stare at the thing standing between us, the ruddy length intimidating and enticing all at the same time. Veins stood out along it, the place where his knot would swell already bulging on the sides. I knew I could take it, it's what omegas were made to do, but my core still clenched at the thought of that thing lodging within me.

Wrapping a hand around the base, Sebastian stroked it up to the tip, squeezing a thin stream of sticky fluid from the slit. The scent hit the air instantly, the salty, musky virility making my mouth water as I let out a whine.

I wanted to taste it. Needed to.

My knees hit the carpet before I consciously made the decision to move. Tongue slipping out to wet my lips, I shuffled forward as I looked up to meet Sebastian's dark gaze. A rumble left his chest, but he angled his erection toward me, offering what I wanted.

My tongue met the tip of him, lapping up the glistening fluid on the crown. His flavor flooded my mouth, teasing my senses and making me want more.

Unlike pure humans, the head of him tapered to a point, the shape more triangular than the mushroom tip I was familiar with. He also had a more defined edge along the base of the crown, so when I slid him into my mouth it was easy to take him deep into my throat, but harder to pull away.

Ice slid down my spine when I tried to move my head but found myself stuck with my airway blocked. My eyes widened, throat constricting with fear as my lungs began to burn.

"Easy, Brooke."

Sebastian's hand cupped my cheek, directing my attention back to his face as he let out a purr.

"Relax and swallow."

The warmth of his hand and the soothing sound allowed me to focus and do as he said. My first attempt to swallow failed but the second try flattened the ridge enough for me to pull off with a gasp.

Blinking away the sting of threatened tears, I sucked in another breath as I studied his cock. Adrenaline still coursed through me, blended with the arousal from my heat and a growing curiosity.

Licking my lips, I leaned forward again, raising a hand to wrap around the head and glide down before pulling up. I toyed with the ridge as more fluid leaked from his tip, tempting me further.

"Brooke."

There was an edge of warning in the way he said my name, sparking some need in me to challenge him. Taking him between my lips again, I made a few shallow bobs before easing him further into my throat. I experimented with using my tongue to flatten his ridge, satisfied that it was easier to do than it had seemed in the moment.

I released my grip on his length and slid my lips all the way down again, until my nose pressed against the hand still squeezing over his knot. When he said my name again it was all growl and sent shivers through my body, causing slick to puddle beneath me.

"Brooke, don't test me."

I stared up into his black eyes as my tongue writhed against him. The hand not holding his erection still cupped my cheek, but the touch was less gentle and more controlling. His claws pricked my scalp just behind my ear.

His muscles strained, standing in sharp contrast as his jaw worked as if chewing on words he refused to say.

Swallowing, I hollowed my cheeks as I pulled away and sucked in a breath before taking him back into my throat again. He growled, his cock kicking the only warning I received before lava spurted from his slit.

Leann Ryans

Chapter Ten

Sebastian

My dick was so deep in her throat my seed poured straight into her belly as I came. Brooke had shocked me when she took me in her mouth after the first time when she panicked. The way she met my gaze, challenging me while she sucked me, brought my orgasm on with a rush.

I strangled my knot, keeping it from swelling as I continued to come. Brooke pulled back after the first few pulses, bobbing on the head as she swallowed jet after jet of my release. She teased every last drop from me before letting go with a pop.

I stared down at her as I panted, chest heaving as I tried to catch my breath. It was hard to reconcile the geeky good girl I remembered with the sexy omega on her knees in front of me, licking my seed from her lips. The sight kept me hard, my erection in no way abating despite the release. Our pheromones filled the air and there was no way I was stopping before I was locked deep inside her.

"On your feet."

I countered the rough order by offering my hand to help her up. She held onto it until she was steady, her knees seeming to not want to support her. Moving my hand to her chin, I tipped her head back and claimed her lips with mine, unable to resist the lure. They were red and puffy from what she'd just done, and it only made me harder.

I slid my fingers back into her dark locks, controlling her head and the angle of the kiss. I plundered her mouth, taking everything, just as I planned to do with all of her.

She was panting by the time I released her, her body molded to mine, my cock trapped between us. The slight friction of her breathing was just enough to tease me and make me impatient for more.

"Are you ready?"

It was hard to keep my head, but I was trying to remember this was about Brooke. I was helping her through her heat, not trying to slake my lust on a random female I'd picked up at a bar. I had to be sure she had everything she needed.

Brooke nodded as much as she was able with my hand cupping her skull. Dropping a quick kiss on her mouth, I released her before it could go any further and let my arms drop, watching as she blinked until the dazed look cleared.

"Then bring me into your nest, omega."

Her lips parted, eyes darting to the bed. As soon as they landed on the corner where she'd disturbed the blankets, she was reaching out to smooth them again.

While I couldn't claim Brooke was the first omega I was going to bed, the others had all been one-night stands, and never during their heat. I'd never seen a true nest before, and the thing in front of me left me in awe. She'd taken the crappy old blankets and pillows I'd left for her and turned them into something that looked so comfortable I was dying to crawl inside it.

When she continued to hesitate, I took the few steps to the side of the bed, purring to show my approval. I couldn't tell where the opening was, and I wouldn't enter uninvited anyway, but I was curious as to how we were going to get in without making a mess of her work.

Small fingers tangled in mine as I studied what she'd built. When I swung my gaze to her, I could see the pink flush on her cheeks as she gave my hand a light tug toward the end of the bed.

"You enter from the bottom."

Her words were so quiet I almost couldn't hear them over my heartbeat thundering in my ears, but once I realized what she said I let her pull me around to the end of the bed. She folded back a portion of the blanket, leaving a gap barely large enough for my shoulders to fit.

"You first."

My gaze darted to her again, my breath catching for a moment. I was surprised she'd want me to go into her nest first, but I carefully lifted the fabric.

"Are you sure?"

She quirked a smile as she nodded.

"That way I can fix anything you mess up."

Leann Ryans

My eyes narrowed but my lips twitched with amusement. I was going to tease her until I noticed her hand going to her belly, signaling the return of her cramps. Orgasms would stop them for a period, but the only way to really soothe them was me spilling inside her while she was locked on my knot.

The thought caused my cock to jerk, reminding me what I was delaying. The sooner I was in her nest, the sooner I could sink inside her.

Careful of the edges, I slid under the blankets, wriggling to the top of the bed and rolling onto my back. Pillows surrounded my head and shoulders, creating the perfect cushion. The way she placed them kept the blanket lifted so there was still space above my face, but the fabric dimmed the light and left me feeling wrapped in soothing coziness.

For a moment I let myself relax, enjoying the gift of comfort she'd created, knowing I was bound to destroy it before her heat was through.

The blankets over my legs lifted as Brooke climbed underneath, pulling my attention back. When I looked down to where she crawled up my legs I was met by a naughty smirk as her head dipped and she placed a nip to the inside of my thigh.

Mock-growling, I let my canines lengthen as I curled a lip in threat. If she kept teasing me her nest would be destroyed sooner rather than later.

The next dip of her head was to the other side, her tongue darting out to swipe at my leg before she moved up. Kisses, licks, and nips followed her slow path up my thighs. My cock was weeping and twitching by the time she reached it, begging for attention, only for her to pause before touching it.

The growl that left me was no longer play, the rumble warning the omega that she was close to pushing me over the edge. I could only take so much before the urge to take control won out.

Her eyes flashed in the dim light shining through the bedding, the lovely green swallowed by her black pupils. Meeting my gaze, she extended her tongue, dragging it up the length of my cock before hovering above it once again.

"Brooke."

My fingers tangled in her dark hair, set to pull her down to take me into her mouth properly, until she dipped her head and sucked a different part of me between her lips instead. Frozen in shock, I could do nothing but watch as Brooke took first one, then the other of my balls into her mouth, licking and suckling in a way that had me throbbing on the edge of coming again like some untried boy.

I yanked her away, my erection pressing into her belly as I pulled her up before I shamed myself. I was supposed to be focusing on her needs, not trying to figure out where she'd learned to do such things.

Claiming her lips with mine once I had her atop me, I took her hips in both hands and pressed her down over my cock, rocking her on it as I ground myself along her sodden folds. I could feel her hard little bud dragging against me, sending shudders through her body with each brush. I kept her there, rocking her faster, until she cried her release into my mouth.

Her slight weight collapsed against me, her breaths coming fast, her heart fluttering where our chests pressed together. I dragged my mouth along her jaw and down her throat to the pulse point, letting my teeth scrape against her.

"No more teasing, Brooke. You wanted me to tend you through your heat, and you need more than my tongue in your cunt or my cock down your throat."

She trembled as I ran my hands down her back, but she had that naughty smirk on her face again when she lifted her head to look down at me.

"Teasing seems to be working fine for me. And having your cock in my mouth is just as good as having it in my cunt."

I had us flipped before she knew what was happening, my hand curled around her throat to pin her to the bed. She writhed beneath me, sending delicious zaps of awareness through my body as her breast brushed my chest and her wetness smeared my abs. The blanket sagged against my back and I knew I'd pulled something loose, but I no longer cared.

"If you believe that, then your previous partners were lacking. Nothing is as good as having my cock in your cunt, my knot locked deep, keeping us together as I flood you with cum."

Though her eyes had widened when my fingers wrapped around her throat, she relaxed and smiled up at me. Tilting her hips, she ground against me as she replied.

"Prove it."

Brooke hadn't seemed so sassy when she came to the garage, or when I went to her house, but I secretly loved the attitude. Letting my own lips tip up in a smirk, I lined the head of my cock up with her weeping entrance before leaning down. I sucked the lobe of her ear between my lips, flicking it with my tongue before releasing it and whispering into the shell.

"I will."

I didn't give her a chance to respond. I thrust forward, entering halfway before her tightness forced me to stop and pull back. Her eyes flew wide, mouth opened on a silent gasp, and when I shoved the rest of the way in her hands pressed against my chest, trying to force me back.

"Wait!"

I couldn't help my chuckle as I licked her ear before nibbling along the edge of it.

"It's too late now."

She groaned as I rolled my hips, grinding against her but keeping every inch lodged inside. Her channel fluttered around me, trying to force my length from her but succeeding only in making me throb harder. The need to move, to snap my hips and make her body rock, was strong, but I resisted to give her time to accommodate me. I wanted her sore enough to remember what happened, but not so much it actually hurt.

"So full."

I lifted my head at her gasp, watching her eyes roll to the back of her head. Her teeth worried at her bottom lip, and I leaned in to lick it before capturing it for my own. Moaning into my mouth, her tongue darted against mine, dueling me for command of the kiss.

She lost.

Pulling my hips back, I kept to a slow, even pace, withdrawing until the head of my shaft rested at her entrance once again.

"What are you, Brooke?"

Her eyes fluttered open, a rim of green showing me she wasn't completely lost to instinct.

"An omega."

Her brows tipped in question and a purr vibrated from my chest to assure her she answered correctly.

"And what am I?"

"Al—"

The word was strangled by her gasp as I hilted myself in her again. Sitting up, I let go of her throat and trailed my fingers over her collarbone to circle one puckered nipple as my other hand grasped her hip.

"Again," I commanded as I dragged my cock from her once more.

Brooke's eyes narrowed, and she bared her teeth at me even as her hips tipped and she tried to take me back into her.

"Alpha."

Chapter Eleven

Brooke

I spat the word, expecting him to surge deep once again, but all he did was grin. Twisting my nipple between his fingers, his gaze trailed over my chest before coming back up to my eyes.

"That's right."

He purred the words, sending a shiver through me as he entered me once more. Unlike the first two brutal thrusts, this time he moved slow.

So slow!

I felt every hard ridge and bump slide past my entrance at a snail's pace. My core stuttered in confusion, having braced for impact only to be confronted with steady pressure. A cramp gripped my belly, leaving me writhing and trying to press myself down his length.

"Sebastian."

My whine grated against my own ears. It was getting harder to focus, harder to recall the name of the alpha poised over me, torturing me with his deliberately soft invasion. I wanted him to do what he was here for and ease my pain.

"Yes, omega?"

His eyes were black when I met them, his brow more pronounced, cheekbones sharp. His face was locked in concentration, his jaw flexing as one inch after another entered me. The nails of the fingers abusing my nipple kept extending and retracting as if he struggled to control the wolf inside him.

I wanted to see him lose that control. The idea of his wolf taking over should have terrified me, but instead it sent a wave of heat through my body, pushing me deeper into instinct.

I needed his cock.

I needed his seed.

I needed his knot.

And I wanted his wolf.

Pressing my heels into the mattress, I lifted my bottom from the bed, causing him to slip in further. We both gasped as he froze, his lips pulling back in a silent snarl that exposed his canines.

"More."

His gaze snapped to mine with my demand, his nose crinkling even as it started to lengthen. His shoulders shuddered as dark hair rippled down his arms before he pulled it all back and took control again. With a sharp twist of my poor nipple that sent a bolt of lightning straight to my clit, he finally released it and moved his grip to my other hip.

"As you wish."

The words were almost mangled around his growl, but it didn't matter. I was flipped to my belly, hips raised in the air, and filled with cock in one smooth move. Hands fisting in the sheets, I cried out as his hips pulled back before snapping forward again.

"I'll give you everything I've got. We'll see if you still need *more*."

Sebastian pummeled into me, each thrust sending my body rocking forward with the brutality of it, delicious tingles spreading from my core as he wound me tighter. I was hurtling toward the hardest orgasm of my life with nothing more than penetration, and every cell in my body chanted *Yes*!

This was what I wanted. What I needed. I could give in to the need and ask for what I desired without fear, because no matter how rough it seemed, I trusted the alpha at my back to keep me safe.

I never could have done that with Arik.

I screamed out my release seconds before Sebastian snarled behind me, his cock jerking within the spasming grip of my channel. His knot swelling inside me was an uncomfortable pressure that grew and grew, my first instinct to try pulling away until he yanked me back on him, locking it behind my pubic bone. I wailed as another crushing orgasm spread through my limbs, my entire body coated in sweat and quivering as he emptied himself in my womb.

As the sensations died away, I melted into the mattress, bones turning to putty as weakness overtook me. Just keeping my eyes open and lungs heaving took every bit of effort I had left, so I made no protest as Sebastian rearranged me until I laid on my side with him tucked close behind, his knot keeping us joined. The random flutters of my core pulled answering spurts from him, my belly bloated with the amount of seed he'd released, yet he kept giving more.

My whine as he raised my thigh and dipped a hand between them was pitiful, the begging tone going ignored as his fingers found my swollen bud. Just a soft brush over the top had me shuddering and clenching on his length, an answering growl vibrating through my spine where it pressed to his chest.

Avoiding direct contact, he began to circle the nub with his fingertips, occasionally dipping down to where he filled me to collect the small amount of fluid that leaked out, using it as lubrication to continue teasing me. I tensed and writhed, gripping his wrist with both hands to try stopping him, to no avail. I was quivering on the edge of another crest, the painful zing threatening to overtake me once again, when he finally spoke.

"Do you still need more, omega?"

I whimpered, shaking my head, though my hands now prevented him from removing his from my sex. I was split in two, one half wanting him to push me over while the other quaked at the thought of what would happen if he did. I couldn't possibly survive another release. My heart would simply give out.

Sebastian hummed as his nose stroked the side of my neck, his fingers slowing to a maddening tease. Just enough to keep me throbbing on the verge, but not enough to go over. I didn't know which way I even wanted it to go, I just needed the tension to ease.

"I think you do."

The sharp scrape of fangs followed the path his nose had just taken back up to my ear before his lips latched onto my neck just below it. Sucking the flesh between his teeth, he bit down just enough for me to feel the sting without breaking skin.

"I think you need a lot more."

His tongue laved the spot as he released another growl, his finger moving to stroke straight over my straining clit. My nerves were wound so tight they must have crossed somewhere because it felt like a second tongue between my thighs, and my spine arched as I finally fell over the edge into orgasm.

The second spasm of my core forced Sebastian's receding knot from me, the gush of fluid barely registering as my limbs twitched and I panted for breath. The world spun around me, the amount of light revealing how much he'd wrecked my nest, but I couldn't find the will to care.

A hand gripped my shoulder and I was pushed onto my back, legs flopping open in a way I'd have blushed at if I was lucid, but I was too far gone to care. The next thing I knew there *was* a tongue between my thighs, lapping up our mixed release in between sucking my lower lips into his mouth. I twitched, trying to close my legs around his head, but he held me open easily, continuing his feast until the gush slowed to a trickle.

I couldn't help the sigh of relief when he finally raised his head and I blinked open eyes I'd clenched shut to stare up at him. Slick shone on his chin and cheeks but the hungry look he gave me kept me from being self-conscious as I had with the other alpha I'd been with. Sebastian clearly enjoyed what he'd done, and I was willing to bet he had plans to do it again by the way his lips ticked up in a grin.

"Are you satisfied?"

The deep rumble sent a shiver through me, but I couldn't move more than that. My muscles were goo, I was high on endorphins, and my cramps had eased once he'd knotted me. Nodding my head the tiniest fraction, I attempted a weak smile, but instead of lying down beside me, Sebastian leaned forward and covered my body with his.

"Are you sure?"

Hardness pressed into my belly as his head dipped to scent me. Teeth dragged along my flesh, raising goosebumps in their wake before being soothed by the swipe of his tongue, and my body responded as if I hadn't just been wrung dry. My sex pulsed, fresh slick seeping out as he rocked his erection against me.

"How?"

The gasp was all I could manage. Sebastian only chuckled, moving to the opposite side of my neck to give it and my shoulder the same treatment. Coarse hair brushed against my pebbled nipples as he scooted down, the friction sending zaps of pleasure through my belly until I felt the tapered tip of him at my entrance once again.

"You. You do this to me."

The words were whispered against my collarbone as he rocked his hips. He entered me only a fraction, the flared edge of him still resting outside my opening. Where seconds before I didn't believe I wanted more, I was suddenly hungry to have him inside me again.

"Sebastian."

His teeth raked harder, claws pinching my nipples and pulling a squeak from my throat. His grumble was all displeasure, and it took my confused mind a moment to realize my mistake.

"Alpha!"

As soon as I breathed the word he entered me, seating himself to the hilt once again, grinding his pelvis against my sensitive clit. It tore a cry from me as I clutched his shoulders, trying to pull him even closer. He reversed and thrust again, my entire body jolting from the force. His mouth covered where my neck met my shoulder, teeth providing delicious threats as his claws dug into my backside where he gripped my hips, but it wasn't until I felt the burn of my channel being forced wider that I realized my fingers tangled in fur on his back.

He was shifting.

Each thrust caused a fresh sting as Sebastian grew within my hold. His already muscled form broadened, the slight give he'd had before disappearing. Coarse hairs like the ones that covered his chest sprouted everywhere, growing longer.

I pulled my head away until I could see his face. His nose had elongated into a snout, his mouth full of fangs sharp enough to rend flesh from bone. His ears had moved up the sides of his head and grown pointed, both of them pinned back as his thrusts slowed. His black eyes had a golden sheen as they met mine, and while many human women would be terrified of the sight confronting me, a secret thrill coursed through my belly. He'd been large in his human-form, but in his were-form he was massive.

Including the shaft still working in and out of me.

"Brooke."

My palm cupped his cheek, thumb stroking the short fur there. He closed his eyes, brows kitting, the fight going on within him obvious.

"Sebastian."

Those dark orbs met mine again as his hips snapped forward, my mouth popping open with a gasp before I could continue.

"Relax."

It was the only word I could get out, but it was enough. Tension drained from the quivering muscles under the hand still wrapped around him and his strokes became longer again. Faster.

His head dipped back to my neck, tongue tasting my skin followed by his fangs sending a wave of goosebumps down my chest before he bit down and growled.

My orgasm swamped me as his knot swelled and locked in place. I couldn't stop a scream from ripping out of my throat as every muscle in my body spasmed, ice followed by lava flowing out from my center. My eyes stung with the light that burst behind my lids, lungs straining as I gasped for breath.

And then he came.

Leann Ryans

Chapter Twelve

Sebastian

It took every bit of will not to break skin and claim Brooke. Especially once she began to writhe beneath me in the throes of her release.

The walls of her channel rippled around my knot, choking it, forcing me to come as I held onto her flesh and fought my wolf. I flooded her depths, the amount of cum leaving me causing my head to spin even as I continued grinding into her.

I'd never expected to feel this way, never meant to shift to my were-form, and damn sure hadn't planned to claim her. Yet the animal side of me seemed to have other plans.

Closing my eyes, I tried to block out the sweet sounds Brooke made as her orgasm eased. There was no way to get her scent out of my nose with it buried in her hair, but I forced my hands to release her plush bottom, moving them to tangle in the bedding. I thought of the guys at the shop, the threat of the Purists, everything I could to ignore the sensations of being locked inside her as I pushed the shift away.

My skin twitched as fur receded, bones aching as they returned to normal. Shifting didn't really cause pain, but the discomfort of it helped me focus more and finally release Brooke's neck.

Dark pupils rimmed in green stared up at me when I raised my head. She stroked my cheek again before letting her hand slide down to rest on my chest. I knew her heat wasn't over, but it had eased enough for her to relax and be lucid for a bit. I should be making my knot shrink so I could get us some food and water while I had the chance, but I didn't want to release her.

The little grunt at the end of her breath let me know I was squishing her, so I rolled us over until she was situated atop me. I tried to be careful of her nest, but I'd already pulled the top sheets loose and knocked some of the pillows out of place. She didn't seem to mind. Snuggling her cheek into my chest, she let out a sigh as I wrapped my arms around her.

"You were right."

I frowned as I tried to figure out what she was referring to, but was too distracted by the feel of her. I rocked my hips without thinking, making her gasp and clamp down on me again. We both groaned but I forced myself to hold still and give her a chance to rest.

"What do you mean?"

"My previous partner was lacking. Nothing has ever felt that good."

Her body bounced as I chuckled and I ran a hand down to cup her ass, giving it a squeeze. While a small part of me was still waving red flags saying this was a bad idea, I didn't mind her stroking my ego.

Or other parts of me.

My cock flexed at the thought, blood rushing back to harden it further despite still being locked inside her. At the rate I was going, I was going to have an erection the entire time we were stuck in this room, and I found myself fine with that. My brain didn't need that much blood anyway.

Leaning my head down, I let myself enjoy the scent of her as I whispered in her ear.

"Why do you think so many women prefer shifters?"

Brooke huffed, tipping her head until she could meet my eyes, one brow lifted. I loved seeing her relaxed and willing to show me who she really was, instead of the meek, formal girl who'd shown up at my shop. We still needed to talk about what had happened to drive her to me like that, but there was no way I could concentrate on something that serious with her naked body atop mine.

"I don't know, maybe they like the smell of wet dog. Reminds them of Fritos."

My jaw dropped as she tried to hold in a laugh. Vincent had teased me about smelling like a dog plenty of times, but I hadn't realized she'd paid attention to us, or that she'd remember he said it was the same scent as Fritos.

Or maybe it was because she had the same sense of smell as her brother.

Mock growling, I hooked my fingers and dug them into her ribs, remembering something else Vincent had said. Brooke squealed, struggling to push my hands away when there was no way for her to get out of my reach. Her laughter filled the room until the contractions finally forced my knot loose and a hot gush of fluid soaked my balls.

We both froze as the scent of us saturated the air. My shaft was instantly aching to be inside her again, focus shifting back to the reason we were here. The lack of green when she stared up at me proved it affected her the same.

Her body slid down mine, nipples brushing against my stomach and thighs as she moved to kneel between my legs, causing me to shiver in anticipation. There was no hesitation as she took me in hand, tongue slipping out to wet her bottom lip before tasting the tip of me. Taking my head in her mouth, she made us both groan, all laughter and teasing forgotten.

Hands fisting in the sheets to keep from taking her head and ramming myself down her throat, I reminded myself again that this was about her.

What she needed.

I was only seeing her through her heat.

I shouldn't get attached.

But when she looked up, lips wrapped around me as she swallowed my length, I feared it was too late. It was getting harder and harder to see that awkward girl that was my best friend's little sister. The one we knew was destined for better things. The one I shouldn't want to claim and keep locked in this room forever.

Brooke sucked me clean, tongue laving every bit of me until there was nothing left of our fluids except the wet spot on the blanket beneath me. When her lips finally popped off me and she sat back, I couldn't resist any longer.

Sitting up, I pulled my legs beneath me and took her by the hips, spinning her around and flipping her so her ass was in the air. Her fingers curled over the end of the mattress as she tipped her hips, presenting for me, and for a moment I was frozen by the sight. This little omega who barely knew me, who trusted me to protect her and her family simply because she remembered I had been friends with her brother, who was far too good for me, offered herself so freely in the most primal way when she was at her most vulnerable.

Something inside me broke. I'd never thought to claim a mate, but looking at her now, I knew she was the only one for me. She was mine. If I couldn't have Brooke, I'd never take another, and I just might kill anyone who tried to claim her in my place.

Her cry rang in my ears as I buried myself inside her, claws and teeth bursting free in my need. I could see the marks she already had on her bottom from our previous coupling, but instead of making me feel like I needed to be gentler, it only spurred me to want to leave more.

Tangling my hand in her hair until her spine arched, I drove myself into her over and over, her cries pushing me to be more brutal with each thrust. Humans were supposed to be weaker than us, the females more delicate, but Brooke met me each time, her core clenching around me. Her body tensed, poised on the edge of release, and I sent her hurtling over when I took one tender nipple between my claws and pinched.

I released her hair, hand slipping down to her nape as my pace increased. Her body trembled as I pinned her down, her channel trying to suck me deeper and keep me there. My knot was already swelling, tugging at her lower lips each time I withdrew, her entire body shuddering when I forced it back in until I was finally trapped. Roaring my own pleasure, I gave in to her body's coaxing, filling her with my seed once again.

Taking the pressure off the back of her neck, I moved her hair to the side, kissing her there before rolling us to the side. Wrapping my arm around her I pulled her close, a purr vibrating from my chest without thought as her ribs heaved beneath the weight of it.

Distantly I heard an insistent pounding, a part of me stirring at the noise, but I was too spent to care what it was unless it came closer. Letting my eyes drift shut as Brooke's breathing slowed, I shook off the concern and drifted into sleep.

Chapter Thirteen

Brooke

I scraped a hand through matted hair, grimacing as my fingers caught in tangles of dried fluids. My heat had begun fairly mild, until it tipped over into debauchery that had me blushing to think about. It wasn't as if I'd been a virgin, but Sebastian had shown me how innocent I'd been. There was clearly a difference between what I'd done with my friend out of instinct, and what happened when I was attracted to the alpha tending me.

My core throbbed at the thought of how many times he'd knotted me, in both his human-and were-form. At the peak of my heat, I'd begged him to shift and force me open around the were's girth, and my thighs clenched at the remembered stretch. It had been painful, and glorious, and something I'd never be able to forget.

My groan as I tried to roll toward the edge of the bed must have woken him, because a hand reached out and pulled me back against a hard chest and a harder erection digging into my bottom. I couldn't help the way I squirmed against him. I wouldn't have minded more of him, but my bladder was screaming for attention, and my rumbling stomach claimed a close second.

"More?"

His sleep roughened voice rumbled in my ear as something hot and wet laved the edge of it, sending a shiver down my spine, and for a moment I considered staying in the bed, but my stomach reminded me there were other needs now that my heat had passed.

Sebastian must have scented the change, or perhaps my body language warned him, because he pulled away and rolled me onto my back, dark eyes searching my face before he ran a hand through his own tangled hair.

"It's done."

It wasn't a question, but I gave him a nod anyway. Opening my mouth, I was cut off before I could speak by pounding coming from the front of the house.

Sebastian's snarl filled the room, his body tensing against me. A second later I heard the distinct sound of a phone vibrating, and he climbed from the bed to grab his jeans from the floor where he'd left them. I vaguely remembered hearing both noises throughout the duration of my heat, but we'd been too wrapped up in each other to care.

Curses spilled from his lips when he looked at the screen, but he didn't answer the call. Instead, those piercing eyes landed on me again and he leaned over the bed, claiming my lips in an unexpected kiss that left me gasping when he straightened.

"I'm going to handle that and grab us something to eat. Why don't you go to the bathroom and clean up?"

Brain still scrambled, I nodded and watched as he turned around, smooth muscle disappearing as he pulled up his jeans. It wasn't until the door closed behind him that the real world came shoving itself back into my thoughts.

Who was banging on the door?
Who'd called?
Why hadn't he answered?

I climbed from the mess that had become of my nest. Pillows and blankets were scattered on the floor around the bed from where they'd been shoved off during our activities. I'd rewrapped us the best I could a couple times while locked on his knot, but I'd been distracted enough most of the time not to notice the destruction.

The red dress I'd arrived in was easy to spot amidst the wreckage, but there was no way I could fix the rip down the back. Wrapping myself in the least dirty sheet I could find, I cracked open the door to peek out into the main area. I couldn't spot Sebastian or anyone else, though I could hear the low rumble of male voices nearby.

Darting across to the open bathroom, I eased the door shut behind me and glanced around. It was larger than I'd expected considering the age of the house, with that shiny new look that suggested he'd recently renovated it. Considering the state of his dining room, he likely had. Even in my distracted state I'd noticed the tools and buckets of paint.

Leann Ryans

There was no tub to sink into to soak my aches away, but the shower was one of those large affairs with three showerheads poking from the walls well above my head. A towel hung from the bar on the front of the sliding door, and a quick sniff let me know it was clean.

Dropping the sheet, I stepped inside the enclosed space. There were two knobs beneath the center showerhead, the lower one with a thin blue and red arrow going in opposite directions from the middle. Clearly the temperature dial, I used it to turn on the water and braced for the impact of frigid liquid, but apparently he had a better setup than the apartment I shared with my parents because the water that hit me was pleasantly warm.

Cranking it a little hotter, I looked from the flowing center head to the two on the sides, and back to the second knob. An experimental twist had them dripping before I turned it up and they sprayed full blast.

It was amazing.

The tension in my muscles melted away as I stood underneath the deluge, simply letting the water run down me. The pressure had my hair soaked in moments with no effort from me, something my pitiful shower at home was incapable of.

Eyes closed, I enjoyed it for a few long minutes before worries began to prod at me again. The first thought to intrude was wondering how long I'd been at Sebastian's. My heats generally lasted four to five days but could vary by a day or two.

The second thought was what would meet me when I went home.

Different scenarios rushed through my head, stilling my hands before I took hold of the shampoo bottle on the shelf beside me.

Had Arik gone there looking for me?

Did he go alone?

Was anyone home?

What if he'd gone when mother was there alone?

Where my parents okay?

Fingers trembling, the bottle almost slipped from them as I poured the shampoo, no longer willing to linger in the shower. I gave my hair a cursory scrub, getting out what tangles I could with my fingers and promising myself I'd do a better job when I got home and was sure everything was okay. My body got the same brisk treatment with the bar of soap I found sitting beside the shampoo, and I was already wrapped in the towel when there was a knock on the bathroom door.

"Brooke?"

Sebastian's voice filtered through the wood, releasing the sudden ball of fear that had fisted my heart at the unexpected sound. I had to swallow twice to get the lump out of my throat before pulling the door open.

Sebastian's eyes raked down my body, sending a wave of heat in their wake. Topless and still smelling of our time in the bed, he was almost irresistible. I had the insane urge to drop the towel and wrap myself around those thick muscles until I smelled of him again, but I reminded myself there were more important things than my suddenly ravenous libido.

"I thought you'd want something clean to wear. Though now I'm regretting letting you out of the bed."

He held a set of folded clothes toward me as he spoke. My sore core clenched at his words, but I ignored the pooling desire in my belly and reached out to take the bundle.

"Thank you."

We both stood in silence for a moment, staring at each other until he shook his head and took a step back.

"I've got food once you're dressed."

He gestured toward the living room, but I shook my head. I'd already wasted enough time, and now the unknown was gnawing at me.

"I need to get home and check on my parents. Arik could have—"

"Your parents are fine, and you're not leaving without eating something first."

My instant reaction was irritation at his highhandedness, but I let his words sink in.

"You know they're okay?"

"The Knights have watched over them since we left the bar. I promise nothing has happened to them, and nothing will."

I searched his face, not sure if he was being truthful or simply trying to placate me, but the seriousness I found there reassured me. My parents had treated him as one of their own when my brother had been alive and Sebastian was at our house all the time. I'd counted on him at least feeling a shred of gratitude for it when I'd decided to come to him.

I studied his face a moment longer before nodding. Clutching the clothing he'd brought me to my chest, I stepped back into the bathroom again, finally looking away as I closed the door between us. My mother would be worried and would question where I'd been, but I trusted him to know she'd still have that chance when I returned.

The clothes Sebastian had given me were a simple black pair of sweats with a white t-shirt. Both were much too large, but I did what I could, folding over the top of the pants before rolling up the hem. I tied a knot in the side of the shirt to help keep the excess out of the way, though there was nothing I could do about the neck being so large it hung off one shoulder.

Or the way my nipples poked through the thin fabric since I hadn't worn a bra beneath the dress.

Shrugging, I reminded myself he'd already seen it all. It was more modest than the dress I'd been wearing at the bar, and while I was sure I'd get a raised brow from my mother, it was better than riding his motorcycle in nothing.

I stepped out into the short hallway and turned into the main room, looking around for Sebastian. I was half expecting to see whoever had been pounding on his door, but it seemed as though they were already gone since he was the only one I spotted.

Looking up from the kitchen sink, he stopped what he was doing and grabbed a glass off the counter beside him, striding over to me and holding it out. He'd put on another t-shirt, this one a dark blue, with his leather vest overtop it, but the sight of him still made my mouth water.

Accepting the glass, I raised it to my mouth to hide the way I'd been ogling him, but the tip of his lips suggested he knew. Once the cold liquid hit my throat though, downing it was all I could think about. My heat always left me feeling dehydrated, and I'd taken a few mouthfuls of water in the shower to quench the worst of it, but what he'd given me was the best lemonade I'd tasted in my life. It disappeared too fast, but Sebastian just smiled as he took the glass and went back to the kitchen, refilling it from a pitcher he pulled from the fridge.

"Once you eat I can take you home, unless there's somewhere else you'd like to go?"

I shook my head as he returned with the refilled glass, forcing myself to take small sips instead of chugging it again.

"No, I'm sure Mom is worried, and I need to get ready for my next shift anyway."

Sebastian nodded as he led the way around the couch so we could take a seat. He already had a pair of sandwiches laid out with a bag of chips and some sad looking bananas that were just this side of perfect for making bread.

He ran a hand through his hair as I reached for the fruit, a slight grimace crossing his face.

"Sorry, it's all I had that was still good."

Shrugging, I peeled the banana.

"It's fine. You didn't exactly have time to prepare."

I glanced at him as I took the first bite. His eyes were locked on my mouth, the look on his face fanning the flames I was still trying to put out.

"I would have if I'd helped you when you asked me to."

Despite how soft the banana was it almost got lodged in my throat. Unable to keep looking at him, I ducked my head as I forced it down and cleared my throat.

"I know it was unexpected and a bit strange, especially after…"

My voice trailed off as I thought about what happened to my brother once again. I was too young when it happened to have gotten all the details, but suddenly I needed them. I needed to know if Arik really was the murderer Sebastian had labeled him when we buried Vincent.

Leann Ryans

Chapter Fourteen

Sebastian

The look on her face when she raised her eyes to mine again told me exactly what she was about to ask even before the words left her mouth.

"What happened? Why do you say Arik murdered him?"

I bit back my groan, dropping the sandwich I'd lifted from the plate again as my stomach soured. I didn't know how much Brooke knew of what we'd been up to, but she deserved to know why her brother died.

Especially since it was due to me.

I just hoped she didn't hate me after I told her.

"Your brother was part of the Purists for about a year."

Her lips parted, eyes going wide. It was hard to escape association with the gang when you lived so close to their territory, but she obviously hadn't known Vincent was an actual member.

I raised my hand before she could speak, continuing with the story before I decided against it.

"I know he didn't hold with their beliefs. He was doing it for the money, so we could start a shop together."

I paused, swallowing the emotions trying to choke me. I had always been working on cars back then, happy with the distraction it provided. I didn't come across motorcycles until later, but once Vincent realized I was good at repairs he latched onto the idea of us running a shop together to get out of the slums. He'd learned to do basic things like oil changes, but he'd never had the talent for figuring what was wrong with an ailing engine. He was the one supposed to run the business since he was better at numbers than me.

"He'd worked for them while I kept my shitty job, and we saved every penny we could. We'd bought a few tools here and there, but he was adamant we buy our own place before we started getting too much. We were too young and broke to get a loan, so we needed cash to buy property."

I didn't mention I'd tried to talk him out of joining the Purists when he first mentioned his plan. It didn't matter now. Clearly, I hadn't tried hard enough, because, like him, I'd been in a rush to see our dream made real and escape the nightmare of going home to my father every night.

"He did his best to keep it all separate. He'd walk miles out of the way before heading where he was supposed to meet them in an effort to keep you and your parents safe. Plus, he couldn't exactly be seen associating with me or he'd be questioned about his loyalties."

My chest burned with the pain I'd caused.

"It worked for a while, but after a few months he started getting the feeling he was being watched. He ran into some of the other members near your home more often than could be called coincidence when they had never been in that area before."

Brooke remained quiet, the banana drooping from her fingers as she listened. I studied her face for a moment, wanting to commit it to memory before the look in her eyes changed.

"Anyway, he never figured out if he was right or not. He was called to do a job at a warehouse, and when he showed up, Arik and the kiss-asses who followed him around had a family of shifters tied up inside. They wanted him to torture them for some bullshit information or something. He tried getting out of it by saying that stuff wasn't his job, but Arik wouldn't let up. Ordered him to do it anyway to prove his loyalty."

It felt like Bill's old truck was sitting on my chest, each breath a struggle as I remembered the horror I'd heard in his voice when Vincent told me what happened.

"Vincent left. They tried to stop him, but he got loose. Ran straight to where I worked in his panic. He didn't realize the other members had followed him until Arik walked up and asked what he was doing running to a dog when he was supposed to be ridding the world of them."

My throat burned with the bile churning in my stomach. Brooke's eyes sparkled with the shimmer of building tears. I was sure she could guess the rest from there, but she'd asked what happened, so I kept going.

"He played it off, saying he was trying to buy something from me and hadn't realized I was a shifter with all the other scents in the store. They claimed to have seen us together before, but we both denied knowing each other. They harassed us for a bit, but the owner and a few others showed up and ran them all out. I wanted to follow him but knew it would make things worse.

"He called me later, saying he'd been forced into a meeting with some of the leaders of the gang. Arik's father was one of them. Vincent thought everything was fine when Arik got chewed out for calling him instead of one of the men they used for such things, and he was allowed to leave."

My throat tried to close on the next words. Tears streamed down Brooke's cheeks, and I wanted nothing more than to comfort her, but I doubted she'd accept. Her brother's association with me led to his death, even if I hadn't been the one to kill him.

"Your mother called me that night when he didn't come home. She begged me to tell her where to look for him, but I knew it was too dangerous to let her or your father go anywhere near the Purists. I told her he'd probably gotten distracted and didn't notice the time, but she knew something was wrong.

"I went out and tried to look for him, but the usual places were empty. After a few hours I realized I couldn't find any known members of the Purists, so I thought maybe something else had happened. Something big that required all of them, and Vincent would come home when it was over.

"I didn't realize he was the reason until I headed into work the next morning and the building was trashed. Windows busted, goods scattered and destroyed, graffiti all over the front."

I had to stop and suck in a deep breath before I could finish. Brooke didn't need the gory details, but the images played in my mind anyway.

"That's where I found Vincent. It was too late to save him. Medics said he'd been dead for hours."

My head dropped, hanging with the weight of guilt and loss I still carried. There was no reason to tell her about what I'd done after. How I'd blown up and gone on a rampage straight to the heart of the Purists, and then been laughed away. I was lucky to have escaped with my life, but they'd thought letting me live with the pain was worse than killing me.

They were right.

I lifted my head again to stare at Brooke, fearing what I'd see. It had taken years to get over the worst of my grief and move on. I'd been careless and taken risks that should have killed me, and I raged at the world when it wouldn't put me out of my misery. Eventually I'd accepted I had to live on, and it was better to do it celebrating Vincent's memory instead of wasting the chance I'd been given.

And maybe I still had another purpose to serve. Another way for me to show my friend the thanks he deserved for being there for me when I'd needed it most. For offering friendship when I was broken.

Brooke drew in a stuttering breath, bringing my focus back to her. If I hadn't been so selfish when Vincent passed, I'd have been there to protect her, and she'd have never had to face the issue with Arik, but that wasn't the way things turned out. Maybe being there to watch her grow up would have made it easier to keep hold of my plan to do nothing more than help her through her heat, but seeing her now, knowing how she tasted, it was impossible not to want her.

Those big green eyes stared at me, lips trembling as the light sparkled from the tear tracks on her cheeks. Her nose was red, hair still wet as she sat in my oversized clothes, and yet she was the most beautiful woman I'd ever met.

The prick of my claws digging into my knees was all that kept me in place, my muscles quivering with the urge to close the distance between us. As scared as I'd been that she'd hate me for my part in her brother's story, all that met me in her gaze was shared sorrow.

Her hand moved toward me, and it took a moment for me to realize she was holding it out for me to take. Whether to offer support, or ask for it, I wasn't sure, but it didn't stop me from wrapping my fingers around hers and letting the space between us fill with my purr.

It took a few minutes for the sound to penetrate, slowly relaxing her muscles as she clung to my hand, and then the soft sound of hers rose to join me. The tears slowed, then stopped, and she never once looked away.

Until the piercing sound of my ringtone ripped through the air.

Brooke startled, pulling her fingers from my grip as our purrs stuttered to a stop. For a moment I was frozen at the loss, but I shook my head and focused, reaching for where I'd left my phone on the table. Carl's name was written across the top of the screen, so I had no choice but to answer.

"Yes?"

I'd already been informed of the issue. Arik had been nosing around our territory. He'd gone by Brooke's home the day after she went into heat, and since he'd arrived while both of her parents were gone my men let him go to the door and waste his energy banging on it. After that he'd sent his lackeys by every few hours, waiting for her, until the third day passed and Arik figured out she wasn't coming home.

Carl and a few of the guys had to intercede when Arik showed up again with other members of the Purists set on questioning her parents about where she was. They managed to keep him from her parent's door, but not without a fight breaking out between the two groups, and he'd shown back up shortly before Tim had been sent to bang on my door and see if Brooke's heat was over yet.

"He's gone and I don't think he's coming back. He's figured out he won't be getting through us without a fight and by now her heat should be over, but our presence gives away that she's with one of us. There's going to be retaliation. She's probably better off home than at your place now."

"Understood."

I disconnected, shaking off the lingering mood of recounting the incident that had set me on the path my life had taken. Glancing at Brooke, I could see she'd pulled herself back together as well. She offered a small smile that didn't quite reach her eyes, but I knew she was strong, and she'd deserved the truth of what happened now that she was old enough to understand. Her parents hadn't even known my part in it.

"Thank you for telling me."

I shook my head at her whisper, reaching out to catch her hand again. When she didn't pull away from my touch my heart gave a painful twist, but I ignored it.

"You were too young to hear it then, but it's past time you knew. I'm not sure your parents know all of it, and it's probably still too hard for them to talk about."

She sniffed and ducked her head, bobbing it in a nod. She looked so small I wanted to wrap her in my arms and never let go, the wolf inside me perfectly agreeable to that plan, but I knew it couldn't happen. Brooke deserved more than I could offer.

Pushing to my feet, I gathered the uneaten food, knowing neither of us could stomach it any longer. When she looked up at me, I cleared my throat and tried to focus.

"Grab your things and I'll get you home."

Turning, I put my back to her and walked to the kitchen, reminding myself I had to keep distance between us. Despite what we'd done the past few days and the grief we shared over her brother, she was still too good for me. Heading for better places than this shitty city, while I was tied here by my shop and my bond to the Hell's Knights.

No matter my sudden longing, Brooke wasn't for me.

Leann Ryans

Chapter Fifteen

Brooke

Everything was numb.

Not just my body from the ride, though the air had chilled me despite Sebastian giving me his jacket for the trip.

No, everything inside was numb too. Too much had happened. I'd learned too much. And now I was trying to process it.

Sebastian walked me up to my apartment after I collected my purse from his saddlebag. The dress had gone in the trash, and I hadn't been able to find my panties, so it was all I had with me.

Blinking at the door, it took a moment to realize I needed to dig out my keys to get in. Mom would be at work already, and while Dad was home, he'd still be sleeping in their room since it was only late morning.

Turning the key and stepping through the doorway, it seemed like it had been forever since I'd been there. Everything looked the same, yet it all felt different.

I felt different.

Leann Ryans

I wondered if my parents had known Vincent was part of the Purists. I had a feeling they didn't, at least not while he'd been alive, but had they found out after? Did they know he didn't hold with their beliefs and he'd died because he wouldn't take the life of another, even one deemed less than a pure human by some? That he'd only joined to reach his dream?

A lump rose in my throat, threatening to choke me. I'd seen the wariness in Sebastian's eyes as he told the story, along with his own pain. It had been too deep and raw for me to think he'd been lying about anything. Plus, he had no reason to. He'd been distant and uncaring up until my heat, and as soon as he told me what had happened to Vincent, he'd clammed up again, giving me no reason to believe my thoughts mattered to him.

My chest ached at the way he'd pulled away. When I'd left the bathroom, he'd seemed so open, if a bit distracted. It felt as though there might have been something there, something beyond what we'd done, but his blank expression as he stood in the doorway had me questioning whether I was projecting my own feelings.

Learning why my brother had been killed had quenched any desire I'd had, but there was still a pull to the alpha staring at me. The way he'd held my hand and purred to soothe me...

I swallowed again to clear the lump, trying to find my voice. Things were always a bit awkward with my friend after my cycles, until we got a bit of space, cleaned up, and could pretend it never happened. It was worse with

Sebastian since he'd been a practical stranger, yet our history didn't allow me to treat him as one, and I wanted so much more.

"Tha—"

"Brooke—"

Both of us stopped, waiting for the other to continue since we'd started talking at the same time. My heart raced though I tried to ignore the sudden surge of hope I felt. Just because I was an omega and he'd helped me through my heat didn't mean he wanted anything more, and while he'd protected my parents during the course of it, that didn't mean he would continue to do so. We weren't his responsibility.

That thought was like a bucket of cold water, and my shoulders curled in as I imagined the next encounter I'd have with Arik. Upset was too light a word for what he'd be since there was no way he hadn't figured out I'd gone into heat without informing him.

My eyes dropped to Sebastian's chest, but he reached out and tipped my chin up, forcing me to meet his gaze.

"Be careful. Let me know if Arik comes back, and make sure you don't answer the door if you're home alone. Hell, don't answer it at all. You can't trust him."

I nodded as much as his grip allowed. His brow furrowed as he stared down at me, dark eyes intense as they dug into mine, and for a moment I thought he was going to lean down and kiss me.

And then he let go, taking a step back.

"Close and lock the door. Keep it locked at all times. If he keeps bothering you and you need the Hell's Knights to help, we're here."

I blinked, processing his words.

The Hell's Knights.

Not *him*.

It was like someone punched me in the stomach. Bile rose up to choke me, my lungs seizing around the sob I refused to let out in front of him. I knew what I'd asked for, what he'd agreed to, but it had felt like more, and now I was the one left looking like a fool pining after an alpha.

I'd blame it on hormones. Once I was done crying into my pillow.

Shutting the door, I did as he'd ordered, locking the knob and the bolt despite knowing Arik could get through them if he really wanted to. My only hope was that he wouldn't want to make that much of a scene in an area that wasn't part of the slums he ruled. The police wouldn't arrive in time to save me even if a neighbor called.

Sucking in a stuttering breath, I pressed my back to the door as the tears started again. It was too much. The financial strain, the fear of Arik, the fresh pain of losing my brother, and now the confusion over Sebastian.

I slid down the door, wrapping my arms around my legs as I rested my head on my knees and cried. I'd had so many hopes when my brother was alive. A drive to do well, go to college, and move somewhere safe. Find a good alpha and settle down. Raise a family.

Yet here I was, still living with my parents. Still working a dead-end job. Still trying to do good, but just spinning my wheels as my life passed by without much participation from me.

Even my plan to escape Arik for my heat was only a temporary fix, one I knew was likely to come back and haunt me. He knew where I lived. Where I worked. And if he decided I was worth the effort, he could destroy me and any hopes I'd ever had.

If he didn't just kill me.

I wasn't sure my parents would survive losing both their children. My brother's death had been a blow that left them less than they'd been before. Less happy. Less involved. I knew they still loved me, but everything was stilted after Vincent was gone.

The tears slowly dried up, my body incapable of maintaining the loss of moisture when I was already dehydrated. Dragging myself upright, I forced one foot in front of the other to the kitchen, pouring a large glass of water that I stood at the sink and drained before filling again and shuffling off to my bedroom. I had every intention of taking off Sebastian's clothes and hopping in my tiny shower for a proper wash, but all the energy I had abandoned me.

Pulling back the covers on my bed, I crawled underneath. I was still recovering from my heat, so the lack of a male's scent was unsettling, and after a few restless minutes I tugged Sebastian's shirt up over my nose, inhaling the tiny, lingering scent of him.

Muscles relaxing, I drifted off only to be startled awake sometime later when my phone rang. Eyes too blurry to focus, I dug it out of my purse and blinked at the picture of my mother on the screen, but I didn't get a chance to answer before the door to my room swung open and her head popped around the edge.

"There you are! I've called every day. What happened? When did you get home? Why didn't you call me back?"

Scrubbing my face, I tried to rub away the fog of sleep, the pull to drift off still strong. I forced myself to sit up, clearing my head enough to form words.

"Sorry, I didn't take my phone out till I put it on the charger before laying down. I got home this morning."

My mouth was dry, the glass of water sitting forgotten on the nightstand. I snatched it up before my mother could say more, chugging it down. Her worried eyes still rested on me when I sat it aside, gaze missing nothing.

"Are you okay? I didn't know you were so close to your cycle. Did anything happen?"

Being a beta, my mom theoretically knew about my heats, but she didn't understand the all-consuming need that could take over, and how I couldn't think enough to be able to call. She'd been aware of my arrangement with my friend, and she knew he'd moved away, so there were likely a myriad of questions she'd like to ask but was doing her best to hold back.

As much as I loved my mother, I didn't go into details about what happened when I disappeared for a few days.

"I'm fine, just tired. And hungry," I added as my stomach rumbled.

I'd only had a bite of the banana before Sebastian told me what happened to Vincent, and afterwards I'd lost my appetite.

"You don't usually disappear so suddenly."

Her voice held a touch of reprimand, but I knew it was based in worry. Despite me being more than old enough to make my own decisions, she still had the tendency to forget I was no longer a child. I never made much fuss about it considering I still lived with them, but it could get frustrating.

"I wasn't paying attention and it came on faster than I'd expected. I thought I had another day. You and Dad have been busy, so I didn't say anything about it because I thought I was going to spend it at home, but then I found someone to help."

Her lips thinned, the disapproval on her face obvious. She may not want me stuck with an alpha I didn't care for, but she also never liked the way I chose to spend my cycles. She was a bit old fashioned, believing I should do my best to wait for the right alpha. As if it was that easy to ignore instinct.

"Are there any leftovers in the fridge?"

I asked the question more to redirect her than anything. I didn't have the energy to handle the direction I could see the conversation going. Emotions flickered across her face, letting me know she knew what I was doing, but she let it slide. I'd always loved my parents for not being the type to pry.

"I'll go make us some dinner while you get cleaned up."

She sniffed but I knew her sense of smell was nowhere as acute as mine or an alphas. Betas didn't rely on scents the way the other two dynamics did.

"Thanks."

She closed the door and I let out a sigh, flopping back onto the bed. I wanted nothing more than to curl up and go back to sleep, but I *was* hungry, and I did need to shower again. My hair had finished drying while I slept and there was no way I'd get the mess under control if I didn't.

I dragged myself out of the covers and stripped on the way to the bathroom. It was impossible not to be disappointed in it after using Sebastian's, but I reminded myself this was my only option. I likely wouldn't see him again, and it was for the best.

I was trying to keep my head down, save up, and go to college. He was already settled, owned a repair shop, and ran a motorcycle gang.

Our worlds were different.

Sighing again, I stepped under the cold water, scrubbing the remaining scent of him from my skin and hair. It sent a pang through my belly, but the sooner I moved on and forgot about what it was like to be in Sebastian's arms, the better off I'd be. I still had to figure out what to do when Arik showed up.

The thought of the other alpha had my blood running just as cold as the water dripping off me. I may have escaped spending my heat with him, but that didn't mean I'd escaped *him*. I knew there'd be a price to pay for avoiding him, but maybe I could still play it off as another alpha keeping me away.

My mother's voice broke me from the paralysis my thoughts brought on. Slushing off the remaining suds, I stepped from the tub and shoved the worries into a box in the corner of my mind. I was too tired to deal with them coherently, and I needed what energy the shower had given me to face my mother. I'd save the problem of Arik for morning.

Leann Ryans

Chapter Sixteen

Sebastian

I lingered in the parking lot of Brooke's apartment, hidden between another building and the dumpster. The scents confronting me were terrible, but there was nowhere else I could sit and be out of view from her window and the road.

Shaking my head, I went to start my bike again. Hours had passed and I was needed elsewhere, but I hadn't been able to bring myself to leave. I'd been on the verge, but seeing her father come down the stairs and head toward the train he took to the warehouse district convinced me I needed to stay.

It was tempting to head back up to the apartment. My cock throbbed at the thought of entering her home and taking her in her nest. Not the one she built for her heat at my house, but *hers*. Her parents were gone and there was nothing to stop us.

Except the worry that Arik may show up while we were distracted.

Sighing, I rubbed a hand through my hair and down my face, noticing the thick stubble. I'd given myself a quick wash in the kitchen sink while Brooke showered at my place, but I kept catching hints of her scent still on me when the wind blew the stench of the dumpster away. I needed to go to the shop and talk to Carl, but I'd have to go home and actually clean myself first.

Huffing out a breath, I kicked the bike to life. Carl was convinced Arik would come after us instead of Brooke, but I wasn't so sure. It all depended on whether he thought she'd avoided him on purpose.

Teeth clenched, I shoved off, turning the wheel back toward my place. I needed to check on the shop and get the details of what happened during the confrontation with the Purists. I couldn't sit outside Brooke's apartment forever.

The wind had been chilly when I drove Brooke home, but the day had turned warm, heat rising from the street and making the wind buffeting me anything but refreshing. I was already tired from the lack of sleep over the last few days, and the heat just made me drowsier, and it was hard to resist the urge to forget it all and go to bed. Knowing I'd be twice as tempted by the scent lingering in my house, I decided going home to wash wouldn't work.

Pulling into the lot at my shop, I parked my bike at the end of the row of others already there. I'd had a shower installed in the back when I was living out of the building and always had a change of clothes in the office. Working on cars was a messy business and I couldn't count the times I'd needed to clean up and change before touching my bike.

Carl was standing at the counter when I jerked open the front door, his head raising to give me a once over. He must have sensed my intent because he only grunted at me, tipping his head toward the bathroom in the back.

"It's empty. I'll keep the guys away."

Giving him a nod as I passed, I didn't stop until I closed the bathroom door behind me. As reluctant as I was to lose Brooke's scent, I didn't want anyone else to smell her on me. Her pheromones would put everyone on edge, and I wasn't sure how I would handle another alpha scenting her slick.

Stripping, I stuffed my clothes in one of the trash bags under the sink and tied the top. It was the best I could do to contain the scent with no way of washing them at the shop.

Warm water blasted me as soon as I turned the knob, my skin stinging from it. This one was nowhere near as large or nice as the one I'd installed at the house, but it got the job done. I was out and drying off in a matter of minutes.

Toweling my hair before pulling it back into my typical ponytail, I grabbed the bag of clothes and stepped out of the bathroom. I hadn't expected anyone to be in the back and hadn't bothered covering myself, so seeing Carl leaning against the wall across from me made me pause.

His brow rose, lips twitching.

"Looks like you got in a fight with a cat. And lost."

He straightened, pushing off the wall and tossing a bundle of clothes at my chest as I looked down to see what he meant. I hadn't noticed the scratches scattered across my skin, and my chest swelled at the evidence of Brooke's pleasure littering my flesh.

"Shut up, old man. Not my fault you haven't gotten your dick wet in so long it's likely shriveled up and dropped off."

He barked out a laugh, turning to stride down the hall to the front of the shop.

"I'll be in your office, whelp."

I huffed out a breath, lips ticking up as I stepped back into the bathroom again. I had no problem strutting through the shop in front of the guys, but I didn't know if there were customers out front, and I didn't need the headache that would bring. I'd worked too hard to build the business to risk ruining it all because I was being careless.

I tugged on the pants and pulled the shirt over my head, feeling naked for a moment without my vest. Wearing it had become habit, though not all the members chose to, but it carried Brooke's scent just as much as my other clothes and needed to remain in the bag.

Rolling my shoulders to settle the unease, I stomped back into my boots and headed out to my office. It was in the front of the building behind the main desk, and I was glad to see no one was waiting in the lobby for service.

Carl was sitting in the single chair opposite my desk when I opened the door. He held a beer in one hand, another open and waiting in front of my seat. Even though it was already evening, it was unusual for him to start drinking so early, and especially while the shop was still open.

"All of the cars on the roster were taken care of, and bills settled except the Mercedes. Jackass broke the thermostat housing when he removed it, so we had to order the part and are still waiting on it. Going to have to give them a discount for the wait."

He started speaking before my ass even hit the chair, but it was one of the reasons I trusted Carl to run things in my absence. He might like to give me hell, but he knew when to get serious. 'Jackass' was the nickname he'd given Jackson shortly after we first hired him and the man knocked down a pile of parts in the storeroom. Something so minor wouldn't warrant a beer, so I knew there was worse to come.

"Martha brought over a potpie and a cake the day after you holed up. I let the boys eat it since I knew it'd go bad before you came out."

I couldn't stop my nose from curling.

"It was probably already bad when she brought it."

Carl chuckled, shrugging one shoulder. Some of the other guys seemed to have no sense of taste and frequently ate things I'd never touch.

Like Martha's cooking.

"I'll send her a thank you card tomorrow."

"Already done."

I tipped my beer toward him in a small salute before bringing it to my lips. Everyone knew how dehydrated an omega could get during their heat, but an alpha lost almost as much fluid, and I was parched. I chugged the whole bottle in four gulps, accepting the second Carl passed me from the mini fridge behind his chair. He waited until I popped the cap off and took another swig before going on.

"There's going to be retaliation."

I stared across the desk at him, trying to figure out if there was a way to avoid what was coming.

"What happened?"

"He showed up while Tom and Knox were there. They blocked him from getting to the building and he backed off before things got physical, but came back with his groupies. Knox had called me and I knew it was going to happen, so I'd headed over with a few more guys. Things got heated. Frank's arm was broken, and Tom got his canine knocked out, which he's still pissed over."

Carl paused to take a drink before going on. I'd already known we had a few minor injuries, but it was what the Knight's did to Arik's men that would make the difference between petty revenge and all-out war. Broken bones healed fast for shifters, and while the loss of a tooth was permanent, it wasn't serious.

"No one died, but one of Arik's men will be crippled the rest of his sorry life. And Arik is sporting a nice new scar across his pretty face."

I couldn't stop the groan that rose. Arik may have overlooked an injury to someone else because the bastard had always been self-centered, but to him? He'd never let it go.

"Has anything else happened besides the one fight?"

"They've been seen snooping around and a few words were exchanged, but nothing else physical."

The *yet* hung in the air. We both knew there would be more to come. It was inevitable. We generally tried to avoid fights with other gangs, keeping to ourselves, but there were times it was impossible.

"The guys know?"

While most of the Hell's Knights worked for the shop or The Hangout, there were a few members who were scattered a bit further and therefore more vulnerable. I didn't want anyone becoming a target without knowing who to watch out for. The Purists had grown over the years to a group large enough to be wary of. We'd already been keeping an eye on them, but this meant stepping up our watch.

"Everyone's up to date and keeping an eye out. The ones who can't be pulled in have been warned to keep their bikes and loyalties under wraps for a bit so they don't become targets, and to holler if there's trouble."

I sighed and took another gulp of beer, wishing it was something stronger, and for a moment longed for the simpler days when I only had myself to worry about. The Hell's Knights wasn't a large club by any means, but that made each soul that was part of us weigh heavier on my shoulders.

"Any idea yet what they're going to try?"

I knew if Carl had the information, he would have already shared it, but I couldn't help asking, hoping for some kind of good news.

"You know what Arik's likely to do better than any of us."

Images of Vincent's body flashed in my head for the second time that day. I wouldn't let that happen to another person because they associated with me.

"Maybe I should confront him myself. Let him know it was me, so he doesn't come after the whole club."

Carl's lip twitched but he didn't outright deny the idea. I knew it wouldn't sit well with him because he knew what that would mean, but he also knew the good of many was more important than the safety of one.

"Would it make a difference, really? Everyone knows you're the head of the Knights. He'd likely strike us just to hurt you."

I grunted in acknowledgment. With what happened after they'd killed Vincent, I knew Arik would avoid me while he went after every other member until I was the last standing. I wouldn't put the men through that.

Leaning back in my chair I rubbed my eyes before scratching at the scruff on my face. I still needed to shave but it was low on my list of things to do.

"Was it worth it?"

Carl's question caught me by surprise and my eyes jerked back to his.

"Yes."

I burned with the certainty behind my answer, but I knew he might not understand. I'd told him about Vincent once, long ago, and while I hadn't gone into the details, he was aware of the history behind me and Arik.

"She's Vincent's little sister. Arik found her somehow, found out she's an omega, and planned to take her during her heat."

Carl grimaced. I didn't have to explain what that would have meant for Brooke. Any omega would have been in danger with Arik, but Brooke more so. Carl's own history left him with a soft spot for women in need, but I knew he was also weighing what the cost would be to us.

"Should we keep men on her place then? I figured Arik would drop it but if he had other reasons to go after her than just being omega, he might not stop."

My gut clenched, claws flexing as I saw red. Instinct screamed at me to run out to my bike and get to her as fast as possible to be sure she was okay, but logic fought back.

"That would draw more attention to her. Make her more valuable. Right now, she's just pussy I stole from him."

The words were ash in my mouth but there was no way I could let anyone know she was more than that. It would put her in more danger.

"Then you should make sure everyone knows that, so there's no question. A few of the guys were questioning why you up and ran out on us so quick. *Mate* was being tossed around in public."

My wolf surged at the word mate, agreeing. My skin twitched with the itch of hair growing before I suppressed it.

Carl's sharp eyes didn't miss any of it. Shaking his head, he drained his bottle and stood.

"We should make sure the guys finished up and locked the garage when they left, then you should go to bed. You look like your bike rode *you* here. Guess you're past your prime after all."

His offhand insult as he walked out of my office had a grin breaking out despite the worry gnawing at me.

"If I'm past my prime then what are you, two steps from the grave? Can you even get it up anymore?"

His chuckle reached me as I finished my beer and tossed it in the garbage as I stood. Muscles twinged, reminding me how much physical effort I'd put in the past few days.

"It's not all about your cock, whelp. I feel sorry for the poor girl if that's all you used on her."

Shaking my head I followed him to the garage, pictures of all the things I'd done to Brooke playing in my head, sending a surge of blood to tighten my jeans. As much trouble as it was going to cause, I'd never regret it. I only hoped the guys would forgive me if things went as bad as I expected.

Chapter Seventeen

Brooke

I spent my entire shift looking over my shoulder, watching the door for any sign of Arik. My muscles were so tense by the time I left they ached as if I'd been working out all day, and my temples pounded with a stress headache. I didn't breathe easy until I locked the apartment door behind me, and even then, I couldn't completely relax.

"Hey, Sweetheart. Everything okay?"

I startled at the masculine voice until my dad's form swam into focus in front of me. Glancing at the clock above the dining table, I realized he was probably trying to get out the door I was leaning against.

"Oh, hey Dad. Yeah, just... long day at work."

His brow creased as his lips tipped into a frown. He'd always felt bad that I had to help them with the bills instead of heading off to college as I'd planned, and I didn't want him feeling any worse because I'd used it as an excuse to cover the real issue.

Leann Ryans

Moving out of the way, I pasted on a smile and straightened my back. Luckily his sense of smell as a beta wasn't strong enough to catch the stench of fear lingering on me.

"Aren't you going to be late? Do you need me to drive you?"

I said a silent prayer he wouldn't say yes. Dealing with my mother the night before had drained my ability to tiptoe around the things I didn't want to discuss, and being trapped in a car with him for the time it would take to drive him to the warehouse he worked at would be torture when I wanted nothing more than to be alone.

His gaze moved to the clock before coming back to me. The frown was still in place but the furrow between his eyes had softened.

"I should be able to make it to the train. You're sure you're okay?"

I bobbed my head, faking an energy I lacked.

"Plan to veg out in front of the TV with some noodles before bed. Tell Mom not to worry if she comes in and doesn't see me, I may already be in bed."

I knew he would message her while he was on the train, so that would take care of having to face her again. Despite the early hour I had every intention of going straight to bed after I stuffed something in my belly to quiet its demands.

"Okay, Sweetie. Have a good night."

He dropped a kiss on my forehead as he had every night when I was little, and for a moment my eyes misted over. Refusing to give in to the surge of emotion, I blinked it away and held the door for him, waving until he disappeared down the stairs outside.

I bolted the door again. Despite being alone, a wave of relief rolled through me. If Arik came for me, I'd rather face him alone than have my parents get hurt because they stood in his way.

Trudging down the hall, I pulled the rubber band out of my hair and let it fall around my shoulders. I stripped out of my uniform once I made it to my room, tugging on a pair of fuzzy pajama pants and a tank top before going back to the kitchen to find something to eat. Usually, I would cook so there was something for Mom to eat when she got home, but I was too tired to make the effort.

Settling on a bowl of cereal since waiting for water to boil seemed like too much, I sat at the table and spooned it up, just the effort of raising my hand to my mouth leaving me exhausted. I still hadn't recovered from my heat, and the stress of waiting for something to happen kept me from bouncing back like I usually did. I wasn't sure how long I'd be able to deal with it.

I toyed with the idea that not seeing him was a good thing. Maybe he'd forgotten about me once he couldn't get what he wanted, and I'd never see him again?

Snorting to myself, I gave up the fight against the need to sleep. I knew Arik wasn't the type to forget. He'd come, I just didn't know when, and that was the terrifying part. At least there would be someone with me during my shift the next day since the truck was arriving to restock.

Leann Ryans

I wiggled into my bed, blankets and pillows heaped around me, and hugged one to my chest. I had every intention of working out what to say when he finally came for me, but found myself blinking into the morning light without the memory of falling asleep.

A look at the time had me surging from bed, already knowing I wouldn't make it to work on time. There were laws in place that prevented employers from discriminating against omegas and forcing them to give us time for our cycles, but I'd found that many would use any other reason they could find to penalize us, and being late right after returning from my cycle was a good way to find myself jobless.

I froze in place at the thought and toyed with the idea for a moment. If I was fired, Arik wouldn't be able to harass me at work anymore. I needed the money and would have to find something else quickly, but it was the knowledge that he'd just come to the house if he couldn't find me there that had me moving again.

I ran out as quietly as I could, careful not to slam the door and disturb my dad's sleep. I was puffing for breath long before I slipped through the door of the convenience store, wide eyes turning to my coworker behind the counter. Technically I was scheduled to run the register and Barry was supposed to unload the boxes, but he shot me a smug look as he leaned on the countertop.

"I already counted in a drawer since you were late. Guess you'll have to stock."

I swallowed my groan, muscles already protesting. I was only eight minutes late but there was no reason to argue and make things worse. Barry was usually pretty laid back, and I doubted he'd rat me out unless directly asked, but there was no reason to irritate him and make it more likely.

I nodded and shot him a tight smile.

"No problem. Sorry."

He shrugged off my apology, standing to pull out his phone and start swiping away on it. I knew that's all he would do the rest of the day, but at least having to stock shelves would keep me busy so I wouldn't be standing around and worrying. I'd have been helping him do it between customers anyway, I just hated having to move the heavy boxes from the back of the store.

Dropping my purse into a cubby in the back, I eyed the stack of boxes, letting out a sigh before getting started. We had a cart I could take things to the front on, but some of the boxes were stacked as high as my head and they could be a pain to get down where I could open and unload them. Nothing was getting done with me standing around though, so I got to work.

I kept going steadily through the morning, falling into a pattern that left me with too much time to think. As much as I kept trying to focus on my task, or anything else, my thoughts kept circling between Arik and Sebastian.

The two alphas were polar opposites. One dark, one light. One good, one bad. One I wanted; one I couldn't stand.

Leann Ryans

Every time I thought of Arik the worry returned, and I couldn't stop myself from looking around the store to be sure he wasn't there. I had no reason to believe he wouldn't show up eventually, and the waiting was distracting enough for me to almost wish it would just happen already.

Thoughts of Arik led to wondering how to placate him, which inevitably led to Sebastian. While I might be able to get away with claiming not to know the alpha who took me during my heat, it didn't stop me from thinking about him and what we'd done. Despite the physical labor awakening twinges of soreness from my heat with Sebastian, I still throbbed with desire whenever my mind slipped down that path.

I shook my head, straightening to stretch my back and neck since I'd been stocking the lower shelves. A glance at the clock told me I'd already been at it more than four hours and my stomach complained about being ignored. I'd ran out of the house without grabbing anything more than a granola bar for breakfast, so I'd have to buy something if I wanted to take a lunch break and eat.

Heading up to the front to let Barry know I was stopping for a bit, he raised his head from his phone just as I opened my mouth to speak.

"Oh, good, I was about to come find you. I'm stepping out for lunch, so you need to cover the register. I'll be back in an hour."

Mouth hanging open, I was left staring after him as he turned and walked out the door without a backward glance. While I usually ate my lunch behind the counter because there was only one employee on shift except for stocking, I'd been hoping to be able to sit down and get a bit of rest for once.

Swallowing the disappointment, I sucked in a deep breath to push away the wriggle of resentment. It wasn't that I was the type to roll over and let people run over me whenever they wanted, it just took a moment to overcome the natural instincts to be submissive, and he was gone before I'd collected my thoughts. I couldn't even purchase anything to eat with him gone since it was against the rules to ring yourself up, though I knew the others did it all the time. With my luck, the one time I did the boss would come in and check, and since I was already hoping Barry would cover for my slight tardiness that morning, I didn't want to take the chance.

The store was still empty, so I went back to stocking shelves. I knew I'd hear the bell if anyone came in, and there was no reason to stand around wasting time. I didn't have too much more to go, but I had to finish it all before I could leave for the day, and I didn't want to delay that any longer than I had to.

A few customers came in as I worked, paying for gas or grabbing drinks, and the hour slowly passed. It was already ten minutes after Barry should have returned when I heard the bell over the door tinkle. I bit my tongue, reminding myself not to say the things running through my head and irritate him. I couldn't afford the potential backlash.

Turning to head up to the counter so I could buy the sandwich I'd decided on for lunch, I came around the corner of the shelf and bounced off a hard chest, stumbling backward until my shoulder collided with the wall. I blinked up into blue eyes, a fresh, pink scab running from his nose to his ear, my blood turning to ice as I gasped for air to replace what had been knocked from me.

"Brooke. You're back."

My throat worked, brain scrambling to remember what I'd planned to say to him. Arik stood watching me, lips crawling up in a cruel smirk when I couldn't find the words. The mark on his cheek only made him look meaner.

"Perhaps the reason you didn't call me as you were told is because you've gone mute? Is that it, because I'm sure my instructions were quite clear."

I couldn't stop the quiver that passed through my body as his face went blank again, malice shining from his eyes and distracting me from his raised hand. The blow to my cheek knocked my head to the side, tearing a cry from my chest as stars burst behind my eyes. If I hadn't been braced against the wall it would have sent me sprawling.

"Hmm. Looks like you're still capable of making noise. I know you're not stupid enough to think you could disobey me and get away with it, so why did you disappear Brooke?"

He closed the distance between us as I tried to blink away tears of pain, my right eye stinging. The skin around it already felt tight, and I knew it was swelling, my lip throbbing in time with my heartbeat letting me know it was in the same state.

"I—I couldn't."

I barely rasped out the words before his hand was clutching my throat, pinning me to the wall and blocking my airway. Face so close to mine we almost touched, he snarled, pupils blowing wide in his rage.

"Don't lie to me, cunt. Those animals were outside your house when I came looking for you. You went to one of them. You let an animal ruin you."

His harsh growl had my belly clenching as fresh tears slipped out. I tried to shake my head in denial, but his grip prevented it, my lungs starting to scream with the need for air.

"I bet it was the same dog your brother ran to. Your family's a bunch of animal lovers."

He leaned back, and for a second, I hoped I would get to catch a breath, until I saw the second blow coming. Caught between his hand on my neck and the solid wall behind me, there was nowhere for the momentum to go besides straight to my skull. The only thing that saved me from blacking out was that he couldn't get the same swing he did when there was more space between us.

My vision went white, teeth aching from the impact as my ears rang. My entire face and head throbbed with my slowing pulse, the grip on my throat the only thing still holding me upright.

And then it was gone.

Leann Ryans

I crumpled to the floor, head spinning as I pulled in a breath filled with alpha pheromones and aggression. The ringing in my ears drowned out the growls, but I could feel the reverberations in the air. My vision kept swimming, opening my eyes a challenge I was losing as products fell from the shelves to pelt against me.

As the ringing in my ears dimmed, snarls took its place, the tears clearing away in the shock of being released so I could see what was happening.

Thick furred legs stood in front of me, separating me from Arik. My gaze moved up, taking in the ripped jeans still clinging to thighs that had almost doubled in size. I knew that dark fur, that muscled form, though it was the first time I was getting a view from behind, and for a moment I was distracted by the fluffy tail standing ridged beside me.

I peered between Sebastian's legs again, his familiar scent calming the panic that had been drowning me moments before. Arik's face sported new marks, three bleeding lines bisecting his previous injury. One hand raised to press against his cheek, blood spilling over though he continued to growl back at Sebastian, his posture tense and defensive.

Barry chose that moment to walk in, freezing when he heard the noise and took in the state of the store. One alpha was enough to command caution, but a pair facing off, especially with one in were-form, was enough to have the front of Barry's pants darkening and the pungent scent of urine seeping into the air.

My body trembled under the strain of the pheromones they were pumping out, but a part of me knew Sebastian wouldn't let anything else happen to me. I was safe, and I gave up the fight to keep my eyes open. Ending my ineffectual attempts to stand, I leaned back against the wall, the world dark around me, and let the growls fade away.

I must have lost consciousness for a few minutes, because the next thing I noticed was silence before Arik's voice broke it.

"This isn't over, dog. You fucked with the wrong person and took what was mine. We let you live once, but it won't happen again, and I'm going to make you watch what I do to her."

When I pried my eyes open as far as they'd go, I saw Arik backing out the door of the store. The legs still standing between me and him were no longer sporting black fur, but covered by jeans ripped at the sides where the seams had split during his shift. They remained in place facing the door for a few more moments before turning, Sebastian's face dropping into my view.

"Brooke? I'm so sorry."

His hand lifted as if he was going to cup my jaw, but his fingers stopped short, a grimace crossing his features. The puffiness I could feel in my face painted an ugly picture in my head since I knew how well my pale skin bruised. I was just glad I could get my eyes open enough to see, and that Arik had left, though the thought of him returning sent fresh terror flooding my system. He wasn't going to let this go.

"I'll be fine," I mumbled as I tried to push away from the wall.

Strong hands wrapped around my ribs, helping me up, though the frown on Sebastian's face told how much he didn't like me trying to move. My head spun with the motion, vision dimming at the edges, but I refused to give in to the desire to close my eyes and let it all go black again. Once Arik got himself back together and called his men, my parents and I were going to be in danger, and I had to warn them.

Guilt welled up before being squashed out by the burning rage that took its place. I didn't ask for this. This was not my fault, and I'd be damned if Arik made me feel like it was. He was the one to blame for ruining my poor excuse for a life.

Clenching my throbbing teeth, I pressed my back to the wall again to hold myself upright as Sebastian continued to study my face. I could see his concern, barely holding back his own anger, and as much as I'd have liked to claim I didn't need his help again, I was going to have to ask for it.

"Sebastian—"

A purr thrummed to life between us, his body moving to block my view when I tried to look past him to see the store. It was hard to hold his gaze with pain gripping my skull. I wanted to curl into his chest and ask him to make it all go away, but I had to be stronger than that.

"We need to go. My purse is in the back."

He held me a moment longer before nodding. Careful to be sure I remained upright when he stepped back, he slipped away.

Leann Ryans

Chapter Eighteen

Sebastian

I was trying my best not to lose it and chase Arik down. The wolf in me seethed, my muscles rippling on the verge of shifting. Every glance at Brooke's face sent a pulse of rage flooding my system, urging me to find the alpha who did this and kill him.

"Wh-Where are you going?"

The puny beta male who'd entered the store and promptly pissed himself at the sight of me seemed to snap out of his paralysis as I guided Brooke toward the exit. I'd retrieved her purse from the storeroom, needing nothing more to prompt me to get her out of there. Arik wasn't likely to come back anytime soon since there was a chance police may show up, but I still wouldn't leave her in her state. No charges against him would ever stick or he'd already be behind bars.

My wolf writhed beneath my skin, demanding things I couldn't do. It didn't want to leave Brooke's side ever again, but that wasn't a feeling I had time to face in the current circumstances.

Leann Ryans

The only reason I'd known where she worked was because I'd been stalking her since I brought her home from my place. I'd followed her the previous morning, keeping watch to be sure she made it safely. I'd spent every spare moment I had watching over her, neglecting the shop and my duties there, but I found myself not caring.

And it was a good thing I'd been keeping an eye on her. I didn't want to think of what would have happened if Arik had come for her when I wasn't there to protect her.

I snarled at the other male, his eyes widening as he flinched away. He'd been between us and the door, but his move gave us a clear shot to the outside, and I wasn't going to waste it. We were stepping through when he called out again.

"Your shift isn't over. Who's going to clean this up?"

With Brooke tucked into my side I heard her sigh before she raised her voice without bothering to look back.

"Not me. I quit."

The words were a bit muffled by the swelling in her cheeks, but a burst of pride warmed my chest. I could see the pain she was in and knew how hard it was for omegas to assert themselves, but I was glad she'd made the decision for herself instead of trying to smooth things over like her instincts were probably urging.

Because there was no way I was letting her come back here again, even if she'd wanted to.

I raised my head to look around the small parking lot that bracketed the convenience store but didn't see her car. I didn't like the thought of leaving my bike there to drive her home, but knew it was a better idea to have her in an enclosed space than to have her lose consciousness on the back of my bike if she had head trauma.

Raking my eyes across the pavement a second time, I paused when I noticed her green orbs looking up at me. My heart contracted at the mottling already marring her skin, the tear tracks on her cheeks making me want to slash my claws through Arik's face again.

I carefully raised a hand to cradle the back of her head, her eyes sliding closed on a sigh as her muscles melted.

"Where's your car?"

"Hmm…"

Her breathing slowed, sending my pulse skyrocketing. I had no way to know how bad the blows to her head were. I'd thought she was okay beyond the superficial injuries, but the way her body began to droop terrified me.

Curling her into my chest so I could hold her up with one arm, I tapped her least swollen cheek until she pried her puffy lids open once again.

"Your car, Brooke. Where is it? I need to get you out of here."

"Home. I walked."

I tried to bite back my growl but all I managed was to muffle it. I'd forgotten she seemed to walk to and from work each day. Her body trembled against me, a crease forming between her brows as she straightened, and she kept her eyes open which gave me hope that there wasn't anything dangerous going on in her head.

"I need to get you checked out. Be sure you're okay."

Her lips were too swollen to turn down into a frown, but I could feel the disapproval radiating off her.

"I'll be fine. Just need ice and some aspirin."

I shook my head, refusing to release her when she tried to pull away. I knew she wouldn't have insurance, and many people didn't trust the local hospitals even if they were willing to take on the horrendous debt of going to one, but my skin crawled with unease at the thought of ignoring her injuries and hoping for the best. The alpha part of me wouldn't allow it, my wolf whining in agreement.

"We need to be sure. If you think you can hold on, I can take you to our medic."

Despite most of the guys in the club being levelheaded, they were still alphas, and Patch was familiar enough with injuries from fights and the signs of head trauma. If he gave her the all-clear, I'd trust his word.

"I trust him."

Brooke still looked as though she wanted to argue but my last words took the fight out of her. Shoulders slumping, another tear trickled down her cheek as she gave a short nod.

"No hospital."

I didn't wait any longer, sweeping her into my arms. It was only a few strides to my bike, and I had her deposited on the back and was taking my place in front of her in moments. Pulling her arms around my stomach, I kept one hand over hers to be sure she didn't let go as I kicked the motorcycle to life.

"No promises, but I'll do my best to avoid them unless it's necessary."

The memory of her fear at the bar the first time I tried to get her on my motorcycle came back, but Brooke didn't fight me. Leaning against my spine, she rested her forehead on my vest, her muscles tight but not in a way that suggested she was scared. She'd still been tense and clutching me in panic when I'd taken her home after her heat, but she seemed to have overcome her aversion to riding with me.

Pushing those thoughts aside, I pulled out into the street. It was a little awkward to steer with only one hand, but I'd done it before when I'd been stupid and broke my knuckles. My only concern was how long the trip to Patch would take, and if Brooke would be okay.

It was impossible to talk with the roar of the engine and the wind whipping around us as I flew down the streets as fast as I safely could, but the feel of her chest expanding against my back and the way she held onto me reassured me she was still conscious. I knew there was something about head injuries and going to sleep, but I didn't remember specifics and didn't want to be responsible for making her worse if she did have a serious injury.

Brooke's little whimpers of pain when I turned and her face rubbed against me felt like someone ripping my claws out one by one, and I breathed a sigh of relief when Patch's building came into view. We rolled into the parking lot, pulling into the space beside a custom chrome and enamel beauty already parked there. The bike was an eye-catcher, the artwork on the tank and saddle bags exquisite, but I didn't have time to admire it the way I usually did. Releasing Brooke's wrists so I could stand, I had her back in my arms, tucked against my chest, and heading toward the door of the tattoo shop before she could protest.

"Where are we?"

Patch's shop was deeper in the city proper than my garage. The skyscrapers of downtown were visible, though still far enough away they didn't loom over the single story building we entered. Backing through the door so I didn't have to put her down, I told her the only thing that mattered.

"Somewhere safe."

Most people pictured tattoo shops as dim lit, noisy areas, with walls covered in tiny examples of cheap, crappy artwork that was easy to copy. Nothing about that image fit Patch's business since he'd originally gone to school to be a doctor. His shop was bright and clean, quiet music playing in the background, and the artwork on his walls was anything but small or crappy.

Or cheap. I'd know since he'd done all of mine.

Piercing pale blue eyes met my gaze as I turned around, blonde brows pulling together as Patch noticed the woman in my arms. It was early afternoon, and luckily he didn't have a client. I didn't have to say a word for him to reach for a pair of gloves and gesture toward his chair.

Tempting A Knight

"Patch, this is Brooke. Brooke, our medic, Patch," I said as I sat her down. "He'll let us know if you need the hospital."

The way she clung to my shoulders when I tried to release her sent blood rushing below my belt. It was impossible not to feel smug about her seeking safety with me in the face of an unknown alpha, but I swallowed the surge and peeled myself away, letting her cling to my fingers as I moved behind the chair so I was out of the way.

"She took a couple blows to the head. I'm concerned about brain trauma."

Brooke eyed Patch with the same wariness I felt about letting another male touch her, but my concern was stronger than the possessiveness. All I could do was assure my wolf it was necessary.

"Headache? Vision problems? Loss of consciousness?"

Patch approached with a penlight clutched between his fingers, attention split between Brooke and the way I hovered. I knew he'd have questions about why I was bringing in a beat-up omega, but he held them in, focusing on the business at hand.

"I think I blacked out for a few minutes. Definitely have a headache. Hard to open my eyes, but I can see normal otherwise."

He nodded, reaching out to take hold of the wrist resting on her thigh. Just seeing the two fingers he wrapped around to take her pulse had my claws extending and canines dropping, but I locked my muscles and didn't interfere, choking on a growl.

He released and moved his hand to Brooke's forehead, tipping her head back with careful pressure as he raised the light to shine in her eyes. She squinted and fresh tears leaked from the corners, visions of painting Patch's shop in blood playing through my head until he stopped.

When a quick press against the swelling along her cheekbone made her gasp, I couldn't hold back the snarl that ripped from my throat as I surged around the chair, shoving him back. For a moment his pupils slitted, fangs longer than any I sported slipping over his bottom lip before he got control of himself and turned away.

"She might have a minor concussion, but she'll be fine. Rest, ice, anti-inflammatories. Take her to a hospital if the headache continues more than three days or gets worse and she has any vision changes or starts slurring. The swelling should go down in a couple days, but the bruising will last a while."

My teeth ground together as I pushed back my wolf, dark fur fading from my arms. I knew it was irrational to get angry over him touching her when I brought her to him for help, but that was part of being alpha. I couldn't claim we were completely rational, especially when watching another alpha hurt our omega.

Blowing a breath through my nose, I rolled my shoulders and forced myself to relax. When Patch turned back to me with a handful of pills and a plastic cup of water, there was no sign either of us had lost control.

"Two now, then every eight hours as needed."

We never asked how he still had access to medication and equipment many hospitals on the fringes struggled to produce, but I knew every member of Hell's Knights were grateful for it, and so was I. Clasping his wrist with my other hand as I accepted the handful of pills, I gave him a nod.

"Next time you need a tune up or new mod, it's on me."

That's how it worked with the Knights. We all had different talents, though a majority of the guys worked for me at the garage, and we took care of our own.

Patch nodded back as he slipped off his gloves and tossed them in the garbage.

Turning back to Brooke, it was hard to resist moving in and taking over, but I knew she needed the chance to do things for herself. I couldn't smother her, especially after what happened at the store. She hadn't reacted yet, but I was expecting her to break at any moment.

Passing her the pills, I waited as she put them between her lips before handing her the cup of water. It was painful to watch her try to drink, the water spilling out the corner of her swollen mouth and fueling the anger still burning in my gut. I'd let Arik get away, but that didn't mean I was done with him.

Leann Ryans

Chapter Nineteen

Brooke

I looked around the shop as I swallowed the pills. Anywhere but at Sebastian. The worry and pity I could see in his eyes hurt almost as much as my head.

My gaze landed on the other alpha in the room. He reminded me of a Viking, the pale eyes, blonde braid, goatee, and silent demeanor leaving me with the impression of something cold.

With a shiver I looked away. I'd never been in a tattoo shop before, but I had a feeling this wasn't a typical representation of one. The pictures on the wall left me in awe of the beautiful artwork displayed on the photographed flesh, and my attention swung back to the alpha hovering at my side and the dark ink swirling over his crossed arms. I knew how far it went now, and for a moment my body pulsed with lust.

Until the pounding in my head broke through again and reminded me of the past hour.

Was that all it had been? It felt like more time should have passed, yet a glance at the clock on the wall assured me it really hadn't been very long since my world came crashing down.

Bile churned in my stomach, threatening to bring up the water and pills I had swallowed. I'd fooled myself into thinking avoiding Arik during my heat would be the hardest part, and I could smooth things over afterward. I should have known better. I wasn't even sure it had ever been about my heat at all.

"Let's go. You need to rest."

Sebastian's deep voice broke in, startling me out of my thoughts. A spike of pain lashed through my skull when I jerked, and I couldn't stop myself from whimpering as I raised my hands to clutch at the source of pain.

A growl began only to be cut off. I was scooped back into Sebastian's arms before I could move. The threatening rumble morphed into a soothing vibration that soaked into my bones and lessened the steady pounding in my face.

He didn't bother speaking to the other male before whisking me back through the door and out into the sunlight. I pinched my eyes closed before he stepped through the exit, but the brightness still pierced into my brain. I knew there was other things I needed to focus on, but my misery kept trying to block me.

"Where are you taking me?"

The question was all I could manage, my own voice reverberating behind my clenched eyes and further aggravating the massive headache.

"Home."

Sebastian sat me on the back of his motorcycle before settling himself, arranging me to his satisfaction once again. I wouldn't lie and say I didn't appreciate the support, though realizing he steered one handed was enough to have ice flooding my veins. I'd been able to push aside the fear I'd had of riding on a motorcycle after two successful trips, but my nerves were still on edge about it.

I pushed through the distractions, working to express my worry when words refused to cooperate. It was like trying to catch fish barehanded in a cold stream when everything had gone numb.

"Whose?"

His fingers tightened around my wrists where they rested against his stomach. For a moment I wished I could enjoy the feel of him again before forcing my brain back in line. The pills I'd been given had to be kicking in because everything was growing fuzzy, and I wasn't sure my head was still attached.

I felt Sebastian's sigh more than heard it as I let my forehead press into his spine. It was the least painful part of my head and having it tucked against him helped block the light. The earlier ride had shown me I couldn't keep my eyes open or I ran the risk of being sick all over his back.

"Your apartment won't be safe, and you shouldn't be alone."

I knew he was right, but I wasn't the only one I had to worry about. Arik wouldn't hesitate to hurt my parents to get to me.

I marshalled my wavering thoughts, forcing my brain to cooperate to extract another promise from the alpha I'd dragged into my problems. Guilt bedded right next to the childish adoration I'd felt for him, but both were covered by the newer feelings that had grown.

"I don't care where you take me, but my parents won't be safe either."

He'd begun to walk the motorcycle backwards but hesitated at my words. His ribs expanded against me, the steady purr he'd provided tapering off before he grumbled and started the bike. He didn't tell me what he was going to do before pulling out into the road once again, but I trusted him to do whatever he could to assure they wouldn't be harmed.

Relaxing as much as I could, I let the motion of the ride lull me into a daze, the medication finally taking the edge off the pain plaguing me. The skin of my face was still tight, but the steady throb had faded and I found myself not caring about the feeling. My head felt stuffed with cotton and like it was floating above me, but that was better than the way it had felt before.

Drawing in breath after breath of Sebastian's scent, it was impossible not to let the weight dragging on me pull me under.

Cold hands pressing against my cheeks woke me sometime later, the same chilly digits moving to peel back an eyelid and making me hiss at the light that speared into my skull. My mother's voice intruded on the comfortable fluff between my ears, but I couldn't make out what was being said until she repeated herself.

"Brooke, what happened? Why didn't you call me? You shouldn't be sleeping with head trauma without being seen. We need to get you to a hospital."

Her voice rose with each concern, bringing back the throbbing I'd escaped in slumber. Pulling my arm away from her when she tried to sit me upright, I waved at her and turned my head into the couch cushions. I had no memory of getting home, but there was no mistaking the feel of the worn fabric or the scents that surrounded me.

Including the smell of a certain alpha that lingered on my clothing.

It was enough to bring a bit more clarity to my thoughts, and I gave up trying to burrow into the couch.

"I *was* seen. I'll be fine, it just looks terrible. And feels terrible."

I blinked my eyes open just in time to see my mother's face blanche. As a nurse, she knew better than I did what a trip to the Emergency Department for something like this would have cost. The imaging the hospital would have insisted on was more than our household could hope to pay for, yet I knew she wouldn't have left me to suffer if it'd been necessary. Luckily, the pills Sebastian made me take seemed to have helped the worst of the headache, and a quick glance showed me two more sitting on the coffee table next to a glass of water.

Mom's hands fluttered before she clenched them in front of her, her lips pressing into a thin line as she struggled with the appropriate thing to say considering our situation. I didn't hold it against her.

"Don't worry, there won't be a bill. I didn't go to a hospital, but the person who checked me does have medical training."

Sebastian hadn't said as much, but it was clear Patch had known what he was doing, so I hoped I wasn't stretching the truth too far.

Snatching up the pills before she noticed and demanded to see them, I swallowed them down with a gulp of water. My stomach still felt queasy, but I wasn't sure if it was from my head or because I hadn't eaten all day.

"Are you sure this person knows what they're doing? You could have a serious injury. Sit up and let me look. And you still haven't told me what happened. Did you get hurt at work?"

Sighing, I struggled upright. I knew she wouldn't give up till she'd reassured herself, the flood of words showing how worried she was.

The two blankets we kept on the couch had been spread over me and a soggy bag of peas laid on the couch next to where my head had been, and my heart gave a painful squeeze at the thought of Sebastian tucking me in and caring for me while I'd been passed out. Pushing that aside to deal with at a less urgent time, I looked up at the worry on my mother's face. I'd tried to keep what was going on from her, but by doing so I was putting her in danger she didn't know she needed to watch out for. Even though I didn't see Sebastian, his scent was strong enough in the room for me to think he hadn't been gone long, which meant he'd stayed to be sure I was okay, and I doubted he'd gone far, even if he'd left before my mother came home.

She moved closer to peer into my eyes again, assuring herself I wasn't in danger from the damage Arik had done. I wondered how much I was going to do to her when I explained what happened.

"Mom, sit down."

I curled my feet closer to me, leaving the other end of the couch empty for her to sit. The concern on her face turned to dread, and I hated knowing I was the cause. What I had to tell her wasn't going to make that dread go away either, and my stomach sank further.

I told her everything, starting with Arik showing up at work and realizing what I was. I left out the part about Sebastian denying me then going to the bar, but I didn't hide anything else, including that he knew who I was and the threats he made toward me and them. Emotions played across her face, rending my heart as I realized the main one was guilt.

"I was trying to protect you, but now we're all in danger."

I dropped my gaze to my lap as I finished, picking at my fingernails as discomfort wriggled in my belly. Her slim hand reached out and blocked what I was doing, forcing me to look up and meet her gaze.

"It's not your job to protect me. You're my child, I should be the one protecting you."

My stomach clenched, worry intensifying the headache that had been throbbing in the background.

"You can't. It's too dangerous."

Mom nodded as I spoke, patting my hands before returning hers to her lap. She looked around the living room, staring at the place as if seeing it for the first time before she spoke.

"I didn't want to believe, about Vincent. He was a good boy. He didn't deserve… We should have left after that happened, but we just couldn't afford it."

She shook her head and shrugged, her eyes coming back to mine, shimmering with a mist of tears she held back by force of will alone.

"I didn't realize we were putting you in danger by staying or we would have found a way. All our memories are here, but that's not as important as your safety."

She let out a sigh, shoulders slumping before she pulled herself upright once more. She opened her mouth to speak again when a rumble began outside. It took a moment for the sound to click, but as soon as it did, I scrambled off the couch, rushing to the window to pull back the curtains and peer into the darkness beyond.

Tempting A Knight

Headlights swung through the parking lot below, the line of them heading right for my building. They clustered at the base of the stairs, some parking in the middle of the lot, and it wasn't until their lights illuminated the space that I realized why they'd come.

Arik's blonde hair shone in the light. He was the only one who wasn't moving, arms crossed over his chest as he watched what was happening in front of him.

A black wolf darted between five other men, their size portraying them for the alphas they were. I hadn't seen Sebastian's wolf since I was a child, but the dark fur matched his were-form and I knew it had to be him.

The glint of light off a blade sent my heart into my throat. One of the men swung at Sebastian as the wolf launched toward him, a scream tearing from me as I watched. The other Hell's Knights were getting off their bikes and coming to help, but they were moving too slow.

Turning, I was at the front door in seconds, ripping it open to race downstairs. The pounding in my head increased with my heartrate, but it all faded to the background at the thought of Sebastian lying bleeding in the parking lot with Arik gloating over his body.

Distantly I heard my mother calling for me, but I couldn't stand by and watch Sebastian be attacked. He was a target because of me. He was here, stopping Arik from getting to me, because I'd put him in that position. I couldn't hide and wait to see who showed up at my door.

I barreled down the last few steps, stumbling and barely catching myself before I went sprawling on the pavement. The crowd of alphas standing between me and my goal barely registered as my feet kept moving forward, elbows flying to get the space I needed to see what was happening.

Thick arms wrapped around my waist as I tried to pass the last person standing between me and where I'd last seen Sebastian. Snarls and roars from multiple throats already filled the air, but my own screech carried over it all as I clawed at the flesh holding me back.

Even as I fought and struggled to get free, my eyes strained for a glimpse of fur. The first I caught sight of was the wrong color, a grey werewolf holding one of the human alphas who'd been attacking Sebastian in a headlock. Gaze sliding past him, I saw a grizzly send another male flying into a nearby car, the crunch that reached my ears making my stomach quiver and threaten to rebel.

Looking away before the dark smear down the car door could register, I finally caught sight of Sebastian. The black wolf's fur was too dark to tell if the knife had connected, but the way he stood with his head hanging, sides heaving as pink foam dripped from his mouth, had my cry changing to one of worry.

Car tires squealed somewhere nearby, and the arms around me loosened as the wolf's head swung toward me. The headlights of the motorcycles shone off chocolate irises, and Sebastian turned to come closer.

It wasn't until then I noticed the growling had mostly stopped, a voice murmuring over my head for me to calm down. It was hard to make out the words with the pressure in my head making it feel as if it was caught in a vice, but my muscles went slack as I realized the danger was over and Arik must have run again. The only humans still in the parking lot sported a vest or jacket similar to the one Sebastian usually wore, Arik's blonde locks missing from the males I could see moving around.

Focusing once again on the wolf heading toward me, his limp was too obvious to miss, and my heart dropped. Gut clenching, I choked on a sob, my emotions swinging so fast I couldn't prepare.

He'd been hurt, and it was my fault.

Leann Ryans

Chapter Twenty

Sebastian

The toes of my left hind leg dragged on the pavement, my thigh screaming each time I put weight on it. It took far too long to cross the distance to Brooke, my lips lifting in a snarl as Patch's arm remained banded around her ribs. Logically I knew why he'd grabbed her, but logic had little weight in my wolf's mind when another alpha was touching my omega.

My brain stumbled on the claim, but I shoved past it, focusing on her face as she began to sob.

I'd brought her home and sat with her as she slept until it was time for her mother to return from work, unable to make myself leave her alone. Patch may have said she'd be okay, but my instincts didn't want to accept words, I needed to see it for myself.

When I came outside, I'd returned to the little corner by the dumpster, keeping watch. I knew Arik was coming, it was only a matter of *when,* and it was a good thing I'd called Carl when I spotted his car. If he hadn't rolled in with the other Knights when he had, things would have gone bad.

Worse. They were already bad.

I tested my leg again as I stopped in front of Patch and Brooke. Patch ignored my snarls, holding Brooke up so she didn't collapse to the pavement. She clutched her head and my stomach churned at the thought that I was doing more damage to her just by standing there.

I'd been forced to switch from my half-form to full wolf when one of the assholes Arik had brought caught the back of my thigh with his blade. Four legs were sturdier than two, though my reach was reduced as a wolf. I'd already been outnumbered and losing my best defense had brought a second of worry, but there was no way I was letting Arik get to Brooke.

Sucking in a deep breath, I closed my eyes and ignored the pain, forcing my body back to two legs and a lot less hair. When the grinding of bones and shiver of receding fur ended, I opened my eyes again and reached for Brooke.

I had no idea what had happened to my jeans once I transformed into a wolf, but she didn't seem to notice my bare state. She launched herself into my arms, wrapping hers around my ribs and clinging with a strength that surprised me even as it sent warmth burrowing through my chest.

"She needs to calm down. The strain will make her head worse," Patch warned as he let her go.

I nodded, running a hand over her scalp and down her back. I had to clear my throat before the noise that came from my chest sounded like a purr instead of a growl, the lingering adrenaline still affecting me. It was impossible to keep the evidence of its affects hidden when her body pressed against mine, nothing but the uniform she still wore between her and my stiffness, but I tried to ignore it.

"Hush, you're going to make yourself sick."

Brooke sniffled and mumbled something I couldn't make out. Tangling my fingers in her hair, I pulled her head back until she was forced to look up at me.

"Repeat."

Her pupils expanded, her state leaving her vulnerable to my orders.

"It's my fault. You got hurt because of me. You didn't want any of this."

There was no conscious decision to kiss her, just her lips crushed under mine. Her spine stiffened before her arms tightened around me and her mouth opened. Taking the invitation, I dipped my tongue between her lips, taking and tasting until we were forced to stop for air.

Moving my hand to her cheek, I reminded myself she was hurt. Some of the swelling had gone down but her face was still puffy, and darker bruising had set in while she slept. I didn't need to cause her more pain because my wolf was clamoring to stake a claim on her. To cover her in my scent again and drown out the smell of the other alphas on her clothing.

My hips moved without permission, grinding the length of my erection into her belly. Lips popping open, the darkness of her pupils swallowed more of the beautiful green as Brooke let out a moan, so quiet I almost missed it. Marshalling my thoughts back to where they needed to be was harder than taking on five alphas by myself.

"It's not your fault. Arik's a bastard. This is all on him. I'm not going to let him hurt you again. I won't."

Visions of sinking my canines into his neck and ripping his throat out played in my head. I'd never been someone to seek violence unprovoked, but the human had passed my last boundary. He was as fixated on Brooke as I was, and she wouldn't be safe until he was gone.

My body relaxed with the decision finally made. Trying to find a way around him wasn't going to work. Even sending Brooke out of the city wouldn't assure her safety, and I wasn't sure I could stand to watch her leave. There was only one way to be sure. Only one outcome my wolf would accept.

Raising my gaze over Brooke's head, I met Carl's eyes. I'd seen Arik run with two of the men who came with him. A quick glance around showed the other three had either run as well, or the Knights had taken care of the evidence. A few our men were already drifting back to their bikes, waiting for the all-clear.

I nodded, acknowledging what lay unspoken between us. He knew what I had to do just as well as I did. Hell's Knights may not usually deal in death, but it wasn't foreign to us. Some dangers were too serious to leave in the world.

He dipped his chin slowly in response. If the worst should happen to me, he would take care of it. That was what being a member of Hell's Knights meant. We had each other's backs. We were the family we'd chosen, a pack, and we protected those who couldn't protect themselves.

He turned away to send the extra men off with other tasks before walking back and handing me a bundle of cloth from his saddle bag. A fight like this would lead to more retaliation, and we needed to be prepared. Only Patch lingered with us, giving my thigh a pointed look as he waited with his medical kit in hand.

Staring back down at Brooke, I dropped a kiss on her forehead before taking a step away. Her tears had stopped but I didn't miss the confusion in her eyes as I let her go. It was hard to keep myself from pulling her against me again, but now wasn't the time.

I was opening my mouth to reassure her when I was cut off by a voice from the past.

"Sebastian Borros."

Spine snapping straight, I clutched the bunched fabric I held over my groin, a shiver of dread rolling through me. I'm not sure I'd ever lost an erection so fast in my life.

"Mrs. Frost. You look lovely. How are you?"

A delicate eyebrow rose, her lips pinched, though I could see amusement warring in her pale gaze. I was struck by how many similarities I suddenly noticed between her and Brooke.

Mrs. Frost gave me a pointed look, shaking her head before pulling Brooke against her side and turning them back toward the stairs.

"Come up once your leg is taken care of and you've covered yourself, young man."

I swallowed, my mouth suddenly dry. I'd faced terrible odds after being wounded, yet I was more worried after a single sentence from the woman I'd seen as my mother for most of my life than I had been before the other Knights arrived. Considering I was a full-grown alpha wolf in my prime, this human beta shouldn't have an effect on me, but despite the years of separation she still mattered to me, as did the omega under her arm. I was only beginning to realize *how much* they mattered.

"Yes, Ma'am."

As the women disappeared up the stairs a chuckle came from my right. I glared at Carl, and he wisely kept his mouth shut as I yanked the shirt he'd given me over my head. I wanted to pull the pants on too, but I knew Patch wasn't going to quit lingering until I let him take care of my leg, which he couldn't do if I stuffed it in the sweats dangling from my fingers.

Sighing, I walked over to the stairs. Using the fabric to keep my bare ass from touching the rough surface, I folded the end of a leg over my junk and waved to the other alpha. I had to contort a bit to make the injury more reachable as Patch knelt beside me.

He was silent as he opened his kit and pulled on gloves, pressing the edges of the wound to see how deep it went. Shifters healed faster than humans, so for it to still be painful and oozing was a sign it had been a bad slash. Still, I could put weight on it and walk, so I knew it would eventually heal.

Clenching my teeth, I turned my head away and got caught once again in Carl's gaze.

"You know—"

"Yes, I know. I'll take them back to my place once I get them calmed down."

Carl's head was shaking before I even finished.

"Your place is too obvious. He knows the two of you are connected now, and it won't take long for him to have all your information. That's the first place he'll come looking for her."

Growling at the thought of Arik on my property, I was temporarily distracted by the pinch and pull of Patch placing stitches in the back of my thigh. He worked quickly, and by the time I'd calmed myself enough to speak, he was finished and wiping off the blood.

Waving him away, I stood and stepped into the loose sweats. Carl and I may have sported the same broad shoulders, but he was stockier than I overall, and the pants hung low on my hips.

"Well the same goes for any of you. When he doesn't find her at my place, he'll send his people to track down every Hell's Knight, and the men don't deserve to have Purists up their ass, following them home."

Carl crossed his arms over his chest, and I matched his pose. I didn't want to put the men in front of Arik as a target, but I wasn't going to leave Brooke, or her parents, where they weren't safe.

"What about Danger?"

Carl and I both snapped our attention to Patch. We knew Patch wasn't his real name, and unlike many of the others, I actually knew the name he was born with. Danger was the chosen name of one of our members who no one knew much about. He showed up occasionally during the weekend rides we took out of the city to let our animals enjoy fresh air and freedom, but he always wore a mask. I didn't even know what his animal was.

"What about Danger?" I repeated.

Patch's shoulder rose and fell in a half shrug.

"He has connections. He could hide them."

My wolf thrashed at the idea of Brooke alone with another alpha, especially one I knew so little about. I knew Danger was loyal to the Knights because he'd helped during some of our operations, but that didn't appease the possessive side of me that had decided Brooke was *mine*.

Carl spoke up while I was struggling with myself.

"How do you know he has connections?"

Patch focused his impassive gaze on Carl, staring at the other alpha in silence until Carl's eyes narrowed.

"I guess it doesn't matter, as long as he can," Carl finally muttered.

"No."

Both men turned to me. I knew I was being stupid because Brooke had gotten under my skin, but that didn't change the fact that I'd go on a rampage if she disappeared with another alpha. I needed her where I could see for myself that she was safe and okay. *I* needed to be the one protecting her.

"He can stash her parents somewhere, if he can, but not Brooke," I conceded.

"Seb—"

I cut Carl off with a raised hand. I knew what his arguments were, and they wouldn't change anything.

"Not Brooke."

Carl huffed, growling under his breath. Patch must have figured he wasn't needed any longer because he gathered his kit and returned it to the bag slung on his back, walking over to swing a leg over his bike.

When Carl finished his grumbling, I met his gaze again before looking back at Patch. A couple walked by in the parking lot, skirting around us as they watched with a wary gaze. We were starting to draw attention from the people who'd grown brave enough to come out again once it seemed like the fighting was over, the area far too familiar with gang confrontations to let it bother them for long.

"Looks like we need to go to church."

They knew what I meant and what was expected of them. Both nodded. I wouldn't keep making decisions that affected the club without everyone's input, but I wasn't going to back down on keeping Brooke with me. I'd realized I was in too deep.

"Two AM."

They nodded again, Patch's bike coming to life with a quiet purr that belied the power held between his legs. Carl turned away to mount his motorcycle, phone already in his hand, though I knew he wasn't going to leave. He'd remain as my backup until everyone was out of the apartment.

Sighing, I turned and looked up the stairs, knowing it was going to hurt like a bitch to climb three flights with stitches in the back of my thigh. I just wasn't sure if what I was heading toward would hurt more. I respected Mrs. Frost, but I wasn't going to let her come between me and my omega either.

Chapter Twenty-One

Brooke

My head throbbed, blocking out half of what my mother said as she shut the front door. It didn't matter, I was still thinking about the blood soaked into my clothes from Sebastian, not listening to her.

Gut churning, I gagged, stumbling around the dining table to get to the trashcan. I heaved, though nothing came up since I still hadn't eaten since the granola bar that morning. My body tried to expel anything it could nonetheless, bile burning my throat before I got the reaction under control.

Not caring that my mother stood behind me, I stripped off the shirt I wore, tossing it into the garbage before letting the lid close. The cost of the uniform would come out of my last check if I didn't return it, but I was beyond worrying about that. I likely wouldn't be able to get bloodstains off the fabric anyway.

I couldn't hide the way I trembled as I turned to face my mother, her face drawn with worry. Clasping my forearms, she guided me into one of the dining chairs, murmuring something before letting me go and disappearing down the hall.

She returned a moment later with a wet rag and a shirt from my room, handing me the rag first before helping me into the top. It would have been embarrassing to need help dressing if I hadn't been too drained to feel anything beyond the pain and exhaustion.

"How long has it been since you've eaten?"

What she asked finally penetrated the throbbing fog around my brain and I shook my head.

"On the way to work."

I wasn't even sure what time it was, much less how long it had been since the paltry bar I'd snatched on my way out the door that morning. So much had happened it felt like a week had passed since then.

Cupping my cheek with a cool palm, she tsked at me before moving into the kitchen. She plopped a glass of water on the table in front of me first, demanding I drink it, then came back with a chunk of cheese and an apple.

"Start with those while I cook. We don't need you passing out when you've already had a head injury today."

Mind fuzzy, I did as she ordered, no energy left to rebel even if I'd wanted to.

I rinsed my mouth with a sip of the water and dragged the trashcan to my side to spit it out before nibbling on the cheese. The trembling slowly eased as I alternated bites with swallows of water. I had no idea how long we'd been in the house, only that I'd finished the chunk of cheese and started on the apple, when a knock sounded through the room.

My head whipped to the door, heart galloping as panic flooded my system once again. I couldn't even force words of caution from my throat as my mother headed over and opened it. Choking on fear, I blinked at the large figure standing in the doorway before they stepped inside.

Dark eyes met mine, my muscles relaxing before my consciousness made the connection to who it was. Sebastian's features softened as he moved to take the chair beside me, my mother treating him to a glass of water and apple like she'd given me.

"I'm assuming that had something to do with Arik?"

She returned to the stove, her voice intruding before I could ask him if he was okay. He'd walked in without help, so whatever injuries he'd taken couldn't have been too bad.

"Yes, Ma'am. You're not safe here."

My mother snorted, raising a brow as she leveled Sebastian with the same stare she'd given him and my brother as kids. For a moment I felt small and awkward again, the little sister hiding around the corner watching the boys' antics. Even when they'd been rambunctious and seeming like nothing would calm them, one look from her was all it took to return a modicum of discipline.

"We'd already determined that before the ruckus. I supposed you plan to whisk Brooke off somewhere safer?"

It almost sounded like that was what she hoped for, and my brow scrunched. I wasn't the only one in danger. I opened my mouth to say as much, but Sebastian beat me to it.

"Not just her. We need to get all of you out of here until the situation can be taken care of."

Mom was silent as she stared at him, likely trying to figure out exactly what he meant by that, like I was. Swallowing, I studied his serious expression.

"He's not going to stop until he gets me, or dies."

Sebastian's chocolate gaze landed on me again. I could see the answer there, but instead of being surprised or repulsed, my chest bloomed with fierce hope.

I wanted Arik dead. Nothing less would do.

"It'll be taken care of."

That was all the acknowledgment he needed to give. A tinge of guilt rose to color the other emotions roiling inside me, but with it came relief. I had no hope on my own, but I trusted Sebastian.

My mother cleared her throat, settling bowls of steaming pasta in front of both of us before taking the last chair at the table. There had been four at one time, but the other seat broke and there'd been no reason to replace it when there were only three of us. No one else had been to our home since Sebastian's last visit before Vincent's funeral.

Sebastian dwarfed the table and chair now, when the last time he'd sat there he'd been closer to my size. Still tall and muscular, but slimmer, and not so broad in the shoulders.

There was silence as we dug into the food. Despite getting an almost overflowing bowl, Sebastian was the first done. My mother pushed her bowl away, but when I tried to do the same, they both protested.

Sebastian's low growl sent a shiver down my spine, capturing my attention until a smack broke through the sound. His head jerked, eyes flying wide as he turned to stare at my mother.

"You know better than to growl at my table, boy. I'll handle my daughter. You go put your bowl in the sink like you're supposed to."

If I didn't know better, I'd have thought Sebastian started blushing, and I had to cover my mouth to hide my grin. It made my cheeks hurt, but no worse than the chewing had, and it helped clear the last of the lingering anxiety.

"Now you," my mother went on, turning her gaze to me. My smile disappeared, and I ducked my head back over my food. "Finish what's in your bowl so he can get you out of here."

The fork was halfway to my mouth when I caught what she said, and I dropped it again to argue.

"You—"

"Eat! I know good and well your father and I need to disappear too, but I'm not doing it without him and leaving him to come home to an empty house."

I frowned at her, gripping the fork again but not lifting it.

"You could always call him from wherever we go."

She reached across and patted the hand resting on the table beside my bowl.

"I'll feel better waiting here for him, and that way I can gather our things. I won't leave anything important behind in case we don't come back. Plus, Arik is focused on you. If we're not with you or easy to get to, he'll likely forget about us."

A chill passed through me at her words, and I couldn't help looking around. This apartment was all I remembered, the place I'd grown up. It was the last place I saw Vincent. I'd known I'd leave it at some point, but faced with the prospect of never returning, I suddenly felt lost.

"You'll get to come home, Mrs. Frost. I'll make sure of it. And you'll all be safe."

Sebastian's rumble behind me was soothing, as was the hand he placed on my shoulder. The fist around my stomach loosened, and I forced another bite into my mouth since I wouldn't be allowed up until I ate enough to satisfy them.

I knew there was a chance Sebastian would fail. The idea of what could happen to him was more disturbing than never returning to the apartment, but part of me was still that young girl who thought he was invincible. His wound tonight proved it wrong, but my heart insisted all would be well if he said it would.

He took the seat beside me again, the heat of his touch mocking me when he removed his hand from my shoulder. I wanted him to put it back. To wrap me in his thick arms where I felt safer than I ever had.

Instead, I finished the pasta. When I started to rise to take my bowl to the sink, my mother reached out and took it from me, standing and looking between me and Sebastian. I could see the worry in her eyes, but she was making the same choice to put her trust in the alpha beside me.

"You take care of her. And don't get yourself hurt either. The two of you are all I have left to leave behind when my time's up."

I choked up, the sheen in her eyes showing how close she was to tears. If either of us started, the other would lose their hold, so I forced the lump down and blinked the moisture from my eyes.

Standing before she could walk past me, I pulled her into a tight hug. Sebastian must have taken the bowls from her hands because I felt them on my back, clinging to me just as hard. I was scared to leave her alone knowing Arik wasn't the type to give up, but I had to respect her wish to wait for Dad. And she was right that I would pull the danger away from them if we were separated.

There was a suspicious sniffle next to my ear, but Mom's cheeks were dry when she pulled away.

"You should get going. Be careful and call me when you can so I know you're safe."

"You too."

We both sniffled, tears threatening again until she turned away.

"You should grab a few things to take with you. I doubt Sebastian has clothes your size."

I looked up into dark eyes, getting lost for a moment in the strength I found there. Neither of us had said anything, but there was something between us. Something that grew and pulsed the longer I stared at him. Something that tightened with each breath filled with his scent.

Clearing my throat, I nodded, blinking and trying to pull my focus to what I needed to do. The dull throb of pain still filled my head, though it was muted from what it had been. Fuzz lingered near the edges of my mind, but I was able to keep it away enough to think.

Sebastian stepped back so I had a clear path to my bedroom, and a bolt of heat lanced through my core at the thought of him following me there. As intimate as we'd already been during my heat, having him in my bedroom was different, and for a moment my heart stumbled.

Did I want him there?

My gaze darted back to his before I yanked it away. My heart was racing with the revelation that the idea of him being in my personal space didn't raise a single territorial flag, only desire.

Swallowing the sudden flood of saliva as my traitorous mind played back images of what we'd done together, only this time surrounded by the comfort of my favorite blankets and pillows, I headed down the short hall but hesitated with my hand on the doorknob of my room.

A glance showed me Sebastian still stood exactly where he'd been, and the pang of disappointment that hit almost doubled me over. But I'd seen the acknowledgment in his gaze. The knowledge that we were past being just Vincent's best friend and his little sister.

Shaking my head and trying to push the distractions away, I huffed out a breath and walked into my room. I stopped just inside, looking around the small space I'd made mine since Vincent's death. There was guilt for getting rid of his things and changing it from the way it had been when we shared it, but pragmatism crowded it out. There'd been almost no room to walk with two twin beds taking up the floor, and there'd been no reason to keep his things when we could pass them on to someone who needed them.

Pulling my shoulders back, I dug out a small overnight bag and began tossing things into it. I had no idea how long I'd be gone, and unlike during my heat, I'd actually need clothes to wear

I shivered as part of my mind whispered that I *could* stay naked, but I hushed it and forced myself to keep packing. I'd finally accepted that Sebastian seemed to be interested in me beyond what I'd asked of him, but the timing was terrible.

I could only fit a couple outfits in the bag with a set of pajamas before there was just enough space left for my brush and toiletries. Zipping it up, I glanced around my room again before snatching my favorite blanket off my bed. It may seem irrational to any but another omega, but just holding it in my arms helped my heartrate slow, and muscles relax. If Sebastian argued about it, I'd dump my clothes and stuff it in the bag instead.

I walked out of my room to the sight of my mother's slim frame wrapped in Sebastian's arms, her head resting on his chest with his cheek leaning on her head. The growl that burst from me startled all of us, ending on a jagged gulp as Sebastian jerked upright and released my mother from the hug.

Mom only chuckled as she wiped her cheeks, shaking her head at me with a lopsided smile before turning back to Sebastian and handing him a small bundle.

"Change your bandage before bed and again in the morning, and put the ointment I gave you on it. I know you're a shifter, but infections don't discriminate between wounds."

"Yes, Ma'am."

She patted his arm before looking at me again. Smiling, she shot me a wink as I moved closer, but she walked back into the kitchen before I got within arm's reach.

"Sebastian said he's leaving a man downstairs to watch over me until your father gets home. By then I'll be packed, and we can leave. Don't forget to call when you can."

She bustled around, washing and putting away the dishes from dinner. I wasn't sure what to say. I wanted to apologize for the growl but was still too surprised at myself to express it.

Before I got the words untangled in my head, Sebastian was cupping my elbow and turning me toward the door, pulling it open and ushering me out. I glanced over my shoulder to watch it close behind us, and it felt final somehow. As if a chapter in my life was coming to an end, and if I ever walked through that door again, I would be different.

Sebastian took my hand, looking into my eyes.

"Are you okay?"

I raised one shoulder but nodded. I both was and wasn't, but I couldn't articulate it. Either way, it wouldn't change what needed to happen.

"I'll be better when Arik is dead."

The grin that broke across Sebastian's face was feral and dark, his canines extending as he flexed his claws.

"Agreed."

Leann Ryans

Chapter Twenty-Two

Sebastian

Brooke's arms around me felt right. Having them there as we rode through the streets was more soothing than any other ride I'd taken, and for a moment I considered changing direction and heading out of the city.

We could leave. Just keep going and never look back.

Reality crashed back in as horns blared and people screamed at each other from the safety of their cars. Even though it was late, it was a Friday night, and there were still plenty of others out and about. It was hard to think that it had been just eight days since Brooke pulled her little stunt at the bar and I took her home with me. Less than a week since my priorities changed.

We passed the shop, sitting dark since it was well past closing time. I needed to thank Carl again for stepping up and taking over for me while I'd been preoccupied. He didn't usually work full time, but he'd moved into my position without complaint.

My street was just as quiet, the homes around me mostly owned by older couples like the ones I'd bought from. They'd all been wary of me when I first moved in, but over time they'd realized I wasn't going to cause a disturbance. I hoped I could maintain that reputation through what was coming.

I debated what I should do about Arik. I knew what the outcome needed to be, but getting to that point was a different matter. Going to prison for murder didn't match with what I wanted from the future.

Brooke relaxed and pulled away from my back as I cut the engine and walked my bike into the garage. My wolf complained about even that small distance between us, there was no way I'd be able to handle the kind of separation being behind bars would bring.

Reaching back, I steadied her as she stood and swung her leg over the bike before rising myself. She didn't remove her hand from mine, and there was no way I was going to let her go if she didn't want me to.

I opened the saddle bag and pulled out her blanket, passing it to her before reaching back to unstrap her bag from where it sat behind the pillion. Most of the guys called it a bitch seat, but I refused to use those terms for Brooke.

The sight of her when I turned around, standing in my garage, clutching a blanket to her chest with one hand as she clung to my fingers with the other, looking up at me with those luminous green eyes holding so much trust... It was a kick to the gut. If I hadn't already realized I was in deep, there'd have been no denying it any longer. I'd do

Tempting A Knight

anything for her, including go to prison for killing the bastard who'd hurt her.

"What?"

Her eyebrows scrunched and I realized I must have been staring for too long. Shaking my head, I tugged her hand and moved toward the door. I'd come back and lock up once I had her settled.

The lights illuminated the pile of crap still taking up my dining room when I flipped them on, a twinge of discontent from my wolf reprimanding me for procrastinating on all the things that needed done to the house. Once again, I was bringing my omega into a den that wasn't worthy of her, but I pushed the feelings aside.

"Are you hungry? Thirsty? I could make us something."

We'd just eaten at her place, but I knew she hadn't had anything for hours before that, and I needed to take care of her. To provide for her and keep her safe.

Brooke shook her head, holding her blanket tighter.

"No, I just want to go to bed."

My dick jumped at the image that popped in my head, immediately hard, but I tried to ignore it. Even if she'd been willing, she was still hurt, and it wasn't the time for that. I had a murder to plan.

I walked her over to the little hallway, hesitating in the opening between my bedroom door and the bathroom. The second bedroom was a little further down, but I was done trying to keep my distance.

Watching her as I opened the door to my room, I waited for her to step through before pulling her into my arms. I restricted myself to placing a kiss on her forehead, the only part of her face not puffy or discolored, before forcing myself to let her go.

Her eyes widened when she finally looked away from me, noticing the mess on my bed. I hadn't been able to bring myself to dismantle what was left of her nest or wash the bedding. The room still smelled of us, though it had grown stale, with my scent overtaking what lingered from her.

"You didn't…"

She trailed off and I realized she may not want to sleep in the mess left from her heat. Dropping her hand, I moved to the bed, grabbing a blanket to begin pulling it all off the mattress.

"I'm sorry, I can wash them if you're okay just using the one you brought for now."

I stopped when her hand covered mine. Shaking her head, she raised an eyebrow at me before turning back to look at the disheveled sheets. We'd destroyed what she built at the beginning of her heat, but I'd done my best to recreate it. I'd never slept so well, but it still wasn't the same.

"It's fine. I just didn't realize you were so sentimental."

I huffed, narrowing my eyes at her. It was hard for her to smile with the swelling in her cheeks, but her tone let me know she was teasing me.

"I'll have no sass from you unless you want your bottom throbbing too."

The words came out before I thought about what I was saying. I worried for a moment that I'd upset her, but instead her reaction redirected more blood flow below my belt. Her lips had popped open, eyes going wide as her pupils expanded.

Nostrils flaring, I could scent how the idea of me spanking her excited her, and I had to hold back the rumble that threatened to leave my chest. Closing my eyes, I reminded myself that now was not the time to fuck and knot her, no matter how bad I wanted to.

"Sebastian..."

I peeled my lids open to drink her in. She was beautiful. The bruises didn't matter, she was still the most gorgeous woman I'd ever seen.

I gently cupped her cheek, leaning in to brush my lips over hers. I wanted to tell her how I felt, show her how much I wanted her to be mine, but I couldn't. If Arik somehow bested me, it would only hurt her more.

"Fix it if you need to, then get some rest. I have to leave again in a couple hours, but I'll have someone stay to guard the house."

I'd almost forgotten, but I still had to meet with the members of Hell's Knights. There was no way I would leave Brooke to confront Arik on her own and I'd already dragged the Knights into the fight, but I needed to face them and explain what had happened and what was coming so they could decide if they wanted to help or lay low. The Purists outnumbered us and taking on Arik on my own was suicide unless I got lucky. I hoped they would stand with me, but I wouldn't order it even if I could. They had to decide for themselves.

Pressing my lips to hers once more, I released her and stepped back. If I didn't, I wasn't going to stop until I was locked deep inside her.

I headed out to the kitchen as she focused on the bed, straightening blankets and rearranging pillows. She'd said she didn't want anything, but I still felt the need to provide for her, so I poured a glass of lemonade and grabbed a granola bar from the cabinet. It wasn't much, but I wasn't one to cook and didn't have a lot in the house.

When I returned to the bedroom Brooke was already curled in the middle of the bed, the only sign of her the steady rise and fall of the blankets. I wanted nothing more than to join her in her nest, but I knew she needed rest and didn't want to disturb her when I climbed in or when I had to leave again.

Sitting the snack and drink on the table beside the bed, I dug two more pills from my pocket and placed them beside the glass. It wasn't time for them yet, but hopefully she would sleep for a while, and she'd need them once she woke up. I doubted I'd be gone that long, but it made me feel better to have everything ready for her just in case.

I stood and stared at her form under the blankets for a moment, letting the fresh scent of her fill my lungs. It seemed impossible to feel such a strong tie to her after only a week when we hadn't discussed anything more than a one-time heat, but I accepted it. My wolf was sure, and she seemed open to the possibility. That's all I needed.

Knowing I couldn't stand there watching her forever, I left the room, closing the door quietly so I didn't disturb her. Left with nothing else to do, I started cleaning up the pile of crap in the dining area. I still needed to finish repairs on the house, but some of it was leftover from what had already been done.

I'd worked through a good chunk of the supplies, moving a lot of it to the garage where it should have been, when my phone rang. Carl's name rolled across the screen next to the time. I hadn't realized how long I'd been working, and it was almost time for me to go.

"Hello?"

I hadn't expected to talk to him again before the meeting, and my muscles tensed, waiting for bad news.

"Patch offered to miss church to stay with Brooke. You good with that?"

I had to force my claws back into my fingertips and remind myself it was necessary to have another alpha watch over her. I needed to go, and while I'd considered bringing her with me, she needed the rest, and Patch was a better option than most of the others. He was the only one besides Carl who knew the extent of what was going on, and while I would have liked to have him as a witness to the injuries done to Brooke, there was no reason for the men not to believe me.

"Okay, yeah. He still needs to stay outside."

I could only relax the possessiveness so much, and having another alpha in my home, near my omega's nest without me around, wasn't going to happen. Even if it was someone I trusted.

"Got it. He's on the way."

I hung up and went to the sink to wash off. By the time I finished and went out to walk my bike from the garage, he was pulling into the driveway. A nod was all that was needed as I passed him and rolled out into the street. He settled in front of the closed garage door, and I forced myself to keep going instead of rushing back inside. I knew she'd be okay while I was gone, and I wouldn't be far away, but instincts didn't listen to reason.

It was a short trip to where we held our meetings when one was necessary. When the club was smaller, we'd had them at the shop, but as the members grew, we needed a larger space, and since we didn't have a traditional clubhouse like most motorcycle clubs, we found another space.

A church.

It was an older one with a small parish, but we'd saved it from being demolished to put in a new coffee shop, and the priest had given us permission to use the space whenever needed.

When I rolled around back, I spotted enough bikes to know I was one of the last to arrive. I was fine with that since it meant we could get started right away and I wouldn't be separated from Brooke as long.

Tempting A Knight

I parked alongside Carl's hog and headed in. There was a short dark hall lined with doors, but the one ahead was open, spilling light and sound into the dim space.

Men were sprawled amongst the pews, a few holding beers someone had apparently brought with them. I made sure they always cleaned up their mess before we left so the priest looked the other way at their antics, if he even noticed since he was rarely here when we used the building.

A few heads turned my way as I strode in, the general conversations dying down. We didn't stand on ceremony, and the men only followed me out of respect, and I tried to keep that in mind anytime an issue came up. It was natural for shifters to band together in packs, and most of us didn't have one outside the club, so while I was the de facto leader, I took their concerns into consideration before doing anything.

Already impatient, I jumped right into explaining what had happened with Brooke, including the fact that Arik had killed her brother for refusing an order to torture a shifter family and for associating with me.

"We can't protect her forever if he's set on taking her," Tim stated. He'd been one of the men keeping an eye on her parents and had been injured in the first confrontation. I could understand his hesitance even though his words made my wolf writhe in fury.

"I'm aware of that, which is why I plan to take him out of the picture."

Leann Ryans

The murmurs died as every eye in the place focused on me. The stillness in a room full of alphas would have alerted anyone who stepped in that they were in a dangerous situation.

"I can't leave her to whatever Arik has planned now, especially with the history between him and I. What he'd have done to her before would have been bad, but her association with me has sealed her fate."

Carl and a few of the others shook their heads, but it was Carl who spoke up.

"No one is asking you to sacrifice the omega."

I nodded at him but kept most of my attention on the other men. I knew how Carl felt, it was the others I needed to check with.

"My involvement in this has already brought attention to us. I've tried to keep the focus on me, but Arik being part of the Purists means we'll all have a target on us. I'm not sure if what I plan for him will end that, or make it worse. The men who follow him are low-level underlings, but his father is one of the original members who founded the gang."

I paused to look around and meet everyone's gaze.

"If you want to take off your cut until this all blows over, I understand. I don't want anyone pulled into this who isn't prepared for the backlash. I will be point on this, I will make the blow and take the fall, if necessary, but I could use some backup."

A few murmurs began again as the men looked between themselves. They knew as well as I what this would lead to. We were still waiting on retaliation from the confrontations that had already happened, but killing Arik could lead to so much more.

Carl stood, drawing our attention.

"You know I stand with you. I'll help any way I can."

I nodded. I'd expected nothing less from him.

Jason, Knox, and Jackson all stood, proclaiming their willingness to fight. They were young and hotheaded like many alphas, but I needed all the help I could get.

Patch wasn't there to show his support, but it was obvious from the way he'd been so careful of Brooke. Hopefully we wouldn't need him, but a weight was lifted knowing he'd be there to save our asses if necessary.

I looked around for Danger, remembering Patch's words earlier. I finally spotted him leaning against the wall in the back where the light didn't quite reach, with his arms folded over his chest, his black mask hiding everything but his eyes.

"I also need somewhere safe for her parents to stay until this is over. They're the closest thing I have to family, and Arik knows where they live. He'll use them against me and Brooke, so they need to disappear for a bit."

It was hard to read anything in the little I could see of him. Keeping my gaze locked on his, he finally raised one finger before turning around and exiting through the front door of the chapel. I doubted he would disappear without details, so he was likely going out to the little front room of the church to make the arrangements.

My chest loosened and I barely noticed a few more of the men standing and stating they were willing to help. There were others still seated, mainly the members with families to worry about, and I didn't begrudge them their caution. I'd have been hesitant to put Brooke at risk if I could prevent it.

"All right then. You know what's happening, and more information will be passed on as we make plans so you can stay aware. We'll assume the ones who couldn't make it won't be involved, so take a good look around so you know who not to expose. If anyone wants to disappear for a while and needs help, let me or Carl know, and we'll do what we can."

The men began to shuffle around, knowing they were being dismissed. The ones who wanted to help moved closer while the others began to head for the door. I told Carl to take over for a moment as I moved to intercept the first person going for the exit.

Blake was an older alpha, his head of salt and pepper hair extending to blend with his silver beard. He was one of my first employees at the shop and had his own omega at home with a pair of teens he'd come to us more than once to help keep an eye on, so I knew exactly why he was choosing to lay low.

Seeing me heading for him, he pulled off his leather jacket with our symbol on the back, holding it out to me. I shook my head, clasping his hand instead.

"Take a little vacation on me and keep your family safe. Let me know if you need help with anything."

His hair hid a lot of his expression, but I knew my acceptance was a relief to him. I didn't want any of the men thinking we would hold their decisions against them.

"Thanks boss," he said as he squeezed my hand before passing through the door.

I shook each member's hand as they left, reassuring them they still had a place with us when the dust settled.

Once the last one left, I made my way along the side of the chapel to the door Danger had passed through. Carl would make arrangements with the others, so getting Mr. and Mrs. Frost squared away was my main concern.

I nearly jumped out of my skin when a darker shadow peeled away from the others after I walked through the doorway. I pulled back my claws and swallowed the instinctive growl, swearing under my breath.

My phone dinged before I could open my mouth to say anything to him.

"That's the address. Keys are under the mat. It's clear for a month."

I pulled my phone out to check it. The address was downtown in one of the nicer areas that the police actually kept free from crime, and short of getting them out of the city altogether, was the best place to hide them.

"Thanks. I can cover the rent for the place, and a month should be more than enough time."

I didn't want to rush anything, but I also didn't want to put it off too long. The more time Arik had, the more danger he'd pose.

Danger just huffed at my offer, waving his hand.

"Unnecessary."

I studied him for a moment, wondering who he was to be able to give up a location like that without compensation. I had made the offer and I'd have found a way to pay whatever he'd asked for it, but I knew it was beyond anything I could hope to afford.

"I can't participate in this one, but I may have something for you in a few weeks that can help."

With that, Danger turned and walked into the little tunnel that led around to the back of the church where we'd parked. Left with that confusing comment, there was nothing else for me to do but head back to the members willing to help and figure out what we were going to do.

Chapter Twenty-Three

Brooke

I woke to distant pounding. For a moment I thought it was in my head, but when I covered my ears, it disappeared. Realizing it had to be something else. I pulled back the blankets I'd tucked over myself and sat up. Rubbing the sleep from my eyes, I scooted to the edge of the bed before my head cleared enough to hear the yelling.

"Brooke, wake up! Hurry!"

The masculine voice yelling between the pounding wasn't Sebastian but was vaguely familiar. I remembered Sebastian saying he had to leave in a few hours and he'd leave someone watching the house.

My heartrate doubled as my breath caught in my chest. If whoever he'd left on watch was pounding on the door there had to be an emergency, but I'd have expected Sebastian to call.

Unless he wasn't able.

I stumbled as I lurched from the bed, my blanket tangling between my legs before I kicked it away. Not bothering to stop for my shoes or anything else, I raced to the front door and yanked it open, finding a furious looking blonde alpha on the other side.

The jolt of fear was automatic, even though this alpha was larger, his blue eyes paler than Arik's. I struggled to remember his name, but he took hold of my arm and was pulling me from the house before I could come up with it.

"What's going on?"

My voice was rough between being awoken and the fear clogging my throat, but he understood me well enough.

"They hit the shop. We need to leave in case they're coming here next. We're too close to the fire."

It wasn't until he said it that I realized the orange glow I'd seen wasn't the sun rising. The wind shifted, bringing me the acrid stench of smoke.

I choked, but it wasn't from the fumes. I knew how much the mechanic shop meant to Sebastian. It had been his and Vincent's dream.

And now it was burning because of me.

Tears collected on my lashes as the alpha pushed me toward his bike. Unlike Sebastian's, it didn't have a little seat on the back for a passenger, and I hesitated, unsure what to do. My fear of motorcycles may have lessened but it still rattled around inside at the prospect of riding with someone other than Sebastian, and especially without a seat.

"On the front, I'll be behind you to protect you. Hurry."

Tempting A Knight

The sharpness in his tone told me how serious the situation was, and while having an alpha I barely knew wrapped around my back made me uneasy, there was no other choice.

Patch. I finally remembered his name as I swung my leg over the seat and scooted forward as far as I could go. When he took his place behind me, I was trapped between metal and a hard body, and while it might seem like a great place to be for some, my stomach churned with discomfort.

He moved my feet atop his boots and began to walk it toward the street. Where Sebastian's bike rumbled with blatant power, Patch's made a sleek purr when it came to life, reminding me more of something coiled and poised to strike. No less dangerous, but more hidden, and a brief view of slit pupils flashed through my mind.

A strong arm banded around my middle, holding me secure as we pulled out of the driveway and turned away from the shop. Part of me wanted to see it, to assess how bad the damage was, but Arik was the type to linger to wait for a reaction, and I had no desire to run into him again.

The reminder of what would happen if he got ahold of me made me realize my face didn't feel as tight as it had when I fell asleep. I had no idea how long ago that had been, but I chose to be grateful for it, no matter how small. I could open my eyes all the way, though my lids still felt strange, and that went a long way to making me feel less helpless.

Leann Ryans

I held onto the metal in front of me, making myself as small as possible so I didn't get in Patch's way as he steered. Once he was sure I wasn't going to fall off he let go of my middle, easing some of my discomfort, though my toes were numb from the wind. When we were a few blocks from Sebastian's house he slowed and leaned down to speak in my ear.

"Did you grab your phone?"

I shook my head, unable to speak past the lump still lodged in my throat.

We continued until we came upon a gas station where he pulled in and parked in the shadows on the side of the building. I yearned for the lit area around the pumps, or the comfort of the bright interior, but understood why he'd chosen the place where we'd be the least visible. He moved around behind me but didn't stand, and when I heard his voice I realized he'd been pulling out his phone.

He must have called Sebastian, because he launched right into the problem without preamble.

"They torched the shop. I took Brooke and left in case they were coming for the house, or the fire gets out of hand, but I heard sirens as we were leaving. The shop may have been their only target for now."

There was silence for a moment before he spoke again. "She's fine."

I heard a grunt before a hand holding a phone thrust in front of me.

"He wants to talk to you."

My fingers were shaking as I collected the phone from him. His palm had dwarfed the device, but my fingers had to stretch to hold it.

"Hello?"

My voice wasn't as scratchy as it had been, but it still didn't come out the confident tone I'd hoped for. More like the squeak of a scared mouse, and I was getting really tired of being that mouse.

"Are you okay?"

Sebastian's voice rumbled from the speaker; tempered anger held behind the concern I heard. My chest clenched and I had to swallow before I could speak again.

"Yes, I'm fine. I'm so sorry."

A whisper was all I could manage as emotions surged and threatened to spill over my cheeks.

"It's not your fault, Brooke. None of this is, so stop apologizing. Now hand the phone back to Patch."

I sniffled, passing the phone over my shoulder as I swiped at an errant tear. He was right, I knew he was right, but I couldn't help the guilt. My boring, going-nowhere-fast life had been upended, and now I felt like a tree at the edge of a cliff, knowing the fall was inevitable, but unable to predict which storm would be the one to send me over the edge. And on top of that, I'd tangled my branches with another and was going to take them with me.

Patch grunted, followed by a span of silence. I had no idea what Sebastian was telling him, Patch's stoic façade leaving little to decipher until he finally spoke again, and even then, I was left clueless.

"Got it."

There was motion behind me again, and I shot a look over my shoulder to see him putting away his phone. I pushed past the natural hesitance to draw attention to myself, because I couldn't take not knowing what was happening.

"Are we going back to his house?"

Patch shook his head. When I continued to watch him, he gave in.

"He's going to meet us at my place once he's done with the police."

My eyes widened until I realized what Patch meant. Of course Sebastian would have been called by officials about the fire, and the police would want to question him. I hoped he didn't have any issues with them, but his club seemed to stay on the right side of the law for the most part.

Still, worry gripped me as Patch wrapped an arm around me again until we were back out on the road, riding through the darkness. The area we passed through slowly deteriorated to boarded up, broken buildings, before improving again. The infrequent streetlights became more regular, the road smoother, the businesses and homes we passed in better repair.

Eventually the hulking forms of skyscrapers grew on the horizon. As late, or early, as it was, the city never slept, and the glow of the lights blotted out all view of the stars.

Patch turned into a parking lot in front of a small white building, and it took a moment for me to realize it was his tattoo shop. For some reason I'd been expecting him to take me to his house, and a bit of tension left me at not being at such an intimate location. Whether the feelings of attachment to Sebastian were instinct or something more, I couldn't help how much it bothered me to be alone with another alpha, especially somewhere there would likely be a bed. At least the shop was less conducive to anything... inappropriate.

I snorted at myself, shaking my head as Patch killed his motorcycle and stood. Once he was off, he held out a hand to help me, my legs wobbly after the long ride. His chilly fingers sent shivers up my arm, and I released them as soon as I was stable.

Pulling out a set of keys, Patch strode to the door and opened it, holding it as I walked through. I winced when he flipped on the lights, blinking through the sting until my eyes adjusted and I could look around without tearing up.

I'd been too distracted to pay much attention when I'd been there the first time, so I took the chance to move closer to the pictures on the walls, studying the inked images on the people portrayed there. Each one was beautiful, the tattoos excruciatingly detailed. Some were full body images with the person wearing nothing but the artwork, but they were tasteful, the backgrounds a uniform solid white to make them the focus. I'd never thought of getting a tattoo before, but the pictures had me wondering how much it would hurt.

"It's easier for omegas."

I startled, jerking around to face Patch where he stood a short distance behind me. He nodded at the photo I'd been studying before gesturing to the others on the wall.

"It's easier for omegas, as long as they have an alpha to help them. I did that as she laid on her mate's chest, and she slept through most of it thanks to his purr."

I looked at the image again. It was the backside of a woman. Her body was divided by a sinuous line starting where her neck met her left shoulder and crossing to the top of her right hip. Above the line, the upper right portion of her back, was clear, smooth skin, while everything below the line was an intricate tangle of rose vines, all the way to the backs of her knees. There were little butterflies tucked amidst the blooms and vines. Even her bottom was tattooed, and I shivered at the imagined feel of having someone so close to such a sensitive place, even if her mate had been there holding her.

"She's brave," I murmured.

The image of straddling Sebastian, lying on his chest as he purred, with Patch seated behind me tattooing something so delicate on my flesh popped in my head, and I shivered again.

"She is."

When I turned back to Patch, his open expression closed again, brows pinching together before he took a step closer. He reached out to touch my forehead before pressing along my cheekbone, making me flinch away.

"Are you cold? How long has it been since you took anything for the pain and swelling? How does your head feel?"

I shrugged one shoulder. I felt better than I'd have expected to considering it had only been around twelve hours since the incident happened. Whatever he'd given me had worked great.

"I'm fine. The headache is still there but it's not too bad. Sleeping helped."

He nodded before turning away to head back where we found him that afternoon. I noticed a mini-fridge under the counter when he leaned down and opened it, pulling out two bottles of water. He passed me one and I took it, thirst hitting me suddenly.

"Let me know if anything gets worse. Getting more sleep really would be your best option."

He nodded to my left and I spotted a low couch against the far wall at the front of the shop. Leaning down, he pulled a plain white pillow and sheet from another cabinet beneath the counter and offered them to me. I doubted I'd be able to get back to sleep, but I took them anyway, giving them a cautious sniff. Relieved to scent nothing more than bleach on the fabric, I took the hint and headed over to the couch as he settled at a desk beside his tattooing area.

I took a seat on the couch, tucking my legs up beside me and smoothing the sheet over myself more for comfort than because I was cold. The tile floor had been chilly on my bare feet, but otherwise the room was comfortably warm. I supposed it needed to be if someone was going to get undressed for a tattoo.

The couch wasn't the most comfortable, and after a while the hip I leaned on began to protest. Bored with nothing to occupy me, I figured there was no harm in lying down.

I dozed off despite thinking I wouldn't be able to, waking to the lock on the front door clicking open. I hadn't realized Patch locked it behind us, and the sound had me jerking upright, blinking blurry eyes at the dark figure that entered.

Sebastian's scent curled around me moments before his arms. He'd crossed the space between us in a breath and had me on my feet pressed against his chest before my brain had registered his movement.

We stood in silence, my arms wrapping around him as he buried his nose in my hair, before he finally heaved a deep breath and released me. Holding me at arm's length, he raked his gaze down my entire body before dropping a kiss on my forehead and turning to Patch when the other alpha lingered a few steps away.

"They didn't go for the house. Not sure if they haven't connected it to me yet, or if they're saving that for next time. Either way, you made the right move getting her out of there. The Fire Department almost had to evacuate the homes anyway when the wind shifted before they had the fire under control."

Sebastian's voice was rougher than usual, and I noted the stench of smoke lingering under his scent. He'd clearly been there, watching his shop burn.

My stomach flipped, guilt rising to eat at me again.

"How bad is it?"

The question cut through the quiet, and I winced before he even had the chance to answer. Chocolate irises caught mine, a large hand rising to cup my cheek. The pressure on the still swollen tissue was uncomfortable, but not enough for me to pull away.

"There were a lot of flammable things in there. Between the fire and the efforts to put it out, it's a total loss."

He said the words softly, as if it would lessen the blow that way, but tears still welled up and spilled over my cheeks. The guilt stretched to engulf me until his other hand came up to frame my face, his thumbs swiping away tears as he shushed me.

"It's okay. The business is insured, and nobody was hurt by it. That's all that matters."

I gulped, trying to hold back the sobs tearing at my chest. It seemed silly to be crying over the loss of his shop when he seemed fine with it, but I knew it had been more than just a business to him, and the link to my brother on top of everything else that had happened was too much.

Strong arms wrapped around my back, holding me to a warm chest that thrummed with a soothing purr. Combined with the scent of him, my instincts worked to calm the jumble and pull me out of the spiral I'd been heading down.

"Everything will work out. It was just a building. Things. They can be replaced. It already saved me, and your brother's dream won't die because of this. We'll rebuild bigger and better than he ever imagined."

Sebastian stroked my back as he murmured to me, the words breaking through to stem the flow of tears. In a flash the distress flipped to anger, and his purr did nothing to dampen it as I pulled away.

"He has to pay for this. I'm tired of living in fear and feeling guilty for things I can't control. It's not fair that we are the ones suffering when we've already suffered so much."

Sebastian's gaze turned feral, meeting mine with the fury burning in him. His claws extended, his canines elongating as he smiled.

"I agree. That's why I'm going to kill him."

I shook my head, hands balled at my sides. No more sitting back and letting things happen to me. No more hiding and slinking around instead of standing my ground.

"No. *We* are going to kill him. I need to see it for myself."

Chapter Twenty-Four

Sebastian

Was it wrong that her fierceness made me hard? Maybe.

But the sight of her standing there, standing up to me and declaring what she needed, that she wanted to see Arik die...

It was hot.

I took a step toward her, already reaching out to pin her body to mine, when Patch reminded me where I was by clearing his throat. It took a moment to pull myself together and not lunge at him for being so close to my omega. I could scent him on her, and it was driving my wolf crazy. It was all I could do not to rip her clothes from her and rub myself against her flesh to mark her with my scent instead.

The breath I sucked in reminded me that I didn't really smell all that great at the moment though. Smoke and sweat clung to me, making my nose curl as I turned my attention to Patch.

"Was anything decided at church?"

I gave myself a mental shake, reminding myself there were more important things at the moment than sinking inside a certain feisty omega, no matter how tempting she was. Maybe after I was home and showered, but Patch needed to be brought up to speed before I could whisk her away.

Since he already knew what we'd been going to discuss, there wasn't a lot he'd missed.

"Danger had a place for her parents. It's in an area with no Purists that we're aware of, and it's Uptown, so even if they found them, I doubt they'd make any moves. I already sent them the address and Jackson should be sitting on them. He'll stay with them till everything is clear.

"Carl has a list of who's up to help, but I got the call about the shop before we could discuss any ideas. We'll meet up again tomorrow night, once everyone's had a chance to rest and hopefully things from the fire settle down."

Patch nodded, his icy gaze sliding from me to Brooke. It was impossible to hold back the low growl that rolled from my chest until his attention returned to me.

"Let me know when. And make sure she takes more pills before, and take it easy on her."

I huffed at the last part. He knew full well what was going to happen as soon as I got Brooke alone again. My instincts were too riled to accept anything less as reassurance.

I turned to her, wondering if she knew. Her lips were parted, breaths coming in short puffs as her chest heaved.

Tempting A Knight

Her pupils were dilated enough to tell me she was as on edge as I was. Even if she wasn't consciously aware, her body knew what was coming, and was fully onboard.

"I need more."

I'd left two pills on the table next to her at my house, and the rest were there as well. I had no plans on going to my place just yet, and while the swelling had gone down a bit, the bruising reminded me she still wasn't anywhere near one hundred percent.

I listened to Patch walk away before returning. He passed me a bottle of water and four more pills. I pocketed two of them before closing the space between me and Brooke.

Holding the pills to her lips, I continued to gaze into her eyes as I waited for her to open for me. Once she did I pressed them inside, letting my fingers stroke along her tongue before withdrawing them from her mouth and holding up the bottle of water.

She drank and swallowed without breaking eye contact, making my cock twitch against my jeans. It was killing me to hold back, and there was nothing else stopping me from leaving so I could bury myself in her sooner.

Capping the water, I pulled her against me, claiming her glistening lips. I kissed her until she melted against me, all tension leaving her body, before letting her come up for air. Sweeping her into my arms, I headed for the door without another word.

The sky outside was already pink, the sun coming up somewhere behind the buildings blocking the view, and once again I had the urge to put her on my bike and head for the country. My wolf had been too anxious since I met her to go out and roam free in the woods like I usually did, and the constant need to fight back a shift was draining me. We'd be safer outside the city, but that would leave those we cared about in Arik's path, and I couldn't do that.

Taking a seat on my bike, I reluctantly released Brooke, letting her slide off my lap to move around behind me, her slim arms circling my waist. I may not be able to release my wolf, but I could find another form of release once I got her somewhere safe.

I started the bike and pulled out in a rush, Brooke's gasp and the tensing of her body around me forcing me to slow down to a safer pace. I wanted nothing more than to roar through the streets, but I didn't want to scare her. She'd had enough of that.

I was too impatient to go far, though it would have been cheaper to find a room closer to the area we lived. Patch's shop was in a nice part of the city, too expensive for the petty thieves and gang members that plagued cheap motels, so while the one I pulled into cost an eye watering amount to rent a room for two days, the relief in knowing we wouldn't be looked for there was worth it.

Brooke had seemed confused when I'd pulled into the parking lot, but it didn't take her long to realize it was safer to stay in a random motel than it was to return to a house barely a block over from where the Purists had burned down my shop. With her apartment no safer, this was the best option we had.

After paying the desk clerk I took her hand, pulling her back out into the early morning light to find our room. The motel wasn't empty, but it wasn't overly full, and the clerk must have realized things might get a little noisy since he put us at the opposite end of the U-shaped building. If the cars in the lot were anything to go by, there wasn't anyone in the room next to ours, which was perfect by me.

I left my bike where it was in front of the office. If someone spotted it and recognized it as mine, at least they'd have a harder time finding our room.

That was the last thought I spared for the mess we were in. As soon as I closed and locked the door to our room, all my focus turned to Brooke. Her wide green eyes stared up at me, a slight tremor moving through her body and making me pause. I had to remember to take it easy so I didn't cause her any pain.

"How are you feeling?"

The question seemed to confuse her, her brow furrowing. Her hands spread before dropping against her thighs.

"Fine?"

Her answer sounded unsure, so I shook my head and crowded her toward the bed as a low rumble left my chest.

"I need to know where you hurt so I don't make it worse when I take you. Because I'm going to take you, Brooke. I'm going to fill you and knot that pussy till neither of us can think about anything else."

Her mouth dropped open, eyes widening. The sweet scent of slick tickled my nose, letting me know her body was preparing itself for what I wanted to do to her.

"Uh, m-my cheeks and around my eyes still hurts. My jaw a little. The headache is dull and mostly gone."

She licked her lips, the flick of her pink tongue making my dick kick against my zipper again. As much as I wanted to feel it on me, I was marking it off limits until the swelling and pain was completely gone.

"Anything else?"

The backs of her legs had hit the mattress and I stood so close her breasts brushed against me with each heave for air. I let my fingers brush along her sides as I waited.

Brooke shook her head, and I couldn't help the grin that stretched my face. I leaned in, cupping her skull in my hands as I brushed my lips over hers. I wanted to do more but was too conscious of being careful not to hurt her.

"Good."

I reached one arm down and scooped her legs out from under her, crawling onto the bed with her cradled to my chest. Her arms went around my neck, anchoring her there as I moved us to the center of the mattress.

This was no nest. It wasn't even a decent bed she'd done her best to convert to her needs, and I swore to do better by her the next time. Because there *would* be a next time. And a time after that. And hopefully a time after that as well. As long as Arik didn't manage to kill me before I got to him, I'd given up on fighting the draw I felt to the little omega in my arms. I wasn't letting her go unless she forced me to.

I lowered her to the bedding and pressed myself down on top of her, being sure to keep most of my weight braced on my arms and knees where they dug into the mattress. Moving my lips from her mouth, I trailed them down her neck, growling when fabric got in the way of tasting her.

I reared back, both hands moving to grip the neck of her shirt but her fingers wrapped around my wrists to stop me.

"Sebastian, no! I didn't bring enough clothes for you to rip them off me."

Her chest heaved, pupils dilated as she stared up at me. I couldn't stop the growl rolling from my chest and her hips rolled beneath me, letting me know how I affected her. The scent of her slick was calling to me, and my patience had run out.

"I'll buy you more."

That was all the warning she got before my claws came out and ripped through the neckline. The fabric parted, standing no chance beneath the onslaught of my deadly claws, and while she made a little mewl of protest, she released my wrists.

I reached back to pull her shoes off so I could remove her pants, only to find she wasn't wearing any. A part of me wasn't sure if she'd already kicked them off or if she hadn't been wearing any, but I was too lost in lust for it to hold my attention for long.

Leann Ryans

I had to crawl off her to remove her pants, standing at the side of the bed as I peeled them down, revealing her pale skin inch by inch. My wolf wriggled inside me, the demand to mark her and leave no doubt who she belonged to making my mouth water as my canines lengthened.

I wanted to, but it wasn't the time to ask those questions and make that decision. Too much uncertainty lingered ahead of us to take the risk.

Brooke laid on the bed, staring up at me as my hands moved to my own clothing. Her pert breasts rose and fell in a quick rhythm, catching my gaze as I tossed my shirt to the floor with her things and thrust my jeans off my hips. There was no time to go slow and let her look me over when I wanted my mouth on her.

As soon as there was nothing left to keep us separated, I fell to my knees, wrapping my hands around her legs and yanking her to the edge of the bed. Putting one thigh over my shoulder, I let the other fall to the side as I pulled her thighs apart and dove in.

The scent of her, already wet and willing, sent my head spinning as I ran my nose along the inside of her thigh before reaching her center. Swiping my tongue along her outer lip, I groaned as her taste hit me and her hips bucked for more.

Licking along the other fold, I savored her flavor before plunging into her entrance. Brooke moaned, drawing my eyes up the length of her body as I moved my tongue in and out of her, mimicking what I planned to do with my aching cock after I dragged an orgasm or two from her.

I'd never get enough of this.

Leann Ryans

Chapter Twenty-Five

Brooke

My eyes wanted to roll back in my head at the feel of his tongue, but his dark gaze captured me and wouldn't let go. His teeth were extended, his claws pricking my flesh where they had grown from his fingertips, and while it might have been worrisome to have those sharp tips so close to delicate flesh, I knew Sebastian wouldn't hurt me.

His tongue rolled through my folds, seeming to grow as it thrust inside. His features sharpened, the shape of his ears changing as the hair grew thicker on his arms where I could see them as he held me open. He balanced on the edge of control, a fraction away from tipping over.

I fought with the desire to push him. To make him lose the tight hold he kept on himself. While I wanted him to have the release and knew I'd taken it during my heat, I wasn't sure I could handle it without the extra slick and hormones.

A whimper ripped from my throat as his finger moved to press over my clit while he continued to lap at me. The shape of his face kept changing, and he trembled with the effort to hold back.

The tension in my belly curled tighter, warmth flooding from my center. I couldn't focus on the fear of pain from his were-form. I could feel his struggle, and I wouldn't deny him. He'd helped me, and it was my turn to give him what he needed.

"Let go. Take what you need."

His tongue paused its thrusting, his thumb stilling over my little nub. The rumble that had been rolling from him deepened, his hold on my legs tightening as he watched me. What he saw must have reassured him, because he let out a sigh and closed his eyes.

The shoulders holding my legs open grew, the one under my thigh becoming rough with fur. The bones in his face shifted, his cheekbones growing more pronounced as his ears shifted to the top of his head. Nose and jaw thrusting forward into a muzzle, he opened his eyes once the transformation was complete, the same alpha I'd known since childhood staring at me from a face that may not be as handsome, but drew me in all the same.

"Take me, Sebastian. I'm yours."

He released another growl against my folds, tongue moving impossibly deeper inside me. My hips lifted of their own accord, grinding my clit against his thumb as my orgasm surged closer with each lick. I was held on the verge before he shoved me over and I keened my release while my limbs thrashed as he pulled his tongue from me to lash it over my clit.

Sebastian didn't give me the chance to come back down before he was rolling me to my belly, pulling my hips up as he stood. His length laid along the crevice of my bottom, sticky fluid leaking from the tip to glaze my lower back as he made shallow thrusts before pulling back to line himself up with my entrance. He had to crouch despite me kneeling on the bed, his towering height in were-form leaving him too tall.

Pressing the leaking tip of him to my opening, he took both my hips in his hands, pausing for a moment. I pushed back against his pointed head even as my core still fluttered with the earlier orgasm he'd given me. The pressure of him as he slipped inside and stretched my entrance was both thrilling and terrifying. Slick coated my folds, easing his way, but I still felt the burn of opening to accept him as he eased in.

Sebastian pulled back and released one of my hips. I looked over my shoulder to see him running his massive hand up and down his length, his sharp claw-tips carefully held away from the reddened flesh. White fluid dribbled from the slit, running down the flared head to drip onto me and join the growing trail of fluid running down my thighs.

He rubbed his palm over the tip, spreading the sticky wetness around before pressing it back to my opening. The heat of him drew all my attention to that pulsing point of contact, and I whimpered as I tried to push myself down his length but his other hand on my hip held me in place.

"You *are* mine, Brooke. No one else can have you. I'll destroy the world to keep you safe and make sure no one touches you but me."

His voice was different in his were-form. Deeper and more gravelly. It made my core clench, and I pictured him leaning over my back and sinking those long teeth into my neck to truly make me his.

I was almost mindless with the need to feel him inside me. It was nearly as intense as when I'd been in heat, but there were no excess hormones to blame the feeling on. I'd passed the point of having a crush on Sebastian and passed well into being infatuated.

I wanted him to claim me. To mark me for all the world to see. Not *despite* him being a shifter, but because of who he was, and his wolf was part of that.

Moaning, I let my chest drop to the blankets, wiggling my hips. The discomfort of my face pressing into the bed wasn't enough to distract me.

"Please, Sebastian."

I gasped out the words, begging him to complete his invasion. Tension already coiled in my belly once again, the release he'd given me with his tongue not satisfying. I needed to feel the stretch of him inside me, filling me as he'd promised.

Claws touched the back of my neck, trailing down my spine until he reached the top of my cleft. I shivered, holding my breath as his fingers curled around my hip to hold me in place.

"Mine. My Brooke."

The guttural words were followed by a driving thrust that pushed half his length inside me. I cried out as he pulled back and slammed in again, yanking on my hips as he pushed forward to cram more of him in. I felt so full, yet there was still more of him.

Sebastian leaned over my back, the heat of him burning into my back where sweat had cooled in the air-conditioned room.

"Good girl. Relax for me so you can take it all."

He purred the words in my ear, his agile tongue licking along the shell before teeth nibbled along the side of my neck. The vibrations sank into me, loosening muscles and allowing him to move easier as he made small thrusts in and out of my channel. Each time he went a little deeper until I finally felt his hips resting against my bottom.

"Good girl."

My whole body trembled with his praise, another moan leaving me though it was half lost with my face pressed into the bedding.

Sebastian sat up, the shifting of his hardness inside me making me gasp and push myself back up onto my hands to relieve some of the pressure. He made little circling motions with his hips before his grip shifted to my shoulders, one hand wrapping in my hair before the fingers hooked over my collarbone.

"Are you okay?"

I didn't know how he could still think clearly enough to be concerned with my comfort, but it was one of the reasons I trusted him so much. His need was as great or more than mine, yet he was still being careful for me.

I tried to nod but couldn't move my head with his grip on my hair, so I gasped out a "Yes."

His purr turned to a growl as his hips snapped, the only thing keeping me from plowing face-first into the mattress again was his hold on me. I couldn't hold back my cries as he took up a brutal rhythm, pummeling my insides. It burned, it ached, and it threw me into another orgasm I hadn't known was coming.

The room spun around me as Sebastian fucked me through the spasms. He moved impossibly faster, his erection seeming to grow even harder inside me as he used my body for his pleasure. The thought of what we must look like, his monstrous body impaling my smaller form as he held me how he wanted me, had me rising toward another peak before the flutters of the last ended.

Sebastian's grip shifted and he pulled me up until my back rested against his chest. The hand holding my hair slid forward to cup the front of my throat, adding slight pressure but not enough to cut off my oxygen. The other moved across my chest to grip the opposite breast, his claws tweaking the tight nipple and sending sparks of electricity straight to my clit.

"Tell me you're mine again. Tell me you'll still be mine when this is all over."

His growl had my body tightening as he lifted and lowered me on his length. My weight was nothing to his strength, I was a ragdoll in his arms for him to use as he pleased. I had no chance of getting away, even if I'd wanted to.

And I liked it.

"I'm yours Sebastian. I'll always be yours."

My words were nothing more than a whisper followed by a scream as he slammed me down onto his swelling knot. It inflated so fast I didn't have time to adjust, the pressure making the burning of my channel increase as he locked it behind my pubic bone. I was stuffed to the brim, and I spasmed around him as I felt him spill inside me, my own release milking him for more.

When I thought it was over, he groaned in my ear, squeezing me tighter as his cock kicked inside me, the movement sending answering ripples through my core. We were caught in a loop, each twitch from him causing my channel to spasm and pull more fluid from him, making him jerk and begin the process again.

The pressure in my womb built and built until my belly felt rounded with it. It became uncomfortable, and my moans turned to whines.

"Shhh, it's almost done. You did so good. We'll lie down in a moment."

I hung limp in his arms, my body drenched in sweat though he'd done all the work. The slow thud of my headache slowly crept back in, the throbbing along my cheekbones and jaw reminding me what I'd been through. Despite the sleep I'd gotten I was still exhausted, and with the lust for him sated, I wanted nothing more than to let the world go and escape into oblivion again.

The thighs I sat on began to shrink, the arms supporting me losing their fur. The sound of Sebastian's panting disappeared, and soft lips pressed to the back of my neck as the pressure inside me eased enough to not be painful.

"There you go. Let's lie down."

He changed his hold on me and leaned to the side, careful of my arms and legs as he got us situated. I was tucked against him, his body half covering me as he pressed me into the bed. When he flipped the edge of the blanket over us it felt like I was in a nest, shielded from the world, and all the tension in my body melted away.

The shifting of his knot inside me was still uncomfortable, but it wasn't enough to keep me awake. I drifted off to the sound of his purr between one breath and the next, my own hum of contentment rising to blend with his and block out the sounds of the waking city outside.

Chapter Twenty-Six

Sebastian

Brooke's soft snoring took over, her purr fading away. I stroked her hair as I waited for my knot to recede, awed by the woman in my arms. She was so much stronger than she thought she was. It was fairly easy for an omega to take a were's knot while in heat when hormones made her muscles lax and extra slick eased the way, it was quite another for her to take it outside of her cycle. I'd have felt bad about it if she hadn't been the one to encourage me and if she hadn't clearly enjoyed it.

I let myself relax despite the increasing noise outside the room. It was only the typical noise of a city; cars whooshing past, horns blaring, the occasional muffled profanities being yelled at other drivers. As worried as I was over Arik and the Purists finding us, it was unlikely.

A yawn overtook me, making my eyes water. I'd yet to go to sleep, and with the energy my body consumed during the fight and then trying to heal my wounds, I was exhausted. It was almost a relief not to need to worry about the shop.

A spike of guilt stabbed through my stomach at the thought. I loved the shop. I loved working with my hands, fixing something that had been broken. It had filled my days before Brooke arrived in the garage, asking me, a practical stranger at that point, to see her through her heat.

I was still mostly a stranger to her despite the amount of time we'd been together over the past couple weeks. Not a lot of talking had happened, and we still didn't know a lot about each other outside of how we fit together. I resolved to fix that as soon as I was sure I'd be around long enough for it to matter.

Ideas about how to get Arik alone in a place where I had a chance of getting away with what needed to happen occupied me until my knot finally slipped from Brooke, the gush of sticky fluid that followed making my mouth water, but I didn't want to disturb her too much. She still needed to heal as well, and she didn't have the bonus of shifter healing.

Slipping from the bed to the tiny bathroom, I grabbed the washcloth off the folded towel on the counter and wet it with warm water. Brooke was still snoring away when I returned and carefully rolled her to her belly so I could wipe the worst of the mess away so she wouldn't wake to it congealed on her thighs. My wolf protested, wanting to leave it there to mark her as ours, but I knew she wouldn't enjoy it as much as I did.

I tossed the washcloth on the nightstand and climbed back onto the bed. The need to cover and protect her was too strong to fight, so I didn't bother, wrapping her in my arms and throwing a leg over hers to pin her in place in case she woke before I did. I needed to know she was safe and waking without her beside me was unacceptable.

I dozed on and off, occasional noises breaking through and putting me on alert until I figured out what they were. Brooke seemed to sleep through it all until shortly after noon when she began to stir, waking me as she pushed at my arms.

"I need the bathroom."

I grumbled, still groggy from the lack of sleep, but let her go. The sight of her bare body as she walked across the room was enough to have an erection popping fast enough to make my head spin, but the empty gnawing in my stomach pulled my attention away as she shut the door between us.

Sighing, I rolled from the bed and searched for my jeans. Brooke may not have a healing shifter's appetite, but I knew she'd be hungry too. As much as I'd like to lock us both in the room for the rest of the day, we had to get a few things taken care of while we could. The Purists, or at least Arik's branch of them, would be laying low after setting the fire, and I wanted to be safely back in the room before they began to stir.

The bathroom door cracked open, Brooke's head poking out, her hair tousled from sleep and our activities before. It made me want to drag her out and throw her in the bed again.

"Is it okay to take a shower? I can be quick."

I nodded despite my wolf's whine about her losing more of our scent, and she disappeared into the bathroom again. If we were bonded, it would be different. She would always smell of us, her scent changing to warn off other alphas instead of drawing them in. As it was, it was hard not to want to keep her covered in my cum.

A rumble escaped but I cut it off, walking over to the covered window beside the door. Peeking out, I checked to see if there was any sign that someone was waiting for us to emerge. Without knowing which room we were in, if anyone wanted us they'd have to wait until we came out, and it was going to be the most dangerous moment.

I toyed with the idea of calling someone to come check the property, but doing so could draw attention to us if the others were being watched, which was likely. The Hell's Knights wouldn't be able to meet except in large enough groups to deter the Purists from attacking.

Unless...

I turned the idea over in my head before pulling out my phone. We usually only went out of the city on the weekends to let our animals free for a bit, but there was no reason we couldn't go now. We'd be far enough I wouldn't have to worry about us being ambushed, so even if only a few of the men could come, I'd be able to keep Brooke safe, and it would give me an opportunity to talk to the men who wanted to help deal with Arik.

The door to the bathroom opened behind me, Brooke emerging with the towel wrapped around her, her damp hair hanging around her face. She looked so small, so delicate and easily broken. It was hard to imagine her taking my were-form's cock only hours earlier.

I adjusted my erection, not bothering to hide what she did to me. Her eyes trailed down my bare chest, locking on the bulge in the front of my jeans. Her little tongue swiping along her lip was going to be my undoing, no matter what I'd told myself earlier. I had to redirect us before I ripped that towel off her and let her have what we both wanted.

"How's your head?"

I had to clear my throat to get the words out, and Brooke blinked at me without comprehension for a moment before her pupils contracted and she gave herself a shake.

"Better. Still aches a bit, but the stabbing pain is gone."

I dug in my pocket for the extra pills Patch had given me, but Brooke shook her head.

"I'd rather wait and see if it gets worse or not before taking more."

Hesitating, I wanted to insist she take the pills so she wouldn't be in pain, but it wasn't my place to dictate what she did, as much as my instincts might assure me it was. That was the old way of doing things, and I liked to think alphas had evolved beyond that point.

"Okay. Are you hungry?"

Her pupils flared, almost making me groan as my thoughts tried to follow hers, but I pulled them back.

"We can go grab some food, then I need to meet with the others. The sooner we have a plan, the better."

Leann Ryans

The light in her emerald eyes dimmed, making my chest ache as I reminded her of our situation. It was natural to want to ignore it, but that wouldn't fix the problem.

"Okay, yeah. Will we be going back to your house?"

Shaking my head, I reached down and snagged my shirt, pulling it over my head before answering.

"Too dangerous for you. If they found the shop, they'll find my house too. I'd known it would happen. Just thought we'd have a bit more time."

Her shoulders slumped but she nodded, and I realized what the issue was as her nose wrinkled when she lifted her clothes from the floor. I looked around as I remembered noticing she wasn't wearing shoes and sighed.

"I'll have one of the guys swing by and grab your things while we eat."

Her lips pressed into a tight smile and she gave me a nod before turning back to the bathroom to get dressed. I dug my phone from my jeans, wondering if Carl would be up yet or if I should call one of the others.

Shrugging it off, I figured if he didn't answer I'd try someone else, but he picked up on the third ring.

"Hey boss, what's up?"

I huffed, wondering if I still qualified as his boss if the shop no longer existed. I'd meant what I'd told Brooke that we'd rebuild, but it would take time. Until then, the men would need to find work, and another weight dropped onto my shoulders.

"Any issues come up while I was sleeping?"

"Sleeping, mmhmm."

I growled, letting him know I wasn't in the mood for his teasing, though I was glad to know he was in a good enough mood to do it.

"Nothing we weren't expecting. Purists crawling around Brooke's place, though they seem to be avoiding the shop. I've checked in with everyone and they're all accounted for. Just waiting for you."

I scrubbed a hand through my hair, scratching at my scruff. I might not care about wearing the same clothes another day, but the hair on my face was irritating me, and there was no reason to buy the stuff if I was having someone go by my place anyway.

"I need you to swing by the house, as long as it's safe. Take a couple guys with you."

"What do you need?"

"Brooke's bag should be sitting in my room, and her shoes are there too. I need a change and shaving supplies."

Carl chuckled. Facial hair was something we didn't agree on, but he wisely didn't try to rib me about it.

"Where should I bring it?"

I didn't want to lead anyone watching my house to the room, but I didn't want to draw them to anyone else either. I pulled my phone away from my ear, putting it on speaker so I could check the map.

"Roxie's Diner on Beaumont and Fifteenth."

Leann Ryans

The diner was about halfway between where we were and my house, and was far enough from anywhere we frequented that it shouldn't put anyone in danger.

"Got it. Give me forty and I'll be there."

"I think we need to go for a run afterward. Send the word out."

"Today?"

I heard the surprise in Carl's voice. Our usual spot was a bit of a drive, which was why we only went on weekends, but without work at the shop to fill the day it wasn't like there was a reason not to go.

"Yeah. The guys who want to help should be there. We need to talk in a place where we won't draw attention."

Carl made a noise under his breath.

"Alright. You heading out there after we meet up?"

"The sooner the better."

Sighing, he agreed before hanging up. Brooke had finished dressing and stood looking at me, questions written across her face as she held the edges of her torn shirt together. I should feel guilty about it, but I didn't.

"We're going to go eat and Carl will bring us your things. Then we're going to head out of the city for a bit so we can make plans without having to look over our shoulder the whole time."

Her gaze narrowed.

"I meant what I said. I want to be involved. I need to be there."

As much as I wanted to hide her away somewhere safe, I knew she was right. She'd always be waiting for him to reappear if she didn't see for herself that Arik was dead.

"I know. You will be, though you're going to promise me to stay out of the way so you're safe."

She huffed, looking away. I crossed the distance between us, taking her chin between my fingers and turning her back to look at me. I was careful since I knew her face was still painful, though it looked as though the swelling had subsided more, except for where the bruising was worst. It was a strange, colorful mix of mottled colors, and the rage inside me flared at the reminder of what Arik had done, along with a pain in my chest for not being close enough to stop it before it happened.

"You *will* stay safe. I need you to promise me. I don't want you hurt."

I said the words softly, and Brooke's lips trembled before she pressed them together. Chewing on the inside of her cheek, she resisted as long as she could before responding.

"I promise. I'll stay as safe as possible."

I didn't like the way she'd amended it, but it was good enough.

I dropped a kiss on her mouth before releasing her, the surprised little gasp she made making me grin.

"Now turn around."

Her brows crinkled but she did as I said, looking over her shoulder at me. Reaching around her, I tugged the edges of her shirt from her hands, pulling the whole thing off her before turning it around and holding it open.

"Arms in."

She put her arms through the holes, the undamaged back of the shirt now covering her front. The neckline came a little high, but not enough to bother her throat. I pulled the torn edges together in the back, using my claws to create strips in the fabric I could tie together. The shirt was stretched tight, but it would work until Carl arrived with her things.

Turning her around, I picked up my vest and wrapped it around her back, covering the rip as I thought about what needed to happen next.

"I'm going to go out and get my bike. I'll bring it over for you to come out and get on. Stay behind the curtain, but watch from the window. If anything happens, and I mean anything, you get out and run as fast as you can. Don't let them trap you in here. Head for the nearest business with people."

She swallowed, eyes going wide before she squared her shoulders.

"Okay. Be careful."

I shot her a smile, knowing I'd do anything but.

"Only because you asked so sweetly."

Chapter Twenty-Seven

Brooke

The need to constantly be on the lookout was exhausting, and Sebastian's warning not to let them trap me in the room if he got ambushed just added a layer of terror atop it.

I watched out the window as he made a show of walking across the parking lot to his bike, taking his time getting on and rolling it back over to the room. Once he was outside the door I darted out and hopped on the back, wrapping my arms tight around him as the bike roared to life and he took off as if we were being chased. I hadn't seen anyone, but my heart thumped with fear anyway.

After a few turns Sebastian slowed. The way his muscles relaxed helped mine loosen, and I opened my eyes to peek at the scenery as we rode by. The city sprawled so wide I couldn't see the towers from where we lived, and I'd had few reasons to be close enough to downtown to see them, so the view was enticing. It looked so quiet and clean from this distance, but I knew what it was like from stories my parents had told.

Leann Ryans

We wove our way through the streets, and I watched the skyscrapers until they disappeared behind the closer buildings we passed. It wasn't much longer before he pulled into the parking lot of a fancy looking diner, taking a place right in front of the doors. It wasn't until my bare foot landed on a pebble as I tried to stand that I realized it would be strange to walk into a restaurant without shoes.

Sebastian knew my concern as soon as my eyes turned to him.

"Few people look down, so if you act like everything is normal, they won't notice. Carl should be along with your shoes shortly."

I nodded, leaving my hand in his and straightening my spine, trying to look like a normal couple having lunch together and not a pair who were hiding from one of the largest gangs as we plotted the murder of one of their members.

I snorted at my thoughts, Sebastian quirking an eyebrow at me as he held the door open for me to pass inside. The urge to tug my pants lower so they might hide my toes was hard to resist but it would only draw more attention to my lack of footwear.

An older woman in a pink apron with a pile of curls pinned atop her head bustled over to greet us, her eyes widening as she took in the sight of Sebastian. I'd grown accustomed to his size and the way he looked, but had to admit the long hair and tattoos in addition to his size could make him intimidating, even without his leather vest.

Tempting A Knight

"Don't worry, he's a teddy bear," I said with a smile to put her at ease.

She huffed, flashing me a quick smile.

"Smells more like a wolf, and that would make you Red Riding Hood. Do you need rescuing?"

The blunt remark and question startled a laugh from me, and even Sebastian chuckled as he tightened the arm he had around my waist. I didn't realize it, but I likely did look like a kidnapping victim with my damp hair, and bruised face.

"Not from him. He's the one paying, and I'm starving" I added with a wink to reassure her.

She eyed Sebastian again but must have decided to trust him. Pasting on a smile, she picked up two laminated menus and waved for us to follow her to a corner booth.

"I'm Betty. Is there anything I can get started for you?"

I hesitated at the table, debating over whether sitting next to Sebastian or opposite him would look less suspicious before giving it up as pointless. I slid into the booth with my back to the wall where I could see the door, and Sebastian took the place next to me like I knew he would. I tried to assure myself any alpha would position themselves the same and it wouldn't seem like he was trapping me in to anyone who looked.

"Coffee. Cream and sugar, please."

Betty nodded and turned her eyes to Sebastian. Her expression didn't change, so I hoped she wasn't planning to go to the back and call the cops on him for abuse or anything.

"Same."

She sat the menus in front of us and strode away, calling to the patrons at another table as she went. She hustled around behind the counter, pouring our coffee before grabbing plates from a little window in the wall and dropping them off before coming back to us. I'd been so distracted watching her I hadn't even looked at the menu, so I just asked for a club sandwich and fries.

I was still watching her when I felt Sebastian's warm breath on my neck.

"Relax. She probably thinks it was a sex accident."

I started, jerking my gaze to him. His lips were tipped up on one side, brow quirked, telling me he knew exactly what I'd been watching for. He obviously wasn't worried.

I let out a sigh, shaking my head as I sank into his side. I was becoming paranoid, but it was hard not to be. I knew what I'd have been thinking if I saw a little, beat-up omega come in the convenience store with a big biker like him.

"It's hard."

He chuckled, his tone telling me where his mind went, and I smacked him on the arm before he said anything. It was strange to feel so comfortable and at ease with him when I considered our situation, but there were too many other things weighing on me to worry about the one thing making me feel good.

Betty returned with our food and we were digging into it before another burly biker strode through the door. He had the same symbol Sebastian did on the leather jacket he wore, and he seemed familiar, so I wasn't surprised when he headed right for us.

"Someone trashed your place. I've got Tom and a couple of the others getting supplies to paint over the graffiti. We hung sheets so hopefully your neighbors won't notice."

The man I assumed was Carl dropped onto the bench across from us as he delivered his news, setting the bag I'd left at Sebastian's house on the table in front of my plate before passing a smaller bundle to Sebastian. Sebastian froze for a moment, the hairs along my arms raising at the fury emanating from him, and I added another weight to the plate of guilt I carried.

Sebastian's chest rose on a deep breath before his hand squeezed my thigh and he let out a soft purr.

"This isn't your fault either. Let it go. It's just a house, and no one was hurt."

I didn't know how he knew, but his words stopped the building pressure of coming tears. It was ridiculous that I needed to keep reminding myself that these things weren't my fault even though I knew the blame was all on Arik.

I turned my gaze to him, giving him a tight smile before reaching for my bag. I assumed my shoes were inside, but I didn't know how Carl had managed to fit them in when it had been so full when I packed it.

Carl winced a little as I lifted the bag into my lap and noted how empty it seemed.

"Your things were tossed around the bedroom, and some of them were ruined. I collected what I could."

He avoided my eyes when I looked up and I decided I didn't want to know how my things had been ruined. Too many ways played through my head that made the sandwich I'd eaten want to come back up.

I pulled the zipper back and looked inside, my shoes the first things I spotted.

"Thank you. I'll make do with what you saved."

Sebastian let out a breath that sounded suspiciously like a growl he was trying to hold back, but I focused on finding a pair of socks in the mess of clothing stuffed in the bag. Once I did, I wiggled around until I could reach my feet and slip them on.

"Any other issues?" Sebastian asked once I was done and sitting up straight again.

Carl shook his head, leaning back and stretching an arm out along the top of the booth he sat in. He looked the same height as Sebastian, but he was thicker, built more heavily, and the image of the grizzly bear I'd seen during the fight flashed through my head. The man certainly reminded me of a bear, even if that wasn't what he was. I had no way of knowing unless one of them told me or I saw him shift.

"Not yet. Patch is staying back with a few of the guys since he has a client in a few hours and that way we're not all out of reach. The ones who are going are ready when you are."

Dark eyes turned down toward me.

"You still hungry?"

I glanced at the half-eaten fries on my plate. I'd eaten most of the sandwich already and as hungry as I'd been when we arrived, my appetite had died.

Shaking my head, I pushed the plate away.

"No, I'm ready."

Sebastian and Carl slid from the booth, the two of them looming over it from my seated vantage point. Even once I scooted to the end of the bench and stood, I felt tiny beside them. It was mind-boggling that a human, even an alpha, would pit themselves against men as massive as them.

Carl waved for us to lead the way out as he brought up the rear. It felt strategic that they were bracketing me between them, and even though I hadn't felt threatened by anything in the diner, my muscles loosened knowing there were two of them there now in case anything happened.

"I'll follow you. The others will meet us on the highway or at the lot," Carl called from behind us as we stepped out the door.

Sebastian waved a hand over his shoulder in acknowledgment but didn't stop. He was looking all around, watching for any signs of danger as we took our places on his bike.

He pulled a helmet out of his saddle bag, turning to place it on my head before taking my bag and stuffing it where the helmet had been. It wasn't until then that I realized I hadn't worn one since the first two times on his bike. Every other time I'd been too distracted to notice.

I put my arms around him as he turned the bike and started it. Carl's roared behind us, the helmet over my ears doing little to muffle the noise. Even though Patch's had been quieter, I was coming to realize motorcycles were just loud in general.

We passed through street after street as they headed toward their destination. There were little reserves in the city for shifters to use if they wanted to let their animals out, but I'd never seen one larger than a couple blocks, so if they wanted more space, they had to drive quite a way. Eventually we ended up on the highway that led away from all the bustle and press of the city, other men on motorcycles joining us and falling into place on our flanks.

As the buildings grew smaller and further apart, more trees took their place, growing taller and broader, their fragrance filling the air. Something about riding amongst them was relaxing, and I began to understand why Sebastian loved his motorcycle. The wind whipping around us was wild, the feeling of flying freeing in a way nothing else I'd experienced was.

I had no idea how much time passed. We continued on as part of the highway branched away and our section dwindled to a winding road with no other signs of civilization.

We'd gone deep beneath the shade of the trees before coming to a gravel turnoff where two other bikes were already parked, their owners standing beneath the boughs of a gigantic pine nearby. Sebastian pulled in beside them, the others who followed us taking their places with a crunch of tires on rocks as engines died.

Loosening my hold on Sebastian, I straightened and pulled off the helmet, relishing the whisper of wind that blew across my face and cooled my scalp. I appreciated the protection of the helmet, but it was certainly more comfortable to ride without it.

Sebastian stood, stretching his neck and shoulders as I waited on the bike. I knew what we were out here to do, but I didn't know how it was going to go, and the presence of so many unknown alphas made my skin crawl as instincts warned me to be careful.

Carl strode over, a few of the other men drifting closer.

"Before or after?"

My brow furrowed and I turned my gaze up to Sebastian, wondering what Carl meant. The look on his face sent my heart racing as his teeth lengthened, fur breaking out along his skin.

"After. This is his place, and I won't be able to focus until he gets his chance to really meet her."

Leann Ryans

Chapter Twenty-Eight

Sebastian

Brooke's eyes grew wider, and I realized she likely didn't know what I meant. A lot of shifters talked about their animals as a separate being, even though they were part of us. It wasn't like we weren't aware or in control in animal-form, but it was different. Priorities were rearranged, thought processes altered, and even in human- or were-form, we could feel the animal side inside us.

It would be just as easy to show her, and my wolf was already impatient now that we were under the trees and away from the noise and smell of the city. The urge to scent her out here where her natural perfume wouldn't be mixed with the lingering stench of everything that went along with too many people living too close together was too hard to resist, so I started stripping, dropping my clothes in a pile on top of my boots.

Muscles stretched and shifted, bones grinding into new shapes with a dull ache that was unavoidable. My skin shivered as fur grew, the itch so intense for a moment I wanted to tear at my flesh. The were-form wasn't as different from the human one, and was easier to change to, though it took more energy to maintain. Becoming my wolf meant every part of me changed.

I tipped forward when my legs and hips altered too much to maintain an upright position. The shift didn't take more than a few heartbeats though it sometimes felt longer, and by the time my front paws hit the ground I was fully wolf. Still me, just, simpler. Also hairier, and a whole lot shorter.

Brooke kept her eyes on me, surprise in her expression but no hint of fear despite facing a wolf who stood as tall as her hips. Shifter animals were always larger than the 'normal' versions, and I was no exception. My were-form may be more frightening, but my wolf was nothing to scoff at.

It was different, looking up at her instead of down, but I found I liked the view. Tongue lolling out in the wolfy version of a grin, I let my thoughts take a backseat and allowed the animal part to get acquainted with the omega.

Brooke held still as I took the few steps between us, and snuffling commenced. I didn't stop till I'd scented every part of her I could reach without jumping up on her, and had rubbed enough of my fur on her to be sure she'd smell of nothing but me if another male tried to get close. Logically I was aware the alphas lingering nearby were friends and had no plans to try and take Brooke from me, but logic wasn't dictating my actions. Animal instinct was.

Brooke was giggling by the time I pulled back, wuffing in her direction before lifting my nose toward the forest. Usually we went for a long run when we came out here, but though I felt the pull, I didn't want to leave Brooke.

"Can we go for a walk?"

Her voice pulled my attention back to her. That seemed the best way to appease both needs, so I focused enough to nod in a way she could understand. I may be able to speak as a were, but wolf snouts just weren't shaped for it.

I glanced at the others, but many were doing as I had and were heading into the trees as their animal. Carl gave me a wave, letting me know he'd watch the bikes as we stretched before reconvening to discuss what we'd come here for.

I led the way to a path through the undergrowth, the old forest closing in around us. It wasn't long before the dense plants blocked out any signs of humanity, and that was exactly the reason I liked the location. At the reserves in the city, you couldn't escape the sounds and smells of civilization. The foliage had no chance to grow large enough to hide the sight of buildings and electric poles and everything that went along with the human world. Out here, you could pretend that world didn't even exist.

Brooke followed behind me, staring around her in wonder as the sunlight shining through the leaves dappled her flesh with splashes of green. I realized she'd probably never even been to a city reserve, much less out to a forest beyond city limits. Like many pure humans, she'd never have had a reason to leave the city.

I nipped at her leg, taking hold of the end of her shirt once she looked down at me and changing direction toward a little clearing nearby. Since spring had finally shoved winter out, it would be carpeted in wildflowers, and I wanted her to see it.

She got the hint so I released the fabric, watching the area around us for anything that would be a danger to her. A hidden snake might not bother a wolf, but human feet were less coordinated, and their flesh was softer. Even a random fallen branch in her path could lead to a major problem out here, especially without Patch.

The trees ahead of us thinned, the light growing brighter as we approached the clearing. Brooke was busy watching where she stepped so she wouldn't trip, so she didn't notice it until we stopped on the edge of the little meadow.

Years ago, there had been a storm that caused an old tree rotted through with fungus to fall over, bringing down three other trees with it. It had created a gaping hole in the canopy, and while the forest was slowly creeping back in, grass and flowers had taken over the sunny spot left behind.

Her quiet gasp made my wolf perk up, ears and tail flagging as she walked out into the opening. There wasn't much of a breeze beneath the trees to stir the knee-high plants, but the flowers in her wake bobbed and swayed, marking her passage through them as she made her way to the middle of the space and spun around.

"It's so gorgeous out here. And quiet."

Nothing was ever truly quiet when you could hear even the bugs burrowing in the nearby trees, but she couldn't, and I knew what she meant. It was hard to imagine how noisy a city was until you left it and didn't have the constant buzz of cars, horns, talking, shuffling feet, and so much more. I was always on alert in the city, but here... I could relax.

I walked to her side and nudged her hand, reveling in the feel of her fingers sinking through my fur. She gave a tentative scratch before growing bolder as I let out what would have been a purr in my other forms. It was a bit different as a wolf, but she could still hear my enjoyment.

Brooke knelt beside me, all of her focus on me as she ran her hands along the planes of my muzzle up to my ears, scratching them in a way that made my eyes close in pleasure. Letting my tongue hang out, I flopped onto my side, rolling to my back to beg for a belly rub like a typical dog. She chuckled, but a howl split the air before she decided whether to indulge me.

Letting out a huff, I rolled back to my feet and nuzzled her neck before turning back the way we came. I was usually the one calling the men back, but we had less time than we normally would have, and we still had important things to handle before returning to the city.

Leann Ryans

Chapter Twenty-Nine

Brooke

The forest had been surreal. Some of those trees had been taller than any building I'd ever been in, their bases too large for even Sebastian and I together to wrap our arms around. The way the meadow he'd taken me to had smelled had made me want to roll in the flowers, but our time there had been cut short by reality intruding once again.

Planning a murder was more complicated than it seemed. At least, if you wanted to get away with it and not bring on an even bigger war with an organization that could swallow yours whole.

It was hard not to think of myself as part of Hell's Knights after the way they'd treated me. I'd have expected a bunch of alpha males to ignore the one little female omega's input, but they'd been willing to listen when I offered ideas about how to get Arik alone, or at least in a small enough group to be able to take him on.

No one had made me feel inferior, though a few had voiced their discomfort with me being involved. It was hard for them to ignore the imperative to protect the weaker dynamic, but once Sebastian confirmed I was allowed to be in on the plan, they quieted.

The wind tugged at my clothing, acting like it would pull me from the bike if I let go of Sebastian. His body produced enough heat to drive away the chill of the ride, but the darkness descending around us left me with little to distract myself. My thoughts kept circling what we'd discussed under those old trees, an unsettled feeling sitting heavy in my belly.

As much as I agreed Arik wouldn't back down any other way, actually planning to kill him made me uncomfortable. I'd still done my best to help, which all boiled down to me playing the sacrificial lamb.

Sebastian didn't like it. None of the men liked it, but in the end, they agreed it was the easiest way to draw him where they wanted him. A fight on Purist turf would lead to more casualties for the Hell's Knights, and I wanted to avoid that just as much as they did.

Carl had mentioned big plans to bring down their whole organization, but that was a worry for the future. For now, I just wanted to be able to live my life without feeling like I was being hunted. I wanted my parents to be able to return home without having to worry that they'd be used as hostages.

I tightened my hold on Sebastian as we leaned into a turn, realizing we were already back in the city. A quick peek back showed some of the men had peeled off and gone their own way when we hit more populated areas, but Carl and two others still rode behind us.

Those two turned off a few blocks later before Carl finally left us as well. I couldn't stop the tension spilling down my spine as fear started to creep in. It had been easy to let it go under the protection of the massive trees so far from all the concrete and glass, but every dark alley we passed felt like it had eyes digging into my back, threatening the budding hope growing inside me.

Sebastian may not have been able to talk in his wolf form, but something about walking with him in the quiet had been intimate. I'd watched his body language, seen the way he carefully guided me to the easiest path, and led me to a spread of flowers I doubted he cared about other than knowing it would make me happy. His comfort in that place had been obvious, allowing him to relax and even be a bit goofy, and I wanted more of that. More of him.

We turned at a light and I recognized the little motel we'd stayed at. He'd approached it from a different direction, and suddenly, fury at Arik once again flooded through me. It was ridiculous that neither of us could go home. That we had to take roundabout routes to get where we were going just to be sure we wouldn't be followed or attacked.

My omega nature meant I tended to be forgiving, but Arik had done the unforgivable. He'd attacked and hurt me after harassing me for so long. He'd tried to force me into a situation I didn't want and would have raped me without a second thought. He'd threatened my parents, destroyed Sebastian's business, and damaged his home.

And more than anything, he'd taken my brother from us simply for being a decent person and refusing to hurt someone who didn't deserve it, just for being different than him.

I swallowed my misgivings about what we needed to do. If anyone deserved it, Arik had a laundry list of people I'd bet would stand up and swear it was him. Life was precious, but we would be saving more by ending one, and sometimes that's what had to happen.

Anger washed the fear away. It almost made me wish we hadn't decided we'd have the best chance if we waited a while and gave things a chance to settle so he wouldn't be as alert. Omegas may be tiny, but we were fierce when provoked, and I wrapped the things he'd done around my heart, hardening it and assuring I wouldn't give in when the time came.

My role was small. We were going to find a place away from others so no bystanders would be harmed, then I was going to stay there 'alone'. I was going to use my car, go to places I used to frequent, and go back to my lonely hideout to wait.

We doubted it would take long for one of the Purists to follow me and Arik to show up at my door. I wouldn't really be alone, of course. Sebastian would be hiding inside with Carl and the others close by keeping watch. Hopefully they would spot Arik coming before it got to the point of him breaking down the door, but that was why

Sebastian insisted he had to be in the house with me. Even the minute or two it would take the others to close in from outside was too long to be alone with Arik.

Sebastian parked his bike in front of the office again after circling the building. He was still on alert as we made our way over to our little room on the end. I knew he wouldn't be so vigilant if it was just him and he wasn't worrying about keeping me safe as well, and I appreciated knowing he was there for me, but I also didn't like having to rely on him for everything.

As soon as the door shut, I rounded on him. One brow quirked, a smile tugging at his lips as his gaze turned heated, and while my core clenched in answer, I ignored it for more important things.

"I want to be able to defend myself."

His other brow rose, the smile melting away as he stared back at me. His eyes slid down my body, but unlike the other times I'd caught him looking at me, it wasn't sexual. It was assessing.

"You're too small to take on an alpha. Your best bet is running and staying out of the way."

I crossed my arms over my chest, straightening my spine.

"I know running is the best option, but what if I can't? What if something like at the store happens again, even if it's not Arik, and I'm trapped? What if they catch me before I can get far enough away?"

His expression said he didn't like it. He ran a hand through his hair, pulling out the tie as he worked out the snags with his fingers before putting it back in. He finally sighed.

"We don't have enough time to teach you to use a gun even if we could find an appropriate one for you. Having it would make things more dangerous for everyone."

I nodded. I wasn't opposed to using a weapon and would look into learning proper gun safety in the future, but that didn't help me now.

"It's the same with a knife. If someone overpowered you and took it, then you're in more danger."

I took a step closer to him. He didn't get it, didn't understand what I was willing to do if the worst happened and it looked like Arik was going to win.

"I'd rather a knife in the gut than what Arik will do if he gets his hands on me. A beating is one thing, but there's a lot more an alpha could use to make what was left of my life a misery. I wouldn't be coming out alive either way."

I could still see his hesitance, so I pushed further.

"And I'd rather not be raped to death."

The growl that he let loose had my entire body tightening, slick automatically flooding my folds in the hopes of distracting the angry alpha. And that was the problem. Even if my brain wasn't on board, my body would respond to an alpha. It was hard-wired into my biology, preprogramed into the recesses of my brain. An omega was meant to take the brunt of an alpha's anger and desire, keeping them from murdering the world by distracting them with sex.

Tempting A Knight

Sebastian sucked in a deep breath, his pupils flaring when he scented what he'd done to me. He tamped down the rumble, rolling his shoulders before closing the space between us and cupping my cheek in one massive palm.

"You're too small to do any real damage to an alpha. The most you can hope for is to shock them long enough for you to get away. Running is always the first option."

I stared up into his dark eyes and nodded, ignoring what his nearness was doing to me.

"You're second option is to seduce them. Get them off-guard, make them think you're going to come easy, then run when they aren't paying attention. This won't always work, but it's the least risky to you."

I huffed, brow quirking as my lips twisted into a self-deprecating smirk.

"Have you seen my seduction skills? That's not really an option either."

His chocolate gaze heated as he grinned down at me. At some point we'd leaned so close together my breasts were mashed against his chest, each breath raking the sensitive tips against him.

He bent down and brushed his nose along my cheekbone until his mouth was at my ear. A shiver raced down my spine as his hot breath washed over it.

"You seduced me."

A noise of disbelief escaped my throat between my panting. Every inch of me was tingling with awareness, my panties dampening further at the way he curled around me, blotting out the world until he was the only thing there was.

"Use their instincts against them. They expect you to be meek and mellow. To bow and scrape and give under their prowess. Inflate their ego until they're so perfect nothing could ever go wrong."

I was having a hard time focusing on the words with the way he was whispering them in my ear, but I knew what he meant. The kind of alpha that would be a threat to me would be the type who'd grow careless if he thought he had the upper hand and there was no danger to them.

"Make them believe there isn't a thought in your head besides worshiping them."

I couldn't help the startled snort I made, but Sebastian's rich chuckle pulled me back under his spell as it washed over me. As important as it was to have a way to defend myself, the ache growing between my thighs was starting to distract me.

So was the hard length digging into my belly.

Shaking my head, I pressed my hands to his chest, pushing hard enough for him to know I wanted space. When he stepped back, he was smirking.

"I can't think with you like that."

"Exactly."

I crossed my arms over my chest, nipples scraping my arms they were so tight. I ignored the way my body yearned for him to come back, understanding what he'd been doing.

"Okay. And then what? What if I don't have time to wait for an opportunity to get away?"

His fingers lifted to press beneath his ribs. "Hit them here." He moved his hand to cup his erection, "Here if there's no better option, or here," he tapped the tip of his nose.

He took my hand in his, curling the fingers and tucking my thumb.

"Hitting knuckles first puts all the force in a smaller area, and hopefully you can drive the breath from them. Put all your might behind it, because you won't get more than one swing."

I nodded at his serious expression. If I didn't manage to hurt them on the first try, I'd only be making things worse for myself. I had to make it count.

He stretched my palm open but kept my fingers curled at the tips.

"Hand bent back so the heel of your palm is in line with your arm. Thrust up, not in. You want the nose to break so his eyes water and he can't see to chase you right away."

I nodded again, swallowing my fear. Having a chance, however small, was better than nothing.

"If you can get a knee or foot to his balls, follow it with a knee to the nose and you should be able to run. Don't waste time to see if he falls or not, just get out."

His worry was palpable. I knew he didn't like the idea of me being in danger when we took down Arik, but he knew I needed it. He didn't like teaching me these things because he didn't want me in the situation to use them, and neither did I, but he did it because I'd asked.

Reaching up to curl my fingers around the back of his neck, I pulled his head down and pressed my lips to his, offering myself to him. His arms wrapped around me, lifting me from the floor.

"Are we safe for a little while?"

My voice was breathy when I pulled away from the kiss, but I didn't care.

"We should be."

It was the best answer he could give me without ignoring the situation we were in, but it was good enough.

"Then distract me," I whispered before kissing him again. I didn't want to think anymore, and he knew exactly how to make me forget everything.

Chapter Thirty

Sebastian

I groaned against her lips, agreeing wholeheartedly with her plan. She may not believe she could seduce anyone, but I was telling the truth when I said she'd seduced me. She'd tempted me more than I could stand, and even though I hated admitting I may fail and she would need what I'd shown her, I was glad she was willing to stand up for herself.

I walked forward until my knees hit the mattress before leaning over to deposit her in the middle of the bed. I stood up and yanked off my shirt, opening my fly before crawling forward to grip the edge of her pants and yank them down with her panties. I'd needed her in an animalistic way that morning, but now I needed something different.

Helping her sit up, I pulled my vest off her as she slipped her ruined shirt over her head and tossed it aside. Her gorgeous body was bare before me, and I needed to worship her the way I'd instructed her to do to another.

Those words had tasted like ash in my mouth, telling her to act like that toward another alpha. My wolf raged inside me, denying there was any possibility of her ever needing to do that, but I was practical enough to know there was a chance. I wanted to lose myself in her just as much as she hoped to forget what could happen.

I trailed kisses from her mouth along her jaw, nibbling her ear before licking my way down her neck. Raking my teeth over the place where the delicate column met her shoulder, I felt her shiver beneath me, and it only made me want to watch her unravel all the more.

My mouth moved over her collarbone as I raised my hands to cup her breasts. I knew she enjoyed when I was rough and used my claws on the tips, but I wanted this time to be different. Trailing my tongue around the entirety of her breast, I slowly shrank the circles until I twirled it around her nipple before pulling the raised flesh into my mouth. Her gasp as I sucked it deep had my cock dribbling precum in my pants, but I didn't care.

I suckled her nipple until it was swollen and red before switching to the other side, laving the mound before latching onto the pert tip. All the while I kept my hands moving with light strokes over her flesh, kneading her hips and thighs as her legs fell open for me.

Releasing the second one, I trailed my lips down her belly, leaving open-mouthed kisses and nips across the cradle of her hips. She tilted them upward, offering herself to me, but I skipped over her core and moved to her left leg.

I made my way down the outside of it until I reached her ankle, kissing and licking the sensitive skin on the inside, just below the bone, until she giggled and tried to pull away. I stared up into emerald eyes, grinning and letting my teeth extend before raking them up the inside of her calf. Brooke gasped and tried to pull away, but my grip held her in place.

There was no escape.

I nipped her inner thigh before soothing it with my tongue. Sucking on the flesh, I released it with a pop and moved an inch higher before doing it again. Closer and closer I came to her core, the scent of her arousal making my head spin and saliva trail from my kisses.

I made it to the crease between her thigh and outer lip, taking extra time to lick up the slick that had smeared there before pulling away and taking the opposite ankle in my grip to tease the inside of it. Brooke let out a frustrated groan, writhing on the bed as I chuckled.

I loved knowing she wanted me. Was desperate to have my mouth on her pussy. I'd never desired another woman as much as I did her, and the alpha part of me needed to show her I could be anything she needed. It didn't always have to be rough and demanding.

Her chest rose and fell with her rapid breaths, her gaze locked on me as I climbed her leg, leaving a trail of marks along her thigh to match the other side. I never looked away, moving my tongue closer and closer to where she wanted it. We were both desperate for that first taste, but

I paused with my mouth hovering above her center, letting my breath fan over the wetness.

"Do you want me, Brooke?"

Her nod was fervent. She was panting so hard I doubted she could speak if I tried to force her to answer with words.

"You want me here?"

I let my mouth drop closer to hers, maintaining a hair's breadth of space between us. It was torture. Each breath filled with the scent of her was sweet, delicious, spikes of torment.

She nodded again, dragging her bottom lip into her mouth to bite down on it. My dick almost combusted at the sight, her pupils dilated with desire not brought on by hormones, but by me.

"Show me."

I challenged her, and she didn't fail to rise to it. Her green gaze narrowed before she reached out and slid her fingers into my hair. She wasn't gentle, yanking me that last bit forward until my face was mashed to her center.

I dove in, thrusting my tongue deep in her channel. The taste of her flooded my mouth and I couldn't hold back a groan. I could stay right there forever and die happy.

Her hips bucked as she searched for more stimulation, the breathy whine she let out telling me how close she was to the edge. Curling my arms under her thighs, I placed a hand over her mound and pressed down on her clit with my thumb.

She shattered, keening into the air as her pussy tried to milk my tongue. The hand in my hair tightened, sending pricks of pain dancing across my scalp that only aroused me further.

My wolf pushed forward, trying to take over, but I held him back. I didn't want to lose myself in the act this time, I wanted to take her apart and help her find herself again in the release.

We still had time before we made our move on Arik, but I'd resolved to live every second until then like it was my last. I wanted to believe she meant what she'd said, that she was mine, but she'd said it in the heat of the moment. I didn't want to waste an instant when there was a chance of her coming to her senses once she no longer needed me. I was going to savor as much of her as I could.

Brooke's movements slowed, the rippling of her channel easing as her release ended. I gave her a moment to catch her breath, removing my thumb from her clit and my keeping my licks slow and easy. Her slick coated my chin, but it wasn't enough. I wanted the scent of her all over me.

Her legs relaxed from where they'd squeezed around my shoulders and her hand loosened in my hair, signaling me to begin again. Releasing one leg, I moved my arm and thrust two fingers into her, curling them upward as I targeted her little pearl with my tongue. No slow build up this time, I drove her straight to the edge as her body tightened around me.

Leann Ryans

Her hands pressed against the top of my shoulders as she tried to get me to slow down. I ignored them, latching onto the bundle of nerves and lashing my tongue over it. Her body shook before going stiff, her cry filling the room and making me spill more precum in my jeans.

Nails raked my shoulders, the sting satisfying a deep part of me that yearned for the omega's mark. The little female found me pleasing, and I was proud to sport the evidence of her joy.

I slowed my tongue and released the suction, removing my fingers from her channel once it relaxed enough to let me. Nuzzling her core, I let her release coat my nose and cheeks before sitting up. Slick ran from the stubble on my chin, leaving trails down my neck before reaching my chest. I used the hand that had been in her to rub it into my flesh before reaching down to swipe up more and spread it on me.

Brooke's eyes had been closed, but she'd opened them when I sat up. Those green orbs watched me, the satisfied expression heating with renewed desire as I marked myself with her fluids.

Before I could stop her, she pulled her legs under her, rising to her knees. She leaned against me, her bare breasts pressing against my chest as she shoved her hand into my open jeans.

"Let me taste you."

I rumbled as her fingers curled around me over the fabric of my underwear. The cloth was rough and not what I wanted to feel.

"Only if you're on top of me."

She hummed, leaning in and putting her head under my chin. Wet heat met my collarbone, her lips closing over the place she'd licked before her teeth pressed into the flesh. It took everything I had not to slam her back into the mattress and sheath myself in her right then.

When she pulled back and released my erection, I slid off the side of the bed, standing and removing the last of my clothing. I was back on the mattress in seconds, wrapping my arms around her and claiming her lips as I rolled to the side and laid down.

Leann Ryans

Chapter Thirty-One

Brooke

I straddled his stomach, more of my slick dripping onto his abs as he kissed me. Something about watching him smear it all over him had lit a fire inside me, demanding that I coat him with my essence and claim his as well.

I wriggled my hips, trying to scoot down so I could feel his hardness, but Sebastian held me in place, taking hold of my hips and grinding me on his stomach. All the while his tongue invaded my mouth, exploring every inch of it and stealing my breath.

He finally released me when I raked my nails down his neck, and I sucked in a desperate breath as my head spun. It was hard to believe I could want him more than I had during my heat when instinct drove me, but every time we were together it was harder and harder not to forget about the rest of the world and lose myself in him. I wanted him to sink his teeth into me and claim me as his forever.

Sitting up, I rocked over his abs but there wasn't enough friction, and the tantalizing scent of his musk still called to me. Sebastian held my hips, but when he realized I was only trying to turn around, not get away, he let me move. I barely got settled before he was grabbing my thighs and yanking me back.

His mouth covered me, agile tongue thrusting into my empty channel before his fingers took its place as his focus moved lower. I was distracted for a moment, but the sight of his stiff cock drew my attention.

The head was glossed with his excitement, the length pulsing with the thudding of his heartbeat beneath me. I stared at it before extending my tongue and swiping it over the tip, collecting the fluid dribbling from him in a steady stream.

His salty musk coated my mouth, making it water as I made another swipe before taking him in hand. I couldn't close my fingers around the base where his knot would expand to lock us together, and my core clenched at the memory of it inside me. The stretch was perfect torture, but it was nothing to the sweet agony of his were-form.

I latched onto him as he added a third finger to the ones he plunged in and out of my center. Squelching filled the room amidst our pants and Sebastian's low growls as he devoured me, and it wasn't long until my moans rose to join the noise. Each press of his fingers into my core shoved me down on his cock, blocking my air for a moment before he pulled back and I could get a sip of oxygen.

I had no idea how long we went on like that, his tongue lapping at me while his fingers plundered, and his shaft invaded my mouth. Every muscle in my body grew tight, quivering on the edge, but unable to fall over.

Sebastian's fingers shifted, gliding through the slippery fluid coating me until the digits circled a new opening. I clenched automatically, a whimper escaping around his length at the unfamiliar feeling, but he didn't stop. Sucking on my clit, he applied pressure to my back opening, the sensations overwhelming me as he pushed inside. I was torn between running away from it, and pressing back into it, all the nerves in my core firing and making my pussy spasm even though it wasn't the one being invaded.

My breathing grew uneven, concentration on the cock between my lips broken as I tried to assimilate what was happening. Sebastian didn't seem bothered, moving his hips to continue thrusting in and out of my mouth, matching the rhythm of his finger.

Drool ran from my mouth, coating his cock and easing its way as he increased his speed. The tension inside me coiled tighter and tighter until I felt like the lightest breeze would make me shatter, yet Sebastian's motions didn't cease. My womb throbbed, my jealous channel clenching on nothing, as the knot I cradled began to swell.

And then he pressed another finger inside.

The world exploded. My vision went white, and my ears rang as my entire body contracted. The scream that tried to rip from my throat was blocked by Sebastian's cock plunging into it, the first pulse of his release going straight down as his free hand moved to hold the back of my head.

Leann Ryans

Sparkles danced at the edges of my consciousness as my orgasm went on. Tingles rushed from my core to my extremities and back, wave after wave threatening to pull me under as Sebastian remained lodged in my throat. Eventually my muscles began to twitch and the hand on my head tightened in my hair, pulling me up enough to suck air through my nose as he continued to flood my mouth. I gulped between breaths, swallowing his release even as mine poured from me. He'd pulled his fingers from my bottom to lap at me, each swipe of his tongue along my sensitized flesh sending lightning through the nerves and making me try to dance away.

I had no idea how long it took for my senses to come back and for his release to slow to a dribble. My stomach felt full, my limbs weak and rubbery from the orgasm, and I was ready to fall asleep atop him, but before I could he spun me around to face him once again.

Sebastian's entire neck and upper chest were soaked, and I could feel the seed I hadn't been able to swallow quickly enough running down my chin, but he didn't care. He cupped the back of my head, pulling me down into a sweet, slow kiss that had my heart melting even as I plastered my body to his. Our breathing slowed as he continued to kiss me, and there was nothing that could have made me move from his arms.

Nothing but the shrill noise piercing the air from somewhere on the floor.

I startled, yanking my head up as my brain rushed to figure out what the sound was. By the time I realized it was a phone ringing I'd slid off Sebastian's chest and pulled the edge of the rumpled blankets over my chest, my heart racing once again.

Growling, Sebastian rolled from the bed, snatching his pants to dig his phone from the pocket. The noise faded away as he looked at the screen, but his voice was still rough with it when he answered.

"This better be important."

I watched his face as he listened to whoever was on the phone, his expression morphing from irritation to shock before he cleared it, putting his back to me as he sat on the edge of the mattress.

"When? Are the others okay? Where are they now?"

The silence between his questions was killing me, the growing knot of dread in my stomach threatening to make me heave. Stomach churning, I clutched the blanket tighter and tried to be patient.

"We can't wait. This has to end. I won't let anyone else get hurt. We'll talk tomorrow."

Sebastian lowered the phone, his shoulders curling forward to make him seem smaller. When I reached out to place a hand on his back, I could feel him trembling, and for a moment I panicked over what could possibly have made an alpha cry, until I realized his fists were clenched and it was a low growl vibrating his chest.

"Jackson's in the hospital. He went back to your place alone to get something your mother mentioned leaving behind and was attacked. Luckily there were a few local shifters who saw it and came to help."

Sebastian's voice was cold and flat, sending a shiver down my spine.

"My parents?"

I couldn't help asking even though I berated myself for the selfishness of it. He's just told me the man who'd been protecting them was hurt, and instead of asking if he was okay, I asked about them first.

"They're fine. They were both at work when it happened."

I swallowed, moving to press against his back when the relief from his answer released me from my frozen state. I wanted to offer him comfort but wasn't sure what to say.

Heaving a deep breath, Sebastian turned and pulled me into his arms, wrapping them around me and burying his head in my hair. I could feel how close he was to losing control, and I felt guilty enough without having to worry about him rushing off in a rage without backup.

"Will Jackson be okay?"

My whisper was barely louder than the breaths sawing in and out of him. His shudder warned me before he spoke that I wasn't going to like the answer.

"If he wasn't a shifter, he'd be dead. They—"

He made a choking noise, causing me to lift my head from his chest to stare up at him. Eyes clenched shut, it took him a few seconds to finish.

"They goaded him into shifting to his wolf. They cut off his tail and tried to skin him."

The last sentence was delivered no louder than my question had been, but it felt like a bomb had dropped in the room. My lungs froze, horror creeping through my veins at the pain I imagined Jackson must be in. I didn't remember meeting him, but it didn't matter. No one deserved to have that done to them.

I struggled with the different thoughts rushing through my head, knowing this was personal to Sebastian. Not only was this one of his men, it was another wolf, and the image of his beautiful wolf bleeding from a stump where his tail had been flashed through my head.

"Will it grow back?"

The tail didn't have an equivalent part in a human body, so I wasn't sure how it worked. Shifters healed faster, but that didn't mean injuries didn't leave scars, no matter what form they were in.

Sebastian's dark eyes held mine as he gave a negative shake of his head. The image of him wavered as tears filled my vision, my stomach revolting. I couldn't understand how anyone could do that to another being, even if they were different than them.

"I'm so sorry."

Sobs clogged my throat, threatening to choke me as I fought to hold them back. Sebastian shushed me, pulling me close again and pushing out a purr. It was low and broken by his own emotions, but it was enough to keep me from dissolving into a weeping mess.

"This isn't your fault. You didn't do this."

Sniffling, I shook my head against him, not willing to even try meeting his gaze.

"If I hadn't come to you, the Hell's Knights wouldn't be tangled up in this. I'm not worth all this."

His purr turned into a growl as he shoved me away and took my chin between his fingers. Startled, I stared back at him as he glared into my face.

"If you hadn't come to me, you'd be dead, and your mother's heart would be completely broken. They only made it through their grief for you. Your life has more value than you give it. This. Is. Not. Your. Fault."

He gave me a shake with the last five words, pausing and delivering each with all the weight of an alpha behind it.

"You are not the one who hurt Jackson. You are not the one who vandalized my house or burned down the shop. You did nothing to deserve Arik's attention, and only sought a way to protect yourself from a vicious alpha who was going to use and abuse you. You. Did. Nothing. Wrong."

He punctuated the last four words again, and despite the fact that I knew he was right, I still felt as though I'd brought this down on them.

"This has gone beyond an alpha being pissy over an omega choosing another male. It was never really that to begin with. He targeted you because of what you are, and your connection to Vincent. He wanted to hurt you. He's coming after me because of my connection to your brother and because of his speciest beliefs. The Hell's Knights were bound to clash with the Purists eventually. Hell, we already have, it was just nothing major enough to make more of it than little tiffs. The time has come to stand up to them."

The conviction in his voice helped calm me. I was the only one blaming myself for what was happening, and it helped to hear it, even if it didn't make the guilt disappear.

"No more hiding and waiting. We're going to take care of this and get back to living our lives. This is not your burden to bear."

His eyes were haunted, my own guilt showing me his. Wrapping my arms around him, I laid my head on his chest and let out my own purr.

"It's not yours either. We'll handle it together."

Leann Ryans

Chapter Thirty-Two

Sebastian

I didn't want to admit how desperately I needed her delicate purr and reassurance. I knew the guilt she carried because I was weighed down by it myself. Yes, the Hell's Knights had been involved in spats with the Purists, but the escalating problems were because I'd chosen to defend Brooke.

But how could I not? No alpha could call himself any such thing if he wasn't willing to defend those who needed help. The ones like Arik gave us bad reps, and I'd thought I was the odd one until I'd met the other alphas of the Knights. They'd restored my faith that we were the ones on the right path, and I was repaying them by pulling them into a fight we may not be prepared for.

Heaving a sigh, I tried to push all those thoughts away. It was too late, and we were too tired to do anything until morning. Scooting back on the bed, I relaxed onto the pillows, pulling Brooke down atop me. Neither of us stopped purring, each offering comfort to the other even as our demons ate at our insides.

Leann Ryans

One minute I was stroking Brooke's hair with her weight comfortably spread across me, her purr stuttering into a snore, and the next there was light shining in my eyes. I jerked upright, thinking we'd been found and someone had burst in the door, only to notice a tiny gap in the curtains allowing the morning sun to fall across the pillow. Brooke was curled on her side next to where I'd been, twitching in her sleep, though my motion hadn't awoken her.

I scrubbed a hand down my face, grimacing at the stiff, sticky feel of the scruff on my cheeks. As much as I enjoyed the scent of her on me, I needed a shower to concentrate on what had to be done.

I rolled from the bed, careful not to disturb Brooke as I tucked the blankets around her before heading into the bathroom. The space was tiny, clearly meant for the average beta and not an alpha shifter, and I was tempted to say screw it and go home to have the luxury of my own shower. Only the thought of Arik arriving while I was unprepared and Brooke suffering because of it had me turning on the tap and waiting as the water warmed up.

Staring into the mirror as the sound of running water filled the space, I tried to figure out the best course of action. I would be safer if I waited for the others to come with me, but then I'd be putting them at risk again. What happened to Jackson was just one of the many atrocities committed by the Purists, and I didn't want to see any more of my men suffer. We all agreed the Purists and their entire mentality needed wiped out, but it wasn't as if we could take them all on, especially with so little planning. Their organization was large enough it would take serious commitment and more than just our club to make a difference.

I knew what the best option was, but it meant breaking my promise to Brooke. There was no way I was going to bring her into a situation where I had no backup to protect her, but it would be easier to get close to Arik on my own. I understood her desire to see Arik go down with her own eyes, but she could accept his death eventually as long as she was still alive to do so.

Stepping into the little stall, I let the lukewarm water pour down my body, accepting what I was risking. If I accomplished my goal she'd be furious with me, but she'd be safe. Even if it meant an end to any chance of the future with her I'd grown to crave, her life was all that mattered. If I failed, the others were still there to protect her. Carl would find a way to get her and her parents out of the city if that was what it took.

The creak of hinges had me whirling around, water slinging from my soaked hair and splashing Brooke in the face. She jerked back, blinking furiously and wiping her eyes.

"I was going to ask if I could join you in there. Seems like a better idea than you trying to splash enough out for me to wash with."

A startled chuckle rolled from me. Reaching out, I pushed the door of the stall wider and snagged her wrist, hauling her against my slippery body. I couldn't help the way my groin tightened, excited at the lack of anything separating us, but we didn't have the time to get distracted.

I leaned down and claimed her lips when she looked up at me and pressed herself tighter against my stomach, trapping my erection between us. Breaking it off before I forgot about not getting distracted, I nipped her bottom lip and turned us around so she was under the spray.

Her dark hair turned nearly black as it flattened to her head. Running my fingers through it, I made sure the water penetrated all the way to her scalp before reaching for the tiny bottle of shampoo on the little shelf beside us. It was hard not to bump my elbows on the sides of the stall, but the lack of space meant she couldn't put any between us, and I found myself willing to deal with cramped quarters for that reward.

I lathered her hair, Brooke closing her eyes and relaxing into my care. Once I'd rinsed it clean, I moved on to washing her body, taking the scrap of a washcloth in my hand and soaping her from her neck down. I took my time, both of us enjoying the act of me cleansing her, though I was careful not to get too enthusiastic when I rubbed the cloth over her tight nipples, or between her thighs where I'd rather have my face buried. Despite the water running down her, I could still smell her slick.

Brooke rubbed her hands through the soap on my stomach from where she was pressed to me, spreading it down my legs while avoiding the one place aching for her touch. I wasn't sure whether to be grateful or irritated by the deviation, a low growl building in my throat as her hands slid up the inside of my thighs before going wide and circling my hips.

"Behave, little omega, or we'll never make it out of this room. I'm already too tempted to drag you back to the bed, but others are relying on us not to forget what we should be doing."

Her face fell, the reminder hitting harsher than I meant it to. Dropping the washcloth, I cupped her cheek and pressed my lips to her forehead, purr vibrating the steaming air around us.

"It'll be okay. Why don't you dry off while I finish up?"

Even as I made the suggestion, I fought the desire to keep her with me. It was a struggle to release her when she nodded and let her slip from the stall, and I stared at the door for a long moment before forcing myself to finish washing so I could get out. I didn't know when I'd have the chance to hold her again, but that didn't mean I could waste the time to indulge now. I had things to take care of before Arik planned anything else.

I shut off the water and stepped out of the shower, taking the rough towel still hanging on the bar and dragging it over my skin to get the majority of the water off. Tucking it around my waist in hopes it would help me forget the raging erection throbbing between my legs, I stepped out of the bathroom to find Brooke already dressed in a simple pair of jeans and t-shirt. Toweling her damp hair, not a touch of makeup on to hide the bruises, she was still beautiful in a way that made my chest ache.

Turning away before I did something I shouldn't, I found the little bag Carl had brought me from home and returned to the bathroom, though I didn't close the door. I dug out the clean clothes, pulling on my underwear and jeans as another deterrent to my wayward desires, though I left off the shirt so I could shave. By the time I finished, Brooke was sitting on the edge of the made bed, hair neatly tied back, the dirty clothes that had been strewn around the room packed away except for my pile sitting on the corner of the mattress.

"So, what are we doing?"

Her expression was so open and trusting, believing I'd never go behind her back after telling her she'd be included. I had to turn away, stuffing my dirty things into my bag as I answered.

"I've got to handle some stuff from the fire this morning, so I'll have to leave you with one of the others for a while. I'm sure Carl would let you hang out at his place."

I hated the uncertainty I saw in her eyes when I turned around. I trusted Carl explicitly, but I wasn't comfortable with her going to another alpha's house either, I just didn't have many options.

Except, once I thought about it, Carl was likely to ask questions I didn't want to answer, so his place might not be the best choice.

"Or I could take you to Patch's shop. I doubt he'd have a client this early, but you might get bored there."

Some of her discomfort seemed to ease, but she looked away from me before answering.

"That's fine, as long as he's okay with it."

I grunted and dug for my phone, shooting him a message that I was bringing Brooke over. I knew he wouldn't deny her, though jealousy rankled inside me. It was irrational since I kept pushing her toward the other alpha, but it bothered me that he seemed to always be the one she went to.

"He won't mind. Let's go."

I sounded brisk even to myself, but I was doing my best to build up a wall between us. I had to, or I'd never be able to do what needed to happen.

By the time we reached the tattoo parlor Patch had already opened up and was waiting at the door for us.

"I've got to go handle some stuff about the fire. She wanted to wait here."

I was bending the truth a little with the phrasing, but Brooke didn't call me on it. Considering I trusted Patch and knew he'd be good to her, perhaps pushing her toward him was a good idea. I was realistic enough to know my chances of coming out of my hasty plan unscathed were slim.

Patch gave me a long look, as if he knew what was going through my head. Perhaps he did. Not much was known about his species since there were so few, and plenty of myths abounded.

He turned his attention to Brooke as she stepped up beside me.

"Good morning. Thanks for letting me come by. I'll try to stay out of the way."

Not a muscle twitched, yet I could feel the way he softened toward her, and the fact that he responded proved it.

"You're always welcome. I don't have any clients scheduled today so you don't have to worry."

He pushed the door wider, moving so he wouldn't be crowding her as she passed by. Casting a wary eye back at me, she headed for the opening.

"Be safe."

I answered her with a small smile, my insides twisting.

She disappeared around the corner of the doorway, and to my surprise, Patch stepped out and let it swing closed behind her. He stared at me, the weight of his gaze growing to the point my wolf began to push at me, trying to rise to the silent challenge of the other male.

"Heroes die needless deaths."

Brows drawing together, I tried to find a response to his strange comment, but he turned and went into the shop, completely ignoring me.

I watched the door swing shut again, mind blank. I was sure if he knew what I was planning he would think it was a mistake. All of them would. But that didn't mean it wouldn't work. It was the best way to keep everyone else from being in the line of fire.

I turned away, walking back to my bike and swinging a leg over the saddle. Would I regret doing this? Maybe. If I lived long enough to have regrets.

I just hoped if I went out that I took Arik with me.

Leann Ryans

Chapter Thirty-Three

Brooke

"He's up to something."

"Yep."

Patch stared back at me, his icy blue eyes reminding me of how cool his skin had been when I'd had to ride his motorcycle the night the shop burned down. Maybe Sebastian did have something to take care of related to that, but that wasn't all he was planning.

"What do we do?"

The blonde alpha shrugged and finished walking to his desk. I followed after him, not sure what to do, but not willing to sit down and accept that Sebastian was likely putting himself at risk.

"Did you ask him what he was doing?"

Patch didn't bother looking up as he shook his head. He stared down at the paper lying on his desk, silent and still until he reached for an eraser on the side and removed a line, picking up a pencil to redraw it with more curve. For a second I was distracted looking at the picture, awed by the delicate lines sprawled across the paper. It was just an outline, but it was still beautiful.

Shaking my head, I pulled my attention back to the current issue.

"Is he going to do something stupid?"

There was no reason to beat around the bush. Patch knew what I meant, and he should know Sebastian well enough to be able to tell me if the worry gnawing at my gut was accurate.

"Probably."

I heaved an irritated sigh, finally drawing that chilly gaze back to me. Patch had never given me any reason to be uncomfortable with him, he couldn't help that he was an alpha, but there was something more that put me on edge around the man. As if there was danger lurking just beyond what I could see.

"Are we going to do anything about it?"

I couldn't help raising my voice, Patch's apparent lack of concern rankling. I cared too much for Sebastian to sit back and let something happen to him when I could have stopped him. The roar of his bike had already faded, so it was too late to run after him, and Patch was the only option I had to work with.

"Do you think you could stop him from doing something he's made his mind up to do?"

My teeth squeaked as I clenched my jaw. My nails left burning crescents in my palms with my impotent frustration, but I knew Patch was right. Sebastian wouldn't listen if we tried to talk him out of something. It would only make him sneakier about doing it.

Unsure what to say but not willing to let it go, I held the alpha's gaze, ignoring the innate need to submit to the dominate male. He waited in silence, his brow slowly rising the longer I held out.

The pressure finally erupted.

"We have to do something!"

I spun around, unwilling to concede defeat, and paced the space between his desk and his tattoo chair. I kept my head down so I wouldn't have to look at him, unable to take any more weight dragging on me.

"Calm, little one. No one said we were leaving him to be stupid alone."

My head whipped up so fast a muscle in my neck protested, but I ignored it. The tiniest little tip at the edge of his lips suggested he was laughing at me, and I couldn't stop a growl from rattling my chest. His brow rose higher until I got myself under control.

"Do you mind telling me what's going on, so I'm not left to worry?"

I pushed the words through gritted teeth. They were still laced with irritation, but it was as polite as I could manage.

"Oh, you'll still worry. Your roles have flipped."

I blinked at him, not processing what he meant. Patch must have decided to take pity on me, because he sighed and leaned back in his chair.

"He's made himself the sacrificial lamb."

My eyes widened as his words sank in. I'd been the one meant to draw Arik's attention and lure him to a place where it was safe to deal with him. It would have taken time to find a place like that, and Sebastian no longer wanted to wait.

"He's going after him. Alone."

My whisper seemed loud in the silence inside the building.

"Of course he is. It was only a matter of time. But he's not alone."

I focused on Patch again, heart in my throat. My swinging emotions left my stomach in a ball, but I dared to let hope surface.

"He's not?"

I needed the reassurance. Needed him to tell me Sebastian wasn't heading into enemy hands with no backup and no plan to call for help.

"Tim and Knox are following him. They'll hold back until they figure out what he's doing, unless he looks like he needs help, then Carl and the others will head in."

My chest hitched as I sucked in a ragged breath. Anxiety I hadn't noticed drained from my muscles, leaving me wilted and too tired to hold myself up. Leaning back against the tattooing chair, I swiped a hand across my face to clear my vision.

"I need to be there. This is my fight."

Patch's brow rose again.

"This is our fight, too. We aren't going to stop with Arik, he's just the immediate concern. The Purists have gained too much power, and that needs corrected before more people are hurt."

I forced myself to swallow, nodding at his words. I might have an issue with Arik specifically, but they had reason to hate more than just him.

"I can't sit here waiting with nothing to do."

The words were thick, and it was hard to push them out. The thought of not knowing what was happening, of not being there if something went wrong, made me want to bawl. My nerves were already drawn too tight, and they'd snap under that kind of tension.

"He'll be furious."

Patch's tone held warning, and I knew if it was up to him, I'd be stuck in that exact situation.

"He promised me."

Blue eyes narrowed, and though I didn't hear a growl, I could feel the alpha's displeasure. I wasn't going to back down though.

"I'll stay out of the way. I'll follow every instruction. But if you try to leave me behind, I'll find a way to follow, and then you won't be able to keep an eye on me."

I couldn't prevent myself from wagging a finger at the alpha, and I was surprised when the irritation left his expression and he actually smiled. Shaking his head, he heaved a sigh and my heart soared.

"I'm sure you would. You're perfect for him."

The comment knocked the air from me, and I gaped for a moment until he continued as if he hadn't just thrown me for a loop.

"We will join the guys when we get the call. You will stay with me, out of the fighting or whatever is going on, until it's all over and I give you permission to leave my side."

The words carried the weight of alpha command, making me bow my head and stare at the floor, nodding in acceptance. I didn't care if he handcuffed me to him as long as I was there to be sure everything went okay. It wasn't even about the assurance that Arik really was gone anymore, it was about being sure the hopes teasing the edges of my mind had the chance to grow.

"Yes, alpha."

Tempting A Knight

Chapter Thirty-Four

Sebastian

The cocky smile on Arik's face as I strode into the restaurant he and his men liked to linger at had me balling my fists, but I hadn't missed the initial flash of fear in his eyes when he first spotted me.

Was it insanity to come here alone? Probably. But I was counting on the fact that he liked the place and wouldn't want to draw attention to it by shooting me on the spot. Murder in public tended to be a little harder to wiggle out of, though it would be one of his men taking the fall, not him.

I strode through the mostly empty dining area to the back booth where he sat. Another of his men sat across from him while more took up the two tables beside it, but it didn't matter how many men he had with him. This was just the set-up.

Taking a seat beside the surprised alpha who was forced to slide over on the bench, I ignored his growl and kept all my focus on Arik. The lapdog beside me wouldn't do anything without his master's command, and Arik wasn't ready to make a move or he'd have already done it.

"What brings you to this part of town, mutt?"

He chewed on the straw clenched between his teeth, smiling like he owned the world. My wolf struggled, trying to shift and claw his throat out right where he sat, but even if I managed to live through it, I'd be in prison the rest of my life.

Brooke made me want to avoid that option if I could.

"You know why I'm here. We need to settle this."

Arik huffed, the men around us muttering and chuckling as if I'd told a joke.

"There is no we. I don't deal with dogs, or any other animals for that matter. Get out of my city and leave the bitch behind. I've got plans for her."

It took everything I had to hold in the growl building inside me. It didn't matter what he called me, I'd heard it all before, but Brooke didn't deserve any of what this man had brought on her.

"The omega has nothing to do with this. This is between me and you. You're still hung up on Vincent choosing shifters over your twisted ideals and fucked up gang. He chose to be a decent person, and you killed him for it."

The smile dropped off Arik's face, his attitude shifting from amused indulgence in something he didn't care about, to cold psychopath in seconds.

"He died because he wasn't loyal. He wasn't man enough to step up and rid this world of the filth infesting it. And what's worse, he went and died too fast for me to play with him. Lucky for me he has such a sweet little sister, ripe for the picking. And she's even an omega!"

The growl burst free, a low rumble building between us as Arik sneered. A vision of reaching out and plunging my claws through his throat filled my head until the crackling protest of the tabletop warned me my control was slipping. It took three deep breaths to get my claws to return to blunt fingertips and stop the growl, all the while Arik's sat watching, amusement written across his face.

"Looks like someone got a little too attached to easy pussy."

I swallowed my reaction, sneering back at him.

"You're the one who wants my sloppy seconds."

Arik snarled, lunging forward in his seat, but I held my place. My wolf would never bow or back down to him, he'd proved himself a coward more than once. I expected him to make another scathing comment, but he surprised me by leaning back again, draping his arm over the back of the booth and smoothing his expression.

"Do you know anything about her family? I know they kept you around as a pet when you were younger, though I doubt you saw it that way."

He paused, trying to let his words take effect, but I knew the Frosts were better than that. They'd taken me under their wing even when they barely had enough to scrape by.

"Brooke's bloodline is pure, all the way back as far as my research can tell. There's not a drop of shifter blood to sully the Frost name, which is why I expected so much more from Vincent. His uncle was one of us, as are a few cousins, and their grandmother came from prime Purist stock. Brooke never had anything to fear from me. I'm not going to hurt her. I'm going to breed her."

Crimson filled my vision. Muscles fluttered, trying to shift to my were-form. I barely held onto my shape, only the memory of Brooke's purr keeping me from tossing the table between us and ending Arik's useless life. I had to calm myself for my plan to work.

Arik's chuckle rolled over me as he relaxed further into his seat. The man beside me remained tense, his hand on what I assumed was a weapon at his hip. I was running out of time, and I still needed to turn this to my advantage, or it would have been for nothing.

Two men at the table beside us stood, moving to block me in, as if I planned to run.

"Tell me why I shouldn't kill you now and go take her for myself? I'm sure she's hidden with one of the other animals in your little club. It wouldn't take long to destroy them one by one until I find her."

The question pulled my focus back to the man across from me. His face was a blank mask once again, though his eyes burned with the glee of someone who thinks they hold all the cards. He didn't realize he'd given me the perfect opening.

"I'll trade her."

Arik's brows rose as he let out a snort.

"I just said I could take her, why would I be willing to trade with a dog?"

I adjusted my posture, mimicking his. My wolf hated it, but I needed to seem as confident as Arik.

"You burned down my shop. I have nothing left to keep me in the city. If I leave, my men will follow me."

I paused to let the words sink in. He'd have no way to call my bluff.

"I'll have the insurance money to start over somewhere else, all I need is your assurance that no one will bother us. A free pass for me and all of the Knights. You get Brooke, and get to claim you drove the Hell's Knights out of the city."

Arik's eyes bored into mine. He tried not to show it, but I could tell he was considering the offer. Hell's Knights and the Purists might have only had a few scuffles, but we kept them out of the area we considered ours, and with us out of the way he'd have the opportunity to move in with no resistance. The area would fall to crime and drugs, turning into another slum surrounding the city.

"If I kill all of you, then you're still gone, and I still get her."

My chest tightened, but I wasn't done yet.

"Yeah, but how long will that take?"

Keeping my voice steady was one of the hardest things I'd ever done, but Brooke and my men were relying on me. If I couldn't convince Arik to wait and meet me somewhere more secluded later, I'd have no choice but to attempt to kill him right where he was, but with three other alphas surrounding me watching my every move, I wasn't likely to succeed.

I leaned forward, bracing both elbows on the table between us. The top was scored from my loss of control earlier, the surface rough beneath my arms as I clasped my hands together. Mainly to keep from reaching out to strangle him.

"You may know where one or two of us are, but what are the chances she's with one of them? Then you'd have to track down the others, when they know you're looking for them, and hope that they're the one hiding her. You already know her parents are gone, so you don't have anything to use as leverage to draw her out."

Arik's eyes narrowed and his lip twitched like he wanted to growl, but he managed to smooth it away.

"I could always use you as leverage."

I snorted, quirking my lips in what I hoped looked like a smile.

"Why would she care about me? She's using me to protect herself from you, just like I'm using her for pussy. If I'm gone she'll just find another available alpha."

I knew Brooke wasn't that type of person, but that was the way Arik thought, and I knew he'd believe her capable of exactly what I claimed. It was the same way he worked, using his men for the advantage it gave him before tossing them aside.

"One of your men will give up her location to save themselves."

My chuckle that time was real.

"First off, they hate you just as much as you hate us. And their egos are big enough to believe you'd never be able to kill them. Plus, we're pack. We wouldn't risk the life of another member to save our own skin, and giving up where she's at would do just that."

I leaned back again as Arik sneered. He was getting irritated, I just wasn't sure yet if that was going to work in my favor.

"There's only two people who know where she is right now. Me, and the person hiding her. You could go after as many of the men as you can catch, but they can't tell what they don't know."

His snarl was pitiful, and while I wanted to grin in triumph, I kept my face smooth, trying to project understanding. Arik was one of those alphas that believed the world revolved around him, so why wouldn't I sympathize with his frustration even though I was the cause?

I gasped in fake revelation, going in for the final blow.

"You know, if you take too long to locate her, he may end up breeding her himself. Even if you disposed of the child, she'd be sullied. Her womb tainted."

Arik lurched out of the booth, growl reverberating around us as I swallowed my laughter. I couldn't take what I said seriously or I'd be in as much of a rage as him, but playing with him was enough of a distraction to keep my jealousy tamed.

"You'll take me to her right now. No filthy animal is going to ruin my mate."

It was then I understood how unhinged Arik really was. If he believed Brooke would ever be his mate, he was delusional, but he'd never been one to credit women with brains of their own, much less think an omega would defy him. He thought them nothing more than slaves to their biology, content to be mastered by whatever alpha wanted them.

I hadn't planned to have him follow me, only to convince him to meet me somewhere at a later time. I didn't have any weapons, but doing this now also meant he couldn't set up an ambush or call for backup. He had five men with him, and I was by myself, but it was the best chance I was going to get.

Standing, I looked down at him, keeping my face serious.

"Do we have a deal? Me and my men are free to leave the city without being followed or harassed?"

"Yes. Take me to Brooke and all you dirty animals are free to leave."

He waved his hand in the air as if he didn't care what he was agreeing to, but I knew him well enough to know if the deal was real, he'd never uphold it. He wouldn't have given in so easily.

That was fine since I wasn't going to uphold my side either.

One of the men standing beside us took hold of my arm, the growl I released automatic. I choked it back, though I didn't remove my glare from him as he tried to turn me and pull me toward the door.

"Let's go, you heard the boss."

I wanted to scoff at him but knew it was better to play along. My wolf was ripping at my insides, not understanding what was going on, but I ignored it and let myself be pulled outside. The other man who'd stood and blocked me in took the lead, with Arik and the others following behind us.

When they went to turn left at the sidewalk I moved to go to my bike, but the man holding my arm yanked it, drawing another growl from my chest.

"This way."

I swallowed my snarl, barely resisting ripping my arm from him.

"My bike is over there."

I tipped my head toward it as Arik moved up beside us, the other men forming a ring around me as if they expected me to run.

"You don't need it," Arik said. My eyes darted to him, brow furrowing as he continued. "You'll ride with us."

My gut churned, but what choice did I have? I couldn't come up with a reason not to get in the car with him, and attempting to would make him suspicious.

I tried to look on the bright side. If I got them to drive to an empty enough area I could kill him in the car before trying to escape. My chances were slim within the confines of a vehicle, but his odds of survival were too.

I could accept that.

Relaxing my shoulders, I shrugged and gave a nod. "Okay."

I was led to Arik's black SUV, the man walking ahead of me opening the back door and leaning the seat forward. It was clear he wanted me to climb into the back after him, and once again my stomach flipped. My idea of taking Arik out as we drove burst.

The man holding my arm prodded me in the side when I hesitated. Shaking off my worries, I squeezed through the opening, for the first time in my life wishing I was smaller. If I'd been Brooke's size, I'd have been able to launch myself over the middle row and have a chance at reaching Arik where he settled in the front passenger seat.

My escort crawled in after me, wedging the three of us in a space definitely not meant to hold so many alphas. Even two my size would have bumped elbows, and if the men on each side of me hadn't been human, there was no way we would have all fit.

The other goons squabbled over who was driving until Arik barked an order to shut up, ordering one to the front and leaving the other two to take the middle row. Doors slammed, and suddenly I was enclosed with five other alphas, all focused on me.

"Where is she?"

Arik's blond hair shone with the late morning sun behind his head as he stared back at me. I scrambled for an address to give him. One where he'd believe I could have left Brooke, but where I'd have a chance to make my move.

And I came up blank.

"Head south. I'll tell you where to turn."

Tempting A Knight

His eyes narrowed and my heartrate kicked up.

"That's what GPS is for. Give me the address."

I huffed, trying to keep my cool as I came up with an excuse that seemed plausible.

"If I gave you the address you could kill me now. Not that it would do you any good since they know to run if they don't hear a special knock. I'll give you the directions and get her out, then you can take her and leave like we agreed."

He stared at me for a long moment, the silence making my skin crawl. My wolf was on edge, knowing we were in a bad position and not liking it.

"Head south."

He gave the order as he turned back to face the front and I let out the breath I hadn't realized I was holding. I was starting to think I may have gotten in over my head by rushing in with a half-baked idea, but it was too late now. I was all in.

And trapped, whether I liked it or not.

I let them go on for a few blocks before telling the driver to turn left. I was still trying to think of a good place to do what needed to be done, but nothing was coming to mind. I knew I couldn't run them in circles, but if I sent them out of the areas I knew I'd have no chance of coming up with a good place unless we happened to stumble into it.

I wasn't willing to bet my luck was that good.

We drove for about fifteen minutes with me giving random directions as I wracked my brain. Nothing I came up with seemed like a good place to kill someone midday without being caught. Even if I provoked Arik and could claim self-defense, I doubted his men would let me live long enough to explain it to the cops.

Telling the driver to turn once again, I noticed Arik's eyes focused on me in the rearview mirror. I didn't catch my mistake until I looked out the window and realized we were coming back down a street I'd already sent them through.

"Put him out."

A split second of hissing was the only warning I got before lightning bit into my side. My vest and t-shirt did nothing to block the taser, my entire body going stiff in reaction to the electricity coursing through it.

I had no idea how long it was held to my side. It could have been seconds, or minutes. My vision greyed at the edges, brightness varying with my pulse.

The weapon was pulled away long enough for frozen lungs to heave in another breath and for them to realize I was still conscious. My claws extended, but not fast enough.

This time the taser hit the bare skin of my bicep. Chest tensing, muscles straining, there was nothing I could do as darkness swallowed me.

Chapter Thirty-Five

Brooke

Every time Patch's phone rang, I jumped, stretching my ears to hear what was said. The voice on the other end of the line was always a muffled jumble of syllables, Patch remaining stoic and untalkative as ever. It was a test of my patience, which was growing wafer thin over the few hours since Sebastian abandoned me for his foolish mission.

This time I caught the change in Patch's body language. The sudden coiling of muscle that heralded our call to action. I couldn't help but think the news was bad when his gaze locked on mine.

"Got it. On the way."

He hung up and stood, my heart hammering in my chest now that the wait was over. Frustration tipped over into panic, the alpha's face a blank mask that couldn't deny my sudden fear.

"It's bad."

I made it a statement, and Patch didn't bother to correct me.

"The guys know where he's been taken. They're moving in now and we'll meet them there."

Taken.

That one word said it all. Whatever Sebastian's plan had been, it seemed to have failed. I doubted he would have let himself be taken somewhere when he'd have been safer on ground of his own choosing.

"Is he okay?"

"He's alive."

That wasn't much assurance, but it would have to be enough since it was all he gave me. Scrambling to my feet, I followed the silent alpha as he made his way out of the shop, turning off the lights and locking the door behind us. I tried to rationalize that it couldn't be that bad if he was taking the time for such mundane things, but it was more likely for him to be buying time so the worst was over by the time we got there. He wouldn't want me in the middle of it, and he was only expected to take care of anyone injured after all was said and done.

Somehow, I found a reserve of calm, managing to climb onto the bike and not recoil as he settled behind me. I even kept my teeth clamped around the scream trying to escape my throat as he maintained the speed limit, acting as if this was nothing more than a pleasure jaunt and not a race to find my alpha before anything bad happened.

I didn't know what I'd do if we were too late. I'd like to say I'd be able to stay rational, but the feelings swirling in my chest, threatening to suck me into madness, were larger than my bubble of calm.

Sebastian had to be okay.

We passed through the area I'd slowly begun to learn, drifting further from anywhere I recognized. Moving deeper into the fringes of the city, we circled around to the west where the river passed by and docks lined the water, attached to warehouses similar to where my father worked.

The engine cutting off beneath me was a sudden shock since we were still rolling down the street, but the reason for it caught my attention before I could ask Patch what was happening.

A row of motorcycles were gathered beside a low building off the side of one of the smaller two-story warehouses. I spotted a couple men wearing the leather of the Hell's Knights lingering nearby, but the others were missing.

It was a dishearteningly small number of bikes. I knew there hadn't been that many with us out in the forest, but I hadn't realized how easily they could be to outnumber. Arik's posse was fairly small, but he had all the Purists to call on for backup.

We *were* Sebastian's backup. There was no one else to come to our rescue if things went south.

I swallowed the lump growing in my throat as we rolled up next to the others and parked. The two alphas standing guard came over, their faces drawn, tightening the band constricting my chest.

"How long?"

Patch's question was terse, but I'd come to realize that was just the way he spoke, and the others clearly understood the same.

"Ten, maybe fifteen minutes. Haven't heard anything yet."

The man who answered him didn't look much older than me, his rumpled dirty blond hair giving him a childish look with his smooth chin. Patch grunted in response, standing and swinging a leg over the back of his bike. Reaching down, he pulled a blade from his boot that was longer than my hand, holding it out hilt first toward me.

Gingerly, I wrapped my fingers around the handle, not sure if it was smart to accept a weapon I didn't know how to handle, but not wanting to say no.

Patch walked to the edge of the building to peer around it toward the warehouse as I studied the knife. It was heavy in my palm, but it helped ease some of the helplessness that lingered. I rose to follow him once I'd accepted the idea of carrying the blade, but those cold eyes landed on me, freezing me in place atop his motorcycle.

"Stay."

I couldn't stop the way my eyes narrowed at the order, but I'd promised to do as he said. I wasn't sure how long I'd be able to ignore the instincts clamoring for me to race inside to find Sebastian, but for the moment I settled back atop the seat, sending up prayers to anyone who would listen to keep my alpha safe as I clenched trembling fingers around the borrowed knife.

Chapter Thirty-Six

Sebastian

I was growling before I even peeled my eyes open, the stench of old blood, fur, and other alphas filling my senses. Sour notes of terror and pain lingered in the air, and I didn't need anything more to guess where they'd brought me.

An idle part of my brain wondered if it was the same warehouse they'd brought Vincent to torture a helpless family. The act that finally drove him to run, but far too late to save him.

I raised my head, the scrape of something hard along my throat jolting me to awareness.

Skull falling back, I stared up the length of my arms, along the chain securing me to the metal beam overhead. I could feel the cold concrete beneath my bare toes, the breeze blowing across my skin from open windows near the roof telling me I'd been stripped before being bound.

Flexing my shoulders, I tested how much play there was in the chain, but already forced to stand on the balls of my feet, I didn't have much room to move. Cold encircled my neck, a band of metal trapped between the column and my raised shoulders, and a shiver ran down my spine that had nothing to do with the temperature.

Collared, I wasn't able to shift. The chains around my wrists could have been broken, but without knowing how thick the metal was around my neck, I couldn't risk taking on a larger form or I could end up strangled by the collar.

I blinked into the dim interior, looking for Arik. I knew he wouldn't be far. He'd want to stand over his prize and gloat, and while it felt as though I'd already been worked over when I was unconscious, he would have saved the extreme stuff for once I was awake.

My mind tried to slip to Brooke. To what she would think when I didn't come back. Hopefully she'd be smart and forget about me and leave the city with her parents. Start over somewhere new, where threats and bad memories didn't hang over her head.

A scuff sounded to my left and I turned my body to look, Arik's bleach blond head coming into a beam of light cutting through the gloom. The smile on his face had my gut tightening, the madness there too obvious for comfort.

"Seems like you'll get to be the first to find out if we can break a Knight."

I huffed, doing my best to look nonchalant despite my predicament. It was hard to relax when you were holding your weight off your wrists with nothing but your toes.

"I doubt you could break a mouse. You couldn't even keep one little omega in hand."

Tempting A Knight

His face clouded as he walked closer. If I could enrage him enough, he might make the mistake of getting within the reach of my legs, and I'd still have a chance of killing him. I could see the others from the car arranged around me, a bit further back, but if I was fast enough and got a good grip, I might be able to snap his neck before they shot me.

I hadn't missed the guns gripped in the hands of two of them. The other three held short black clubs, and there was a suspicious table sitting just a little too far away for me to see what was on it.

Images of what had been done to Jackson flashed through my head. I hadn't been able to go see him, to apologize and offer support, but my imagination had no trouble coming up with ideas about what had happened to him.

My wolf snarled inside me, the sound leaking out through my throat as Arik took another step closer. I choked it back, but the other alpha had already stopped, too far for me to even kick, much less get my legs around.

"Oh, I've broken plenty of rats, and pretty little bitches too. Collar a wolf and it gives doggy style a whole new meaning."

His grin had my vision going red, but there was nothing I could do hanging from the ceiling with him out of reach. I didn't regret my decision to come alone, but I knew Arik planned to make me pay for the foolishness. I could only hope it all ended with me, and the other Knights were left alone. Not likely if he still planned to go after Brooke, but I could wish my sacrifice was for something.

My muscles ached as I stretched them, testing the chain around my wrists again. The links were thick, more than I could break in my human-form, but perhaps I could shift enough to use the were's strength before strangling.

A crackle came from behind me, and I jerked around to spot the man who'd tased me moving in, the tip of the club he held shimmering with blue sparks. Apparently he had a thing for electricity. The wand was about two feet long, and added to the length of his arm he'd be able to stay safely beyond danger when he prodded me.

When, because there was no question about the look in his eyes or the way his lips stretched as he stared back at me.

"Not so big and bad now, are you?"

The man's growl was pathetic compared to mine, but he didn't have an animal inside to back it up. I turned with him as he started to circle me but kept one eye on Arik as he crossed his arms over his chest.

"Animals like you killed Paul's brother. He's going to take a bit of revenge before we get to the good part."

I kept my attention on them both, but Arik seemed content to just watch. The man he called Paul lunged forward, but I managed to swing out of the way before he connected with my flesh, my wrists burning from the bite of the chain as I swung my weight on them.

Snarling, he turned to swing at me again without realizing he was still within my circle. Keeping my weight on my arms, I pushed off with one foot as I lashed out with the other, letting claws grow from my toes as I caught him in the thigh.

His cry brought a fierce smile to my face, but he jumped back out of reach with one hand clutching his bleeding leg. I doubted he'd be foolish enough to make the same mistake again, and it clearly wasn't deep enough to have hit the artery, but at least I could say I hadn't gone out without bloodying anyone.

Too distracted by my momentary triumph, I didn't hear the man who came up behind me, the muscles in my back seizing from the brief contact with the tip of another prod before I jerked away. The one I'd clawed slammed his forward into my stomach before I could steady myself, making me curl around the knot of pain.

More blows came, both physical and electrical as all the men besides Arik moved in around me. It wasn't the first time I'd been beaten. I'd had my first taste as a child under my father's drunken hand, but the prods sensitized my flesh, making each hit feel more intense. Sweat dripped from my brow before long, lungs laboring to draw breath between shocks.

Throughout it all, Arik's laughter drowned out the grunts and growls until he gave the order to stop.

"Ready to tell me where she is?"

I panted, unwilling to admit it was hard to catch my breath, so I maintained a stubborn silence.

"So heroic. Didn't you know the wolf is the bad guy of the story?"

Another zap lanced through my body before I could muster an answer, my teeth squeaking as my jaw tensed. I braced for another as I swung the opposite direction, but before it came there was a yell from the balcony circling just beneath the windows in the second story. I blinked the sweat from my eyes to see Arik and the others look up as the person overhead opened fire.

The steady bang, bang of a handgun echoed in the open space, Arik and his men ducking and running for the edges of the building where there was cover. Before they made it, the doors at both ends of the building opened and more gunshots were fired.

Caught in the middle, all I could do was watch as men I recognized moved through the doorways and took positions behind the support columns holding up the balcony. It was shoddy cover, but it was all there was, and Arik's men fared no better.

Shots were exchanged from all sides, a few coming too close for comfort. Arik's men had clumped around him behind a beam at the side of the building with Knights pinning them in, but no one was making any headway.

And I was still hanging naked in the middle of the building, vulnerable to ricochet.

"STOP."

My roar echoed through the building, all eyes drawn to me. Muscles quivering from being tased, I focused and forced my arms to shift. Bones lengthened, thickened, as shoulders swelled and the collar grew tight around my neck as I strained at the chains binding me. I was about to have to release the shift when a link finally slipped the tiniest bit, and I redoubled my efforts. The metal around my neck squeezed, cutting off my air, but still I flexed until the link spread enough to let my hands drop, pins and needles flooding the limbs as I let them relax back to their human shape.

I took a step toward where Arik hid behind his men, the two with guns swinging them between me and the Knights at each end of the building. It wasn't until I took another step that Arik pulled his own weapon, leveling it at my chest as he hissed to the others to focus on the threats from the sides.

"Stop there or I shoot you now."

"I don't think you're in a position to make demands."

His eyes narrowed but his aim didn't waiver. I didn't have a weapon, and though I could shift my claws enough to rip out his throat, I'd have to reach him first, and that would mean getting closer without getting shot.

The other members of the Hell's Knights still held their places behind the beams, watching the exchange but remaining on alert. I had no idea if there were more Purists close by or if Arik's men were the only ones, but I knew the longer we waited, the more likely we'd be discovered.

I recognized Carl's scent as he moved on the balcony above us, quiet enough that human hearing wasn't likely to pick up his steps. I didn't know what he planned, but I didn't like the idea of him risking himself.

This was my issue to handle. My omega to protect.

I took another step forward and Arik squeezed the trigger. I barely dodged in time, the whistle of the bullet whizzing past my shoulder sending a shudder down my spine.

His shot set off a cascade of more from each side, and I was forced to move back again, or risk being hit. The humans were more familiar with the weapons than my men, who preferred fighting with their natural forms, but since they were outnumbered and taking fire from both sides, it equaled out.

I tried shouting over the noise for them to stop, but it didn't work. Either they couldn't hear me, or they were too worked up to be the first to quit. The shots kept going until more than one gun clicked with an empty magazine.

"You're all dead. It's only a matter of time. I'll get that little bitch and make you regret you were ever born. Get on your knees and I'll make it quick."

The conviction in Arik's voice told me he truly believed he still had a chance. That he wasn't trapped and waiting on his own death to come knocking.

I shook my head, walking toward his clump of men once again.

"Surrender, and we'll let your men leave unharmed."

He scoffed at the offer, but I didn't miss the way the alphas surrounding him shot glances over their shoulders. Any good leader would trade himself to protect those beneath him, but Arik had never been any such thing. His men were out of bullets with nothing left to defend themselves except the prods they'd used on me, yet he still expected them to stand between him and danger.

I changed tactics, addressing the men. The scent of copper in the air told me at least a couple of them were already wounded, and while my wolf seethed at the idea of letting the men who'd been using me like a pinata leave unpunished, my only goal was to make sure Arik didn't make it out of the warehouse still breathing.

"Our current quarrel isn't with you. There's no reason to sacrifice yourselves for someone who wouldn't think of doing the same for you. Give me the key to this collar and leave. My men won't stop you."

They glanced between themselves again, Arik's snarl doing nothing to keep them in line.

"He has it."

The man standing to the right between me and Arik tipped his head toward the blond alpha. He lowered his arms, letting the prod he held dangle and taking a step toward the back of the warehouse as if he planned to do as I said.

Until another gunshot rang out.

Blood misted the front of my body, the face I'd been staring into going slack before his body dropped to the ground. The spreading crimson stain beneath his chest held my attention before I dragged my gaze back up to the man I'd come to hate more than any other.

He turned the gun toward me once again, his features pulled into a scowl that disfigured him more than the marks on his face. The men around him looked as if they wanted to bolt, but they didn't want to be the next one sacrificed by the leader they followed.

Arik's finger tightened on the trigger, tip aimed at my chest, but a shadow behind him caught my attention.

"You shoot me, and you have no chance of getting out of here alive. I doubt you have that many bullets left, and it takes more to take down a shifter than your human there."

"You filthy fucking animals just don't understand. You don't deserve to live. You're polluting the world, stealing our omegas, and forcing them to carry your bastard offspring. It doesn't matter how many have to die, as long as you die with them."

The four men still standing with him shifted, their eyes darting between their leader and the shifters blocking their escape. Any sane person would see they were trapped and take the offer given them.

Yet Arik refused after killing one of their own.

The Knights at each end of the warehouse crept closer, darting between the beams since none of us knew how many more shots Arik had. I was fairly certain his men were out, but he hadn't fired as much as they had.

Trying to keep the attention on me, I took another step as I answered.

"Your men don't seem to agree with you. You killed one of your own just because he was smart enough to see the situation is hopeless and tried to save himself."

"He was a traitor. Weak. The world is better without him."

I huffed, shaking my head.

"There's no shame in admitting when a situation is untenable. And nothing wrong with not wanting to sacrifice yourself for someone who doesn't deserve it."

Arik's snarl echoed through the building, his eyes flashing as he shoved forward to stand in front of me, his cheek a twisted mess of scabs. We were still too far apart to touch, but if he fired the gun, it wasn't likely I'd be able to get out of the way.

I let my claws extend, keeping my hands at my sides and waiting for the right moment. He'd done me a favor by turning on his own man, causing the others to lose faith in him. Given the chance, I was sure they'd run, I just had to cut the head off the snake first.

"Do you know who I am? My father runs this city. One day it'll be me, and I'll rid the whole thing of your kind. He thinks you have uses, but we all know you're better off as nothing but a rug."

A growl escaped me before I could stop it, hands clenching and claws digging into my palms. The movement I'd seen behind him had stopped when Arik moved forward, and I didn't know what Carl was waiting for, but I was running out of patience.

A quick glance to the side to check on where the Knights were had my lungs freezing. Carl's face looked down from above, the gun in his hands aimed at Arik, though he gave a negative shake of his head.

My attention whipped to the shadows behind the blond alpha in front of me, eyes searching. I sucked in a deep breath, digging through the cloying, overpowering scents of the other males and the blood. The breeze through the building was blowing away from me, so I couldn't tell if my fear was correct, but I couldn't risk it.

I lunged, but Arik must have noticed where I was looking. He was half-turned when he fired, the bullet hitting me in the left shoulder instead of dead center. Claws extended, I caught one forearm, but he kept turning with the gun.

A swirl of dark hair, the wind shifting to bring me a scent I'd never want to find in this situation, and I couldn't stop the change.

Chapter Thirty-Seven

Brooke

The gunshots had been the last straw. I couldn't stand by, knowing Sebastian was in danger.

I slipped away as the others stood at the end of the building, staring toward the warehouse and debating what to do. It took longer to go around the opposite side, moving behind stacks of pallets until I was close enough to make a dash for the warehouse wall where I wouldn't be seen by Patch or one of the others.

The open door at the end was too obvious. I wasn't willing to risk running into someone, especially when random gunfire kept echoing from the opening. Windows lined the sides of the building on the top and bottom, but all of the bottom ones I could see had wooden shutters hanging closed overtop them.

I was a little over halfway to the opposite end before I found one still cracked open enough for me to slip my fingers under and pry it back. The hinges were at the top, the shutter meant to be propped open by a bar at the bottom of the window so it still provided shade while allowing airflow. It was stiff and reluctant to move, heavy for my meager strength, but I refused to give up. Working first my hand, and then arm beneath the shutter, I managed to wriggle beneath, squashing myself between the wood and the windowpane.

For a moment I froze, unsure what to do next when I realized I still had another obstacle to get through, but what I could see through the grimy glass spurred me back into motion.

Sebastian, nude, with weird red blotches marking his skin, and a metal band around his neck that looked suspiciously like a collar, stood facing directly at me. Something blocked part of my view, and it wasn't until it moved that I realized it was a group of men.

Arik's blond hair caught the light, fueling my fear and rage as my fingers worked around the edges of the window, searching for a way inside. I finally found the hinges at the top and realized the window opened out the same way as the shutter, and I had to push the heavy wood open more to move back from the glass to tip it open.

"Do you know who I am? My father runs this city. One day it'll be me, and I'll rid the whole thing of your kind. He thinks you have uses, but we all know you're better off as nothing but a rug."

Arik's voice drifted to me through the opening, making my stomach churn. I wriggled my way under the glass, panting from the exertion of being squeezed under the weight of the shutter, but I refused to give up. I still clutched Patch's knife in one hand, the only thought in my head to get inside and bury it in that monster's guts before he hurt anyone else.

Metal scraped my stomach as I pulled myself through the window. There was nothing elegant about the way I was bent over the sill, hands on the floor as I scooted and pulled my legs through. I had just enough sense to keep my foot on the glass and stop it from slamming shut behind me, but once it settled back into its frame I scrambled to my feet, thankful for the shadows along the wall where I stood heaving.

It felt like it had taken an hour to get inside, yet I knew it couldn't have been long. Arik stood in front of Sebastian, both arms raised ahead of him where I couldn't see, but I didn't need to see his hands to know he aimed a gun at my alpha.

I did the only thing I could. I launched myself at the man who'd harassed me for so long, mouth opening on a silent scream as my feet hit the floor in quick succession. I watched him start to turn, the loud bang of a gunshot making me flinch, but I kept moving, blade clutched in my fist as I ran between two alphas looking in other directions.

They thought their backs were covered, the wall behind them seeming solid in the darkness. They didn't expect an omega to slip in and dart between them.

Sebastian's snarl reached me just as light shone off hated blue eyes. Arik was turning in slow motion, his mouth twisted in a vicious grin as I closed the space between us. The arm nearest me kept swinging, gun clutched in his hand, but it was too late to worry about my own safety.

I was committed. I wanted to see that light extinguished, that grin forever fade away.

A gunshot sounded from further away just before I ducked under his arm and impacted with his body, never once trying to slow my momentum. My eyes were locked on his face as the blade slid deep in his belly, the shock I saw there sending a fierce pulse of glee through my frame. The world froze, though heat washed over my fist as I yanked it back as much as I could with my body pressed to his before sending it surging forward again.

Mouth open, brows drawn together, Arik stared down at me until dark fingers curled around his throat from behind, jerking him backward. I lurched with him, releasing the knife handle on instinct to keep from toppling over.

Sebastian's other arm wrapped around Arik, pinning him to the were's chest as the claws of the hand around his throat dug in. Bright red bloomed where black claws sank into pale flesh, Arik's gurgle the only sound that penetrated my brain despite the chaos I sensed around us.

Sebastian's hand clenched tighter as his gaze moved to me. The body between us twitched, heels drumming before muscles went slack, the only expression left on Arik's face that of utter confusion.

Emotions swirled inside me.

Relief.

Shock.

Hope.

Fear.

It was what I had wanted, but what would it cost?

I was brought back to what was happening when Sebastian staggered, dropping Arik's limp body on the warehouse floor before falling to his knees. It wasn't until then that I noticed the blood running from his own neck, an odd hacking sound coming from his throat as his chest hitched in short bursts.

Black hair receded as Sebastian swayed, muzzle flattening and bones shifting. Reaching forward, I tried to brace him, but couldn't stop his fall.

I didn't remember screaming for Patch, only hearing the echoes of his name reverberating inside my skull as I tried to roll Sebastian onto his back. His body slowly finished the change back to human, the metal around his neck no longer a dull silver, but almost black with blood and fur coating it.

"His pockets. Check his pockets."

Voices yelled around me. I was bumped and jolted, but I couldn't pull my focus away from Sebastian. Even though the collar no longer dug into his neck, his chest still wasn't moving.

When someone put a hand on my shoulder to tug me away I snarled, lashing out with a scream that tore at my throat. I fought as hard as I could, but arms stronger than I could resist pulled me away, jumbled words murmured in my ear leaving no meaning behind as my mind clung to the thought that I was being separated from him forever.

"Give her this."

Patch appeared before me, kneeling beside Sebastian's body but holding out something small to whoever held me. I wanted to beg him to do something, to help Sebastian, but all that came out were sobs.

A sharp prick in my shoulder made me flinch, but I was too focused on Patch as he finally rolled Sebastian onto his back to pay attention to what it was. I was still being held back, but they weren't forcing me any further away, so I stopped my struggles to watch.

Patch's fingers worked around Sebastian's neck, the metal wrapped there finally coming open. Desperately searching for a sign that it wasn't too late, my eyes locked on his bare chest, waiting as tears flooded my cheeks.

It was taking too long.

Vision swimming as I refused to blink, darkness crept into the edges. My limbs grew heavy, my head a boulder my neck couldn't hold up. I resisted gravity for as long as I could, and just before the world reached out and swallowed me whole, I saw his chest rise.

CHAPTER THIRTY-EIGHT

SEBASTIAN

The beeping was fucking annoying. Constant, steady, not letting me sleep. Growling in frustration, I tried to roll over to block it out, only to find my arms tangled in something that didn't want to let me move. Even my eyelids resisted my orders, taking far longer than necessary to peel back and reveal the plain, white room I lay in.

Monitors hung by the side of the bed, revealing the source of my initial annoyance. The slow blip of the line assured me I was still alive despite the numbness weighing me down.

I rolled my head to the other side, glancing down at my arm to see tubing disappearing into the back of my hand. My neck felt tight, the motion making it burn, and it took a moment for me to remember why.

Brooke.

I tried to growl but it choked off in a sputtering cough that had fire pouring through my throat. Voices washed over me as I tried to get it under control, but my eyes were watering too much to see whose hand slipped behind my head to sit me up and press a cup to my lips.

I sucked in the tepid water, the liquid doing nothing to quell the flames, but at least it calmed the hacking. Blinking away the moisture in my eyes, I was surprised to look up into Mrs. Frost's concerned face.

I'd barely parted my lips when she cut me off, her concern turning into a fierce glare.

"Don't you dare try to speak. What kind of imbecile tries to shift into a werewolf with a collar locked around his neck? Do you realize the damage you did?"

I knew her rising voice was the worry, and despite the seriousness of it, I couldn't help smiling up at her.

Narrowing her eyes, she took a step back and set the cup down on the little table beside me with more force than necessary. She huffed out a breath, and I got the feeling she was barely resisting the urge to put her hands on her hips and give me a full scolding.

"You're lucky shifters heal fast, otherwise you'd be dead. Burying one son was enough for me, thank you very much. Next time, use the brains I know you have and find another way."

I opened my mouth to tell her I'd done it to save Brooke, but she held up a hand and stopped me before I could make a sound.

"No. No talking. Your throat is still a mess, and nothing you say is going to make this feel any better."

She turned, putting her back to me and fiddling with something on the monitor, but I could hear the way her breath hitched. I reached over the railing along the side of the hospital bed, tugging on her scrubs. She swung her hand at me to get me to quit but I caught it, tangling my fingers with hers.

Her shoulders hunched, but she squeezed back. I'd been wrong to leave the Frosts alone with their grief when sharing it would have helped us all, and I swore I'd do whatever it took to make it up to them. She didn't deserve the stress I brought her, and she certainly hadn't deserved to be abandoned when she'd treated me as one of her own for so long.

We clung to each other in silence for a moment before she turned to face me again, offering a shaky smile before turning serious.

"You're going to survive, but you'll be eating mush for a while. You should refrain from talking as much as possible for a few days until the swelling in the tissues has a chance to recede."

She pushed the little table closer to the side of the bed, moving the cup of water where it would be easier for me to reach. Her face fell, and I knew what was coming next would be the worst of the news.

"There's scarring. There wasn't anything we could do, but it shouldn't affect your mobility or eating or anything."

Lifting my hand, I felt the edges of the bandage around my neck. The wound had to have been deep to still need dressing by the time I was brought to a hospital. It wasn't like we'd been close by, or able to call an ambulance.

"Brooke stayed with you until I forced her to go home and get some rest. I'm sure she'll be back as soon as she wakes."

Bustling around the end of the bed, she tucked in the corner I'd kicked loose, but I was stuck on what she'd said. I knew Arik was no longer a threat, but it would take a while to see what the fallout from that was, and if Brooke was at her apartment alone I had to get to her.

Levering myself upright, I shook my head when Mrs. Frost gave me a sharp look, grimacing when I tried to speak and nothing but a rasp came out.

"What are you…"

Her mouth formed an O as her eyes widened. Raising her hands, she came over to press them to my shoulders, preventing me from getting up.

"No, I didn't mean home. She's not at the apartment."

I stopped trying to shove her aside, focusing on her face as she patted my chest and pushed me back down.

"She's at the condo. Patch took her there after he checked on Jackson. That boy would have made a great doctor."

She offered a smile with the last comment as I slowly relaxed back onto the pillow. I doubted Patch would welcome being referred to as a boy, but her praise would have been appreciated.

"Jackson?"

My voice was broken and rough, the whisper abrading the sore tissue in my throat. I hadn't realized Jackson was at the same hospital since he'd been attacked at her apartment, and it was zoned for a different facility than the one Mrs. Frost worked for. Emergency services would have taken him to the nearest, not necessarily the best.

"I had him transferred here once he was stable. He was hurt because of me, so it's only right I take care of him myself. He wouldn't get the proper care out near the slums. They didn't even have enough pain medication to give him a proper dose for a shifter his size."

Worry etched her face again, so I caught her hand and gave it a squeeze. It wasn't her fault he'd been attacked, but I couldn't explain that without a voice, so all I could do was offer support. We both knew where the real blame belonged, but guilt was something that had a mind of its own.

"Anyway, I've got to check on him and get back to my other patients. You've got someone waiting if you feel up to it. Visiting hours ended a while ago, but so far no one has said anything. I don't want to push it too much though, so you need to be quick."

I nodded, scooting higher in the bed. I couldn't help that I was wearing a stupid hospital gown, but I could at least try to maintain some dignity by sitting up.

It was impossible to miss the way Mrs. Frost shook her head, an exasperated sigh reaching my ears as she slipped from the room and closed the door behind her. It was only a few seconds later when heavy footsteps approached my room and the door swung open again, Carl's bearded face peering at me across the white expanse.

"Took you long enough. I was starting to think I'd have to take your place permanently, and I'm not cut out to deal with these miscreants."

I huffed, even that sending a spike of pain through my throat.

"I also thought you had more brains than to try shifting with a collar around your neck, but you proved me wrong there, too."

My eyes narrowed, lip curling even though I held back the growl. Just the thought of how that would feel to the damaged tissue sent a shiver down my spine that had the urge melting away.

Carl shuffled further into the room, letting the door swing shut behind him. The moment of silence as he stared at me said everything I knew he wouldn't, and I gave him a nod of thanks.

"So, I'm sure you want an update on everything that happened after you decided to go beast-mode and take a nap."

White teeth flashed amidst his dark beard. I rolled my eyes, using my fingers to express how I felt since I couldn't tell him to shut up and get on with it.

"Well, your little stunt meant the authorities got involved once we got you here. You missed the fun part where we were all arrested, but between Brooke and Mrs. Frost, and some benevolent god smiling down on you who sent cops not on the Purists' payroll, we were released again. Pending investigation of course. Hope you don't have any plans to elope with the little omega anytime soon."

My heartbeat had picked up at the mention of authorities, but he wouldn't be cracking jokes if he thought we were in any real trouble. I let out the breath I'd held, waiting for the rest.

"We subdued the others with Arik, though one has since succumbed to the gunshot wound he took. Jason and Knox had stayed behind at the warehouse to hold them, and I guess Arik pissed them off bad enough for them to pin the whole thing on him. I'm sure someone is going to want to get your statement, and you'll have to go to court for it to officially be written off as self-defense, but they already admitted to assisting in kidnapping and torture. Danger said he'd send over a lawyer as soon as you're ready for it."

My brow rose but Carl only shrugged.

"He's the reason you aren't currently chained to the bed with cops breathing down your throat. Whoever he is, that man's got pull."

I filed that information away, making a note to thank Danger for more than just keeping the Frost's away from harm.

Carl sucked in a deep breath, looking around the little hospital room before focusing on me again.

"That's pretty much everything. Mrs. Frost has been handling your care, so she's who you'll have to talk to about getting out of here, but I think they're planning to release you tomorrow if you behave."

I tried to nod but the bandage around my throat pulled. Raising my hand to run my fingers along it again, I watched Carl grimace and glance away.

"That bad?"

My rasp jerked his attention back to me, his nose curling as he shook his head.

"Not like you were winning any beauty contests before. At least Brooke doesn't seem like the type to run because of it."

The thought hadn't crossed my mind till he put it there, but suddenly I worried how bad it really was. She'd been onboard with what needed to happen to Arik, though I knew she'd had reservations about it. Taking a life wasn't an easy decision, no matter how many reasons there were to do it, but now I wondered if the scars would be a constant reminder that she wouldn't want.

My gaze had dropped to the blanket covering me as I thought, fingers still exploring the bandage. The flesh beneath seemed a bit more sensitive than usual, but not as painful as it could have been.

Looking back up at Carl, I watched him shrug again.

"Not much you can do now. Get some rest."

Turning, he abandoned me to my thoughts, worry turning them into an unending cycle.

Chapter Thirty-Nine

Brooke

I jerked upright, heart pounding as my eyes searched the room.

Plain furnishings met my gaze. Simple pictures on the walls that said nothing of the person who'd chosen them. It looked like something you'd see in a magazine, not somewhere people really slept.

The weak light coming through the window told me it was still the early hours of the morning, but I scrambled from the bed anyway. I hadn't wanted to leave the hospital the night before, especially since Sebastian still hadn't woken, though everyone assured me he would be okay.

The time after I was pulled away from him at the warehouse was a blur. There'd been voices lobbying back and forth over my head, but none of it had made sense as my vision faded in and out from whatever I'd been given. The distress at being held away from Sebastian hadn't eased, but my focus had narrowed to the rise and fall of his chest, and being able to watch him breathe had kept me calm enough for Patch to do what he could.

I remembered being ushered into a vehicle, the arms banding around me changing to a restraining hand on my shoulder, but by then I was cognizant enough to know I needed to stay out of the way. Whatever transportation that had been found for us, Sebastian had been laid across the back seat, head lying in Patch's lap with his legs bent and crammed in enough for the door to shut.

I'd claimed the front passenger seat, reaching back to hold his limp hand as Carl took the driver side and raced through the city. I wasn't even aware we were going to a hospital till the bright lights caught my attention when Carl opened the door to yell for a stretcher.

Sebastian's lack of response to anything had sent ice through my veins. Even once I was sure he was going to keep breathing, new worries took over, whispering terrible things about what a lack of oxygen could do to the brain in a matter of minutes.

I slipped my shoes back on. They'd been the only thing I removed before flopping down on the bed however many hours ago it had been. I'd expected to fret all night, and the fact that I'd fallen right to sleep made me suspicious of the drink my mother had brought me before sending me away. Still, I felt better for the rest, but it was time to get back to Sebastian and face what damage had been done.

The one relief in all the worry was that we didn't appear to be facing any charges. I'd spoken with the police at the hospital when they'd insisted it was necessary, explaining the stalking and harassment I'd endured with Arik. It had been impossible to hide what we'd done, that we'd killed him in the warehouse, so claiming self-defense was the only option we had.

I slipped out of the room after searching for my phone. It wasn't on the bedside table or the dresser, so I was hoping I'd left it in the kitchen when I stopped for water before crashing.

"If you hurry, you can catch the bus downtown."

My mother's voice jolted me to a stop as soon as I made it to the bottom of the stairs and stepped onto the smooth tile of the dining room. She sat at the table, dark circles under her eyes, still in the rumpled scrubs she'd worn the day before when she came rushing in to take over as Sebastian's nurse.

"Have you slept?"

The question spilled out without thought, though the sight of my phone on the table in front of her urged me back into motion.

"Not yet, I just got back. Don't worry about me. Sebastian woke last night, and I think he's waiting on you."

My heart stumbled, breath catching in my throat before leaving me in a woosh.

I snatched up my phone and the bus pass my mother shoved across the table at me.

"Take the Five downtown, then the Ten East to the hospital. The stop is right on the corner outside."

The door slammed behind me, cutting off anything else she was going to say. I felt bad for running out on her, but all my focus was on getting to Sebastian and being sure he was okay.

The bus was rolling up as I barreled down the porch steps toward the sidewalk. Waving my arms, I raced to it, chest heaving by the time I crossed through the door and swiped the card over the little machine to let me on.

Impatience ate at me the entire trip, and by the time I reached the hub downtown I couldn't stand the thought of waiting for another bus and sitting through however many stops were between there and the hospital. Finding the sign for Bus Route Ten, I jogged down the sidewalk, dodging the early morning crowd as they made their way to work. I got a few odd looks and muttered curses as I squeezed by anyone going too slow for the urgency beating in my chest, but I ignored it all, eyes searching for the hospital.

I was out of breath by the time I reached it and had to pause to catch it at the desk before I could gasp out my reason for being there.

"I need a pass to the third floor to visit my mate."

Heat flooded my cheeks at the lie, but I didn't try to take it back. It was still a few minutes before visiting time, but I was hoping she'd let me through anyway.

"His name?"

"Sebastian Barros."

She typed away on her keyboard, each second dragging by like nails raking down my back. The longer it took, the tenser I grew, until my heart stopped with her next sentence.

"He's already left. Against medical advice."

The world pulsed around me, walls wavering until I sucked in a deep breath filled with the scent of cleaning agents and recycled air.

"When?"

Her face pinched in concern at my gasp, but she glanced at her screen again.

"They realized his room was empty about an hour ago. He seems to have slipped out during the shift change."

My growl startled both of us, the poor beta's eyes widening as I bared my teeth in frustration. He waited for Mom to leave so he could sneak out, and I had no idea where he'd have gone. Or how he would get there since I hadn't seen his motorcycle at the warehouse with the others.

I ran a hand through my hair, tangles catching and sending zings of pain through my scalp. Looking around with helpless indecision, I tugged on the locks, racking my brain for what to do.

"Miss, I'm going to need you to step aside so I can help others."

The woman looked as if I was freaking her out, her hand under the desk warning me that if I didn't want a situation on my hands, I needed to calm down. Gulping another breath of sterile air, I spun on my heel and walked back out of the hospital, pausing outside the door to pull my phone from my pocket.

Sebastian's number went straight to voicemail. I'd heard enough of what happened before I entered the warehouse to know Arik had stripped him before stringing him up like a hunk of meat, so I doubted he even had the device, and I didn't have anyone else's number.

I snarled as I turned and paced the space beside the doors. He'd been conscious less than twelve hours, why would he leave? Especially when he knew I'd be coming to see him.

My stomach dropped, blood turning to ice as I froze, blank stare aimed at nothing as doubts took over.

Did he leave *because* he knew I'd come looking for him? Was what I'd felt between us all in my head, and now he wanted nothing more to do with me?

My chest spasmed, bile burning the back of my throat. Tears pricked the corners of my eyes as a massive breakdown threatened, but I shoved it back. I refused to believe the insidious whispers.

Spinning on my heel, I marched back into the hospital, slipping past the receptionist desk with a group of people heading for the elevators. When the doors cut us off from the lobby, I pressed the button for the third floor, saying a silent prayer that I wouldn't be stopped by anyone with the authority to make me leave. I didn't have a visitor's pass to stick on my shirt, so I had to be sure not to pass anyone who would notice.

The elevator rocked to a stop two floors up. I could feel the eyes of the others on me as I peeked between the doors before slipping out to walk down the bare hallway. I could hear feminine voices speaking around a corner ahead, but the nurse's desk had been past Sebastian's room, which was right beside Jackson's.

I couldn't help the urge to verify Sebastian was no longer where I'd left him. The room was empty when I poked my head inside, the bed made and waiting for a new tenant, though his scent lingered in the air. Steeling myself, I strode to the next door along the hallway, holding my breath as I spotted the nurses behind their desk. One glance and I'd be busted, but I managed to get inside and close the door behind me without either turning their head.

A steady beep filled the silence, reminding me of the time I'd sat beside Sebastian and listened to the same sound. Swallowing the lump threatening to choke me, I gazed through the dim light and found pain-filled eyes watching me.

"H-hello."

My mind was a sudden blank as I stared at the injured alpha. The sour stink of agony and medications filled the room, making each breath a challenge. His arms and legs were covered with bandages, and images of what he must look like underneath flooded my mind, sending my stomach churning.

The alpha remained silent, not acknowledging my greeting. Pushing past the awkwardness and the pity I tried not to show, I took a step closer to the end of his bed.

"Are you Jackson? I'm Brooke."

His eyes flashed, but whatever emotion I'd evoked disappeared as fast as it came.

"I want to say thank you for guarding my parents and tell you how sorry I am about what happened."

Face clouding, he turned his head away from me, staring at the open blinds.

"I don't need your thanks or your pity. You can leave."

There was so much pain in his voice a piece of my heart broke for him. I was torn between the desire to help and comfort him, and the need to find Sebastian, but the second was stronger. I had to hope he had others to rely on to get him through.

"I would, but I'm looking for Sebastian. He left before I could get here, and I don't know where he went. His phone is off, and I don't have any other numbers…"

My voice trailed off as I realized how selfish I sounded. This man was hurt, had been horrifically attacked for being involved with me despite not knowing me himself, and here I was begging him to help me find the man he'd blindly followed into the danger.

"I'm sorry."

I bowed my head, hands clasped in front of me as I backed toward the exit.

"I won't bother you anymore."

Slipping through the door into the hall beyond, I glanced back as I closed it to find those hurt eyes watching me once again.

A shiver wracked my body as I turned toward the elevators only to bounce off a hard body, large hands reaching out to clasp my shoulders. My first instinct was to jerk away, the action ripping me from the hold and sending me ricocheting off the wall before I steadied myself.

A gasp brought me a familiar scent, but it wasn't until I looked up into the bearded face that I recognized Carl.

"What are you doing in Jackson's room?"

His rumble and narrowed eyes had my shoulders hunching forward before I forced myself to straighten.

"Sebastian left and I need to find him."

I issued the statement as firmly as I could despite the quiver in my gut. I'd already had enough of confronting alphas for the day, and it had only just begun.

"He went home."

Jaw going slack, I stared up at the man in incomprehension. Something so obvious hadn't even crossed my mind, and my cheeks heated as my teeth clacked back together.

"Oh, uh, thanks."

His brow wrinkled, expression softening as he stared down at me.

"Give me a minute and I can give you a ride."

My heart fluttered, and I nodded despite my stomach's antics. I'd been on a motorcycle enough times now that most of my fear had abated, but it still flared when I rode with anyone besides Sebastian.

"Of course."

I stepped out of the way of the door, giving him a wide berth as I moved around to wait beside it where I wouldn't be seen from inside. The vision of Jackson's eyes on me still made my skin crawl, and I didn't want to risk him seeing me lingering.

I was staring off into space, trying my best to be patient, when another body stopped in front of me.

"Did you check in at the reception desk?"

My eyes flew to a pretty face, black hair pulled back in a ponytail, burgundy scrubs telling me she was a nurse even before my gaze dipped to her ID.

"Oh, ye-yes. I must have lost my sticker."

I made a show of looking down and searching for it, and breathed a sigh of relief when Jackson's door opened beside me.

"It's okay, we're leaving."

Carl placed a hand between my shoulders, turning me toward the elevators as he addressed the nurse.

"He's in pain, though he's not going to admit to it, and that room needs aired out. You betas may not notice the stink, but he's not going to get better breathing foul air."

The woman visibly straightened at Carl's admonition. I could see the trepidation creeping into her expression and couldn't blame her. All of the Hell's Knights seemed to be massive, even for shifters, and it was easy to be intimidated by them.

"I'll take care of it."

She glanced at me again.

"Make sure you don't lose the pass next time."

I pinched my lips together, offering a tight smile as Carl hustled me away. As an omega, it was natural to be the one the other dynamics took their frustration out on, and it wasn't like I wasn't in the wrong. Hopefully I'd have no reason to return.

Leann Ryans

Chapter Forty

Sebastian

I sighed as I looked at my blank screen. The guys had thought to grab my clothes when they took me from the warehouse, but they hadn't thought to charge my phone.

Looking around my house, I sighed again. The guys had done what they could to clean up, but I hadn't realized how bad it had been trashed.

My TV sported a spiderweb of cracks, the couch cushions torn, though the fluff had been bagged and put out at the curb. Bits of broken dishes littered the floor under the counters where whoever had swept had missed them, the crooked ceiling fan in my dining room now dangling almost to the tile.

None of that was quite as irritating as the paint splashed across my tools in the garage. At least it had been spilled out there and not on my carpet.

When Carl showed up that morning with the key to my bike, telling me they'd found it and brought it back for me, I hadn't been able to stand another second in that hospital room. There was no reason to wait around to have a doctor tell me the same thing Mrs. Frost already had, and she wasn't there to stop me.

But after a long night of tossing and turning, the sight of the house only made me more exhausted. I couldn't bear the thought of what I'd find in the bedroom, where Brooke had made a nest on my bed. Just the thought of the violation had me wishing I could bring Arik back from the dead to run my claws through him again.

Turning my back on the space, I returned to the garage. I could repair and replace what had been destroyed, but even then, I doubted this place would feel like home again. The memories of Brooke's heat were here, but they'd forever be overshadowed by what happened after.

The house was ruined.

Exhaustion dragged at me, but I wasn't sure what to do. I didn't want to stay at the house, but I wasn't sure where else to go.

I settled onto my bike, looking around at the mess before giving in to the burning need to close my eyes. Crossing my arms over the handlebars, I leaned forward to rest my forehead on them, giving my eyes a break. The only option I could come up with was renting another motel room, but I needed a minute before I could focus enough to drive again.

I jerked awake to the sound of a motorcycle growing closer. My neck and back were stiff, telling me I'd nodded off for more than just a minute or two. Stretching, I tried to work the kinks out as I waited for whoever was coming to arrive.

Carl rolled into view, and as soon as I spotted the little dark-headed body behind him, a growl ripped from my throat. It died on a sputtering cough that felt like shards of glass as I gripped my neck, my possessiveness forgotten in the wash of pain. It helped that Brooke launched herself from his bike as soon as he rolled to a stop in the driveway, her feet bringing her hurtling towards me.

"Sebastian, are you okay?"

Cool hands pressed to my cheeks, deep green eyes searching my face as I tried to get the hacking under control. Carl slipped around me, returning with a bottle of water from the fridge before I could collect myself and wonder what he was doing.

Sucking it down, the irritation finally eased enough to let me draw in a ragged breath, Brooke's scent flooding my lungs and easing more of the tension. I still sent Carl a narrowed glare, but he was already backing out of the garage, lips quirked in a grin that promised I was never going to live this down.

I focused back on Brooke when he threw a leg over his bike, rolling out into the street before firing up his hog. Her eyes were still wide, chest rising and falling with each rapid breath she took as she watched me.

"I'm fine."

The croak set off new ripples of pain, but it was nothing like it had been moments before.

"What the hell were you thinking?"

The explosive question paired with the scowl marring her face had me jerking back, my own brows pinching in return.

"You can't just get up and leave a hospital. You're supposed to wait for the doctor to make sure everything is okay first. I showed up, and they said you were already gone, and then your phone was off…"

I could hear the panic in her voice, the pitch rising with each word spilled from her beautiful lips. Raising my hands, I reached for her, but she batted them away, stepping back to pin me with her glare once again.

"You didn't have to put yourself in danger just to get away from me. I thought we had something between us, but if you didn't want me, all you had to do was say so."

Jerking upright, I stood and swung my leg over the saddle. Her scowl changed to a look of surprise as I stalked toward her, backing her into the wall of the garage. There was nowhere else for her to run when her back met the plaster, and I continued forward until I could pin her in with an arm on each side.

"It's you who shouldn't want me, but I'm not giving you that option anymore. You're mine."

My whisper was harsh, making me long for another drink, but that was secondary to what I needed most. Brooke stared up at me, pink lips parted, and I couldn't wait another second.

My mouth crashed down on hers, the hard edge of teeth pinching before I turned my head and thrust my tongue into her mouth. She was stiff with surprise but melted under the onslaught, her tongue moving to dance with mine as I claimed her with my kiss.

There could be no question that I wanted her. That I would do anything to keep her. If I had to take on the entire Purist organization, I'd do it to taste her lips every day.

I swallowed her moans as her arms crept around me. She clung to me with the same fierceness I felt, the need to be closer overriding all the aches still lingering in my body. It didn't matter how bad I hurt, I wanted her.

But I wasn't going to take her into the house.

She gasped when I released her, her forehead pressing into my chest as I gave her a moment to catch her breath and dropped kisses on the top of her head. Grabbing her hand, I straightened and pulled her toward my bike, taking my seat and helping her slid into place behind me.

"Where are we going?"

"Anywhere but here."

She accepted my answer without protest, and I kicked the bike to life, riding out into the street with a roar. I didn't have a destination in mind, only finding a safe place to lay my omega down and show her how tempting she was.

I knew we'd still have to talk. I'd have to tell her how serious I was about her being mine, and we'd have to discuss what we wanted from the future, but for now, being with her was enough.

The wind rushed through my hair as we rode through the streets, the morning traffic light since most people had already made it to work. As much as I loved the sensation, I was more interested in the sensations I could cause in Brooke, and eventually pulled off the road at the first decent looking motel I found.

Paying for a week, I hustled us into the room and locked the door. I'd left my phone at my house, hadn't even bothered to lock up, but I didn't care. I didn't want any interruptions. We'd had enough of them in our short time together, and it was time to focus on the two of us.

I spent most of four days knotted inside her, filling her as if she was in heat all over again. As much as I wished to mark and claim her, I knew it wouldn't take until her cycle rolled back around, flooding her system with hormones.

I was impatient. I wanted it done. Wanted to know she'd forever be mine.

Brooke called her mother the evening of the fourth day, Mrs. Frost's shrill voice clear despite the phone being on the opposite side of the bed. Brooke barely got a few words in, but the way her cheeks reddened had a grin crossing my face. Mrs. Frost wasn't a fool, and the few words I caught were enough to know she was well aware of how we'd spent the last few days.

I finally reached across Brooke's bare form and snatched the phone from her hand, putting the receiver to my ear and waiting for Mrs. Frost to take a breath so I could cut in.

"I plan to claim your daughter, Mrs. Frost. She's mine."

I heard her huff through the line and could imagine the way her eyes rolled as she shook her head at the other end.

"I'm well aware of that, though I'm glad you're finally admitting it. It's still rude to disappear for days on end and leave others to clean up your mess."

I grimaced at the reminder that just because we wanted the trouble with Arik to be over and done with, there was still more that had to be handled.

"I'm sorry."

She sighed, the sound tired, but full of relief. There was a moment of silence before she switched gears.

"How is your neck?"

The bandage had come loose the day after we locked ourselves in the room and I hadn't bothered to redo it. The wound no longer bled, though they'd been right about the scarring. The pink tissue stood out against my tanned flesh, but I knew it would fade eventually and be harder to notice.

"It's fine."

"You still sound raspy."

I huffed. There was no reason to argue, she was right. With my increased healing the damaged tissue should have been better after so many days, so it was likely the rasp would never go away.

I didn't care because Brooke had already proved it didn't bother her. She'd lavished attention on the scar the first time she'd seen how bad it was, pressing her lips to the sensitive flesh in a way that had me hard just remembering it.

"I'm fine. I promise. Doesn't bother me at all."

It probably helped that we hadn't talked much the first couple days, though Brooke had grown hoarse from her cries of pleasure. Grinning at her, I wriggled my brows and she narrowed her eyes at me, making my wolf wriggle in excitement over the implied challenge.

I'd been hesitant to shift after what had happened, not sure how much worse the damage would be in my other forms. Since it had happened in my were-form, I'd been convinced the scars would be worse. Possibly bad enough to prevent me from using that shape any longer.

When I confessed the worries to Brooke after she asked why I was holding back, she'd encouraged me to give it a try. There was no other way to know, and no reason to worry when I could get the answer so easily.

My wolf looked no different other than a new stripe of white fur around my neck. Howling was a bit harder, but otherwise my wolf-form was unaffected.

It was more obvious in my were-form. In addition to the white fur, the hair was also thinner, the skin beneath gnarled and rough. Where the flesh had been black before, it was now a deep, angry red, pitted and sunken from the collar cutting into me.

I still didn't regret it. I'd do it again in a heartbeat if it meant protecting Brooke from danger.

I missed what Mrs. Frost said, humming in a way that suggested agreement when she paused as if waiting for an answer. Another sigh vibrated through the line.

"When you have enough blood pumping to your brain to actually listen, call back and I'll let you know who to talk to about the trial. You still have some time."

Chuckling, I promised to call again the next day before handing the phone back to Brooke. As soon as she said her good-byes and hung up the phone, I pounced, pinned her to the mattress and devouring her lips. I'd never get enough, and I'd just been given permission to keep going for another twenty-four hours before we had to return to reality.

Leann Ryans

Epilogue

Brooke

I adjusted the pillow again, snarling when it refused to sit how I wanted. Everything had to be just right, and the damn thing kept defying me.

Long fingers wrapped around my biceps, heat scorching my spine as Sebastian pulled me upright. Kiss pressed to my hair, he reached around me and plucked the offending cushion from its spot, holding another out in front of me with the other hand.

Cooing, I took the offering and fluffed it, tucking it into the empty spot and sighing when it stayed. Shuffling within the cage of his body, I made a few more adjustments before the tension finally drained out of me.

"Happy now?"

His rumble vibrated through my ribs, wrapping me in happiness and ratcheting up the heat flooding my body. Slick coated my folds, wetting my thighs where they clenched around the emptiness in my core.

I raised my voice in a purr, words too much effort to find. Turning within the confines of his arms, I tucked my head under his chin, pressing my ear to where his heart beat beneath a wall of muscle. We'd been waiting for my cycle for so long, and it was finally here, yet neither of us were in a rush. Everything would happen at the right time, when it felt natural and our instincts took over.

Fingers trailed through my loose hair, relaxing me further. I'd planned to put a blanket overtop the nest to block out the world, but I didn't need it with Sebastian holding me. He was my protector, my lover, and soon to be, my mate.

Spreading my fingers against his flesh, I kneaded the muscles beneath. I'd already shed my clothing before climbing into the middle of the bed, and Sebastian had followed my lead. There was nothing between us, exactly as I wanted.

I let my hands explore, relearning the body I'd come to know so well over the past few months. Though the self-defense case had taken longer to settle than we'd hoped, we hadn't let it stop us from moving on with our lives.

Sebastian had tried to urge me to go to college outside the city once everything was cleared. Even offered to relocate his entire buisness, just to get me somewhere safer. He hadn't understood all I needed to be safe was him. One place was as good or bad as any other, and we both had ties here we didn't want to lose.

He'd never let me go back into his house. Once he was sure we weren't leaving the city, he sold it to two of the other Knights and used the money for the down payment on our new home. It was bigger, further away from the area where we'd grown up, but right down the street from the condo he'd purchased from Danger when my mother expressed how sad she was to have to leave it. They fought him about it of course, and insisted on paying him back, but we both felt better with them out of the rapidly deteriorating area around the apartment.

It had been bittersweet to go back for our things. Packing had taken twice as long as it should have with the four of us working on it, because we took turns sharing memories of Vincent. It was hard to let go, but we knew he'd never have wanted them to stay because of him.

Sebastian's fingers trailed down my spine, making me arch into him as his fingers dipped lower to test my wetness, bringing me back to the present. Everything was done and settled, construction on the new shop begun, and all that was left was to claim my alpha.

Tongue slipping from my mouth, I licked his collar bone, trailing my tongue up over the rippled flesh of his neck to nibble on his jaw. Though the skin that had been torn was still paler than the rest of him, the scars weren't as obvious anymore, and most of the rasp had left his voice. I could still hear it when he was tired, but otherwise, he'd recovered completely.

I still had moments of panic brought on by lingering memories. I had issues with knives, so Sebastian was the one who prepped our meals, going so far as to cut mine into bite sized pieces before we sat at the dining table. It felt silly since I'd wanted to kill Arik just as much as Sebastian had, and in the end it had been his attack that caused Arik's death, but apparently the brain did weird things in times of high stress that didn't always make sense.

A thick finger plunged into my dripping core, a second joining it. Sebastian was good at keeping me focused in the moment and not letting me linger in the past. I had no idea how he knew, but he always did.

I moaned into his ear, teeth pinching around the lobe and drawing a growl from his chest. I shuddered as he pushed his fingers deeper, knuckles stretching me in preparation.

"I don't want to wait."

There were times when Sebastian would spend hours teasing me, working me into a frenzy of jittering nerves and lax muscles, when I swore I couldn't orgasm again and he sought to prove me wrong, but I didn't have the patience for that now. Held in the circle of his embrace, his bare skin pressed to mine, flesh held between my teeth, I wanted him inside me.

Now.

His chuckle filled the space between us, but he pulled his fingers from my core, shifting his hands to grip me under each thigh. Lifting me and spreading my legs over his, he poised me atop his cock, but paused before entering me.

"Are you sure?"

He asked me daily. We both knew he'd never let me go even if I said no, but my answer never changed. He was mine and I was his.

I let out my own growl, raking my teeth down his neck to take a mouthful of flesh where it met his shoulder. His answering rumble drowned mine out and sent my eyes rolling back in my head, slick flooding from my center.

He yanked me down, the tapered tip always deceiving me into thinking accepting him would be easy, but the head flared quickly, the thick length of him filling me with a delicious stretch that sent goosebumps flooding across my skin.

I cried out around my mouthful of flesh, refusing to let go even when he started working me up and down his shaft. His sounds of pleasure mingled with mine, filling the room and echoing back to us in a sensuous symphony that had me delirious with the sensory overload. I could hear him, smell him, taste him, feel him. My eyes were clenched against the onslaught, but it only heightened everything else.

The tension in my core coiled tighter, twisting around the plunging invasion. Every muscle was stretched tight, trembling with effort despite Sebastian doing all the work.

"Come for me, Brooke. My mate. Mine, forever."

I shattered at his command, my scream of pleasure muffled against his skin. I felt him swell impossibly larger inside me, knot inflating as he snapped his hips up and slammed it behind my pubic bone, sending a fresh wave of exquisite pain radiating from my womb.

My jaw clenched as pointed teeth pierced my shoulder, scalding blood flooding my mouth with the taste of ambrosia. The room spun around me as invisible hooks anchored in my chest, love and possessive need pouring from Sebastian through the bond to fill me with more than I could have ever thought possible.

He was inside me, stuffing my womb as his feelings spread behind my breastbone. The depth of it was awe inspiring, bringing tears to my eyes even as I smiled around my gory mouthful.

As my orgasm eased and his spurting slowed, we both released, licking the wounds we'd left on the other. I'd expected pain, but each swipe sent an erotic shiver down my spine, making me clench on the knot still locked in my core.

"Mine, forever," I echoed, purr vibrating from my throat with a joy that couldn't be matched.

He was mine, and I was his. No matter what life threw at us, we would face it together. He would keep me safe while I kept him sane, tempering the natural aggression of an alpha with the gentleness of an omega.

Two halves of one whole.

Thanks

I want to thank you for reading my story and I hope you enjoyed it!

This thing turned into a beast!

I'm a pantser. I start out with an idea of the couple and what might happen, and jump in with both feet. I never could have guessed this would be my longest story yet. It's twice the length of some of my other books, approaching double the length of my (previously) longest story!

I've never written shifters before, though they've been a favorite of mine to read. I enjoyed the experience of figuring out how to make my world work, with both shifters and humans, while still incorporating the omegaverse I love throughout it all.

Are you interested in more? There are so many alphas left for me to play with, and they all deserve their own Happily Ever After. I'd originally planned for Carl's story to be next in the series, but the events that unfolded in this one have me debating. Should we see what happens with Jackson next? Or are you more curious about Danger? And what about Patch and his mysterious beast?

If you leave me a review, mention who you'd like to see next, or you can email me your vote at leann@leannryans.com

Thanks again for reading my story! If you want to check out more of my books, find me on Facebook or at my website https://leannryans.com

Printed in Great Britain
by Amazon